PAMELA HILL

The Green Salamander

A Historical Novel

D0990561

St. Martin's Press
NEW YORK

Library of Congress Cataloging in Publication Data

Hill, Pamela.
  The green salamander.

  1. Douglas, Margaret, Countess of Lennox, 1515–1578 –
Fiction. 1. Title.
PZ4.H648Gr3 [PR6058.1446]   823′.9′14   76–41856

The Green Salamander

By the same author:

THE DEVIL OF ASKE

THE MALVIE IN

THE INCUMBEN

WHITTON'S FO

NORAH

MARY QUEEN OF SCOTS' marriage with Darnley is well known to history. Darnley himself is less well known, and his mother almost forgotten. Yet she was the link who provided the double inheritance of the English Crown. Visitors pass by her tomb in Westminster Abbey every day and never think of her; visitors to Holyrood Palace see only a portrait of a woman presumed to be a pillar of the Scottish Reformation. That Margaret Douglas was nothing of the kind can be discovered from the lightest research into her story, which stands in its own right as one of the greatest historical romances of the sixteenth century.

In my own research I have to thank, as always, the District Librarians of Dumfries and Galloway; H.M. Constable's Office, The Tower of London; Mr. C. Gilbert, the Custodian of Temple Newsam House, by Leeds; and lastly Mr. G. de Bellaigue, The Lord Chamberlain's Office, St. James's, who has given invaluable help with regard to the Darnley Jewel.

... Over all, on a shield of pretence argent, a man's heart gules crowned or, for Douglas.

Crest – A salamander vert in flames and spouting out fire.

Balfour's *Scots Peerage.*

Prologue

The House at Hackney

A High-Coloured Gentleman, well mounted, his florid good looks no longer boasting youth, but his body erect and flat-bellied, attired modishly in strawberry colour, with a ruff well starched and a plumed cap set on his head at a rakish angle, clattered through the village of Hackney surrounded by his servants. It was the seventh day of March, 1578. The hour was past noon. A small cold wind blew, that made folk withdraw again into their doorways after looking out to see what the stir might be and marvel at such horses, so fine as to be seldom met with in this unfashionable street. Having seen, the folk lowered their eyes, and after the cavalcade had gone by one or two murmured a forbidden prayer to the Virgin. Others expressed themselves more roundly in the privacy of their houses.

"The Queen's Robin! He goes as fine as ever, yet they say she has cast him off."

"The wizard! The poisoner! They say a lady at Court loved him and when he had tired of her, he caused her hair and nails to fall out."

"He murdered his wife, that's for certain. Best not say more now; walls have ears." The ears were those of the Queen's Master Secretary, Cecil, also Walsingham, whose paid informers lurked both within the walls and without. It was even said that they still kept spies in the tumbledown house of the poor old woman at the end of the village, who –

A maidservant came hurrying in, her pail of drawn water

slopping its contents in her haste. "*He* has stopped at her house, poor soul! He'll find small cheer there. They say neither she nor her servants have enough to eat."

"They say—"

Robert Dudley, Earl of Leicester, meantime dismounted and threw his reins to his groom, who wore the device of a bear and ragged staff on his livery-sleeve. The device itself had been filched, like so much else, by the upstart family his employer came of, but neither the groom nor Leicester cared for that. The latter's mind was occupied instead with the probable reason for this invitation he had received to ride over and dine today with the aged Countess of Lennox. She must want to borrow money. Otherwise Leicester would have been surprised to hear from her after so many years. She had never liked him, and she must be in sore straits to apply to him and, having hardly the means to feed herself, undertake meantime to play host to a guest of his standing as well as to his retinue. Charitably, he had brought few men. It occurred to him now, seeing the poverty of her dwelling—the roof leaked and the damp crept up green against the walls from the nearby marshes—that he might well have spared, from his place of Kenilworth, a gift of fish or fowl, though it was not yet the season for the grapes with which, two summers since, he had diverted Her Grace the Queen by piling them on a pedestal during her stay there.

He frowned, surveying the small courtyard where grass grew up between the cobbles. So derelict a place! It was true that the old woman was suffered to keep this part of her property to live in now all her kin were dead or—"Why," he remembered, "her grandson is the King of Scotland; has he no care for her?" Then he recalled that the boy himself had small power, being at the mercy of the Regent, Morton, his grandmother's kinsman and enemy. Morton, now Leicester resurrected it from the capacious places in his mind, had come to some arrangement with this lady's dead lord whereby her inheritance and title of Angus had been sold for money. That last, when all was said, was the necessity without which all else must perish; the wonder was that the old woman had survived with so little for so long. It would be of interest, after all, to see what the years had made of proud Madge, as Her Grace had used to call her, and to hear how she might couch her probable request to himself. It was pitiful, after all, for her to come to this; and the matter would divert his mind meantime from his own problem, that of his forthcoming marriage to Lettice Knollys. He had not broken that news yet to the Queen.

Elizabeth, he thought, surveying the small gloomy entrance to the house where he was to dine today. Elizabeth of England. For so long he had used the first name to her, never any more formal or flattering title such as fools employed; he had thought she loved him. The years had passed and he and she had both grown older, and now that youth and passion and hot blood were gone he realised that she had played with him, too, as she had done with d'Alençon and Savoy and Sweden, France and Austria and Anjou and Philip of Spain. She had held all men and nations aloof while appearing to dally with them, consider them, flatter them, be amused by them, use them. He himself had been used, and squeezed dry like an orange. Now he wanted sons to carry on his name.

He entered the doorway, and beheld an ancient manservant there in a black gown, bowing. The man's face was familiar. Leicester stared at it to down his dismay at the miasma of the outer marshes which arose in the hall, whose hearth lay empty with no fire lit, so that the place smelled of bog and damp and was cold as a tomb. They had not yet taken out the trestles to lay the tables to dine. Leicester thought briefly and without pleasure of the meal, and wondered what my lady's purse could provide; stale fish, perhaps, spiced with lavender, as this was the season of Lent. A flash of recognition for the manservant came to him with the thought of that season, and its meaning. He turned, halting in his brisk tracks upstairs, his short cloak swinging; he had not taken it off.

"Malliet!" He smiled, and extended his hand.

"Your lordship's memory serves well." The man was pleased, but not servile. Leicester continued to question him, delaying his meeting with the Countess abovestairs. This was a kinsman of Zwinglius the reformer, and he had known him slightly from his father's day when such folk were the fashion.

"You are of my lady Lennox's household? I had thought you too stout a Protestant. How do you fare here?" The Countess, he knew well, was of the old faith, and as they said stiffer in her Poperies even than the late Queen Mary had been. Malliet's

15

grey head inclined itself, and he smiled, lending his scholar's features an instant's lightness.

"My lady and I have long since buried our differences by never referring to them. I was Lord Charles's tutor."

The name fell on silence. Lord Charles Stuart, the Countess' younger son, was dead. He had succeeded to the earldom on his father's murder, Leicester remembered, and then —

"My lady's grace awaits you upstairs, my lord. There is a fire lit there, and she desires me to ask if you will take wine."

Thank God for the fire, thought Leicester; the cold here struck one to the bones. He accepted the offer of wine for that reason. When one was as near death as this old woman, no doubt one accustomed oneself to the prospect of the tomb; or perhaps it was some form of mortifying the flesh. The shallow part of Leicester's mind turned over the matter as he came to an upper chamber. The door was opened; inside was a strange greenish light, as though one were under the sea. It filtered through a small paned window outside which grew ivy that had not been cut. Inside, close by the fire which was too low to warm the room, sat an old woman in a black gown. She rose as Leicester entered. She did not advance, but waited, as a queen might do, while he went forward and kissed her hands. These, though twisted with age, were small and elegant, almost transparent, as though she ate no food to speak of. Her gown, he saw, was worn in places and had been carefully mended. It's fashion was that of Queen Mary's day, and her coif was flat and plain, concealing silver hair to which the light conveyed a greenish tinge. Although the Countess wore mourning a large elaborate pendant jewel hung at her breast, which she caressed from time to time so that his eyes sought it; but in the dim light he could see little of its detail. Beside her, a child, a little girl, played unheedingly on the rushes of the floor and when reproved, came and stood by them, regarding Leicester with candid hazel eyes. When told to do so she made an infantile curtsy. The dim light shone on her clear, pretty features and fair curls.

"It was good of you to come so far, my lord," said Margaret Lennox. She smiled a little; her face was not wrinkled but smoothed with age, like the Gothic ivories he had seen in French cathedrals. "You must wonder why an old woman sent for you," she said. "Arbell, sweetheart, go and play with your doll. She

16

will pay no heed to us," she added in a low voice, as the child obeyed. 'I like to have her here by me, and it means also that there need not be more than one fire lit. I must keep close commons, my lord."

It is coming now, he thought, the request for money. He smiled, and waited. She indicated a chair, however, and he seated himself after she had again done so. A different grey-haired servant brought in the wine. He poured it and Leicester drank; the bouquet was faded and the flavour cheap, but it warmed him. Presently he put his wine-cup down, as the Countess still had not spoken. The pair of them sat facing one another, while the low fire smouldered.

"I have had a presentiment, my lord," she said, "that I am going to die. No, do not disclaim –" for he had raised a hand as if to launch forth on some courtly denial "– for it is time, and I am glad of it. I am very weary. You used to accuse me, through the spies you kept in my Yorkshire house, of keeping a witch there; do you remember?'

The transition had been so smoothly made that it took him at a loss. He put up a hand to hide the flush that had come over his bearded face. "My lady –" he began. Then he shrugged a little; of what use to dissemble the matter? It had been, as she should know well, necessary for both himself and Secretary Cecil to keep an eye on Lady Lennox's movements in the north, with the trafficking she had had there back and forth with letters and messengers to France. "My loyalty is to the Queen," he said abruptly. Through his confusion he felt conviction come, and give him strength. It was true enough, he thought; however devious his methods, the truth itself had always been no less, and no more than that. He was still loyal.

"I have no disloyalty to Her Grace in her realm," said the Countess. "England sheltered me when I was homeless; both this Queen and her father showed me kindness as well as cruelty. As I am to die, my lord, I need have no fear what I say; it is a privilege of the dying. There are matters I have been unable to speak of since my husband was killed, for I had none other I could trust." Her eyes, which were red-rimmed as if with constant weeping, gazed at Leicester and he realised that in her youth they must have been blue. The colour was drained out of them, and her, he thought; she was like a study in neutral

17

B

tones such as he had seen painters make before embarking on a great state-portrait. And that ivy-filtered light, making everything in the room seem as if it had died except the glinting jewel, and the child playing by herself ... Had his widow said she *trusted* Lennox? Had she? Leicester downed hard laughter. Yet, he reflected, he had heard it stated that there had been steadfast love between that man and his wife.

It was not, at any rate, money she wanted. Shame flooded him and he spoke harshly, suddenly. "Say and ask what you will, my lady," he told her. "You may live many a day. There is no fear now in plain speech between us. I myself need no longer report what has been said to any man ... or any woman." It was an admission of his own diminished status at Court.

"Then you shall hear it," she said. "It is a tale half a century old. It is, if you will, a story of love and hate; but in the end love triumphs. And at the end I would ask you a question which you alone, I think, can answer. Whatever answer you render shall lie in my grave."

He began to listen, forgetting after a time even the cold, or the child playing beneath the ivy which tapped always against the window.

I

Crowned Heart

"YOU WILL FORGIVE my leaving you now, good ladies, but I cannot trust the serving-maids to busy themselves preparing supper alone; and you will be hungry after your ride."

Lady Strangeways, wife of the castellan of Berwick, a town at present held for King Henry VIII, swept a last dissatisfied look beneath her eyelids at the group of women huddled in the castle's upper chamber. There was something about them she could not understand. Vagrants they looked like, with their gear worn and faded to a uniform dun brittleness and their skins weather-beaten from long exposure to sun and wind; certainly they had ridden in here today as beggars, suppliants – and unexpected at that – for her husband's favour and bite and sup, which he had not denied them. Yet instead of pretending a humble gait in face of this generosity – and to Scots, marauding thieves as they were, my lady thought, it need not have been given – they had continued to bear themselves as though, in fact, the honour were hers to have to find meat enough to fill them, and broach another cask or two of small-ale, and use up the week's baking with no warning given that the ovens would have to be heated again tomorrow! In short, she might have been offering hospitality to the Queen and her Spanish ladies instead of to a scraggy pack of outlaws who had some-how evaded justice in Scotland the best part of two years. But Berwick, though it had belonged to that savage domain until the end of last century, was England's now, and so the vaga-

21

bonds were safe: at least, until word should come from London as to whether or not His Grace permitted them to stay.

"I will have your own man bring up the washing-water," said my lady briskly, knowing that the unshaven serving-man they had brought – he himself needed a good wash, as did they all – would have found a bite to eat by now in the kitchens. The maids were such fools any man's tongue could get round them, and here on the Border few of the common folk seemed certain whether they were English or Scots. As for bedding – "They will be glad enough to sleep five or six to a bed, for I warrant it is long enough since they lay on aught but hard ground or hayricks," she thought, but did not speak aloud. It would have been a waste of breath to do so, with their way of speech so different from her own; in any case, neither to words nor signs would these Douglases vouchsafe much reply, merely staring back long-necked, like the herons which still stood, hour by hour, at times on the river bank now there was less shipping hereabouts to disturb the fish. As for that girl who could be no more than twelve years old and to whom they all deferred, *she* had stalked straight to the window and stayed there looking out, with her back turned. "Queen's daughter?" breathed my lady. "A likely tale, in rags and without even the manners of a gipsy." But the girl spoke now, through the others' silence, without troubling to turn her flaxen head.

"Order your servants by all means," she said in a voice which my lady could follow. "We will contrive till supper is ready."

The castellan's wife bridled, so that the summer sun caught at her fine gold neck-chains, beaded frontlet and rings, for like all Border women she carried her goods upon her. A tall creature who had been sitting amongst the saddle-weary group by the wall rose then, and spoke for the first time in a voice which was commanding but, with its accents of the far north-east, even less possible to interpret than the rest. Yet she seemed more courteous than the girl had been.

"I fear we are putting you to some trouble, my lady. But, as the Earl of Angus my cousin promised, you shall receive due recompense, and meantime we are glad of your roof to cover us." She nodded, as though dismissing a servant, to indicate that my lady might go. Bereft of words – the gesture itself had been clear enough – the castellan's wife went out and down to

22

her duties. After she had gone the tall woman, Lady Archibald Douglas, whose husband had ridden off lately with the Earl, turned to the young girl by the window as if, respectfully, to admonish her. One of the wind-reddened hands went out to touch that slim unheeding back, then let itself drop. The Lady Margaret was upset, she knew, at parting with her father.

"I think," she said quietly, "that my lady's grace should have been more civil a trifle. We trespass on their good-nature here, in an English town, and our plight is not their doing. Such pains as they choose to take meantime on our behalf should be received with gratitude, as we may best show it."

"Small need for that!" A dark fierce woman, her hair straggling loose beneath her hood, burst in, as she was wont. "We need show little gratitude to King Henry's folk! They've caused us dule enough.'

"Not of late. Flodden is an old man's tale, and since then – "

The dark woman continued to shout. "Gratitude means silver to the English, and we've none. They'll get it, doubtless, from their King – " she almost spat – "for sheltering his sister's bairn. That apart, the Earl will pay when he can."

"Be at peace, Isabel; wherever there is trouble you are in the midst," said Lady Archibald sharply to her kinswoman, Lady George Douglas. The altercation made the girl at the window lift her shoulder slightly, as if she were half paying heed.

"Was I not civil?" she asked absently, without turning round. Lady Archibald put a finger to her lips at Lady George, who subsided into silence. A shaft of sunlight at the narrow window rested itself on the girl's thick hair, which was tied back meantime with a leather riding-thong. It was beautiful hair, and should have had the sheen of silver gold; but it had long been bleached almost white by sun and weather and lately dulled with filth, for the summer ways were dusty. The girl spoke quickly, almost scornfully in a low voice to the tall woman who still stood near. "Leave me be, Nan, a while from your governessing! Go and talk with the rest. Go, I say."

After Lady Archibald had left her, Margaret Douglas, only daughter of the Earl of Angus and his estranged wife Margaret Tudor, Queen of Scotland, resumed her rigid staring out of the window. Beyond the mullions, on one side, she knew, would lie the jumbled houses and booths of the market-town; she had

23

chosen the other, because it showed the Tweed on its way to the sea. She would rather look at that; although it was a different Tweed, tamed, broad, and steady, unlike the water she knew: that brown and treacherous torrent she herself had forded many times this year and last, back and forth from Norham as danger on the Scots bank came and went. Ay, brown as stale blood had been Tweed, when she had last seen it run below Norham: deep and strong with a pulling current from last autumn's rains, and the drifting leaves on its surface had clung to the horses' harness as they made across, she among all of them and her father cheering them on from where he guarded the bank they had left.

Where did he ride now, the Earl? Back into Scotland, rife with his enemies? Down into England, to try his fortunes with that glorious royal uncle, the King, of whom she had often been told, and whom she herself had even met once when she was too young to remember? But that had been when she was with her royal mother. It might be a different reception for her father, who had dared to marry a Tudor and think himself as good as she. "God and His Saints watch over him, whichever way he rides," Madge thought. There was no one left now to call her Madge. She longed with an almost physical intensity for her father, then began, as she had been schooled to do at such moments, to pray for him, using her fingers as beads. Often and often she'd prayed for him that way at Norham, standing at just such a slit of window as this, except that there the sill had been fashioned of soft yellow stone still pitted with the marks of Mons, the great gun brought south a generation back by the Scots under King James IV, who had been her mother's first husband. That had been in his earlier war, not the one which had ended in Flodden and his death.

Guns had sounded also lately at Tantallon, that the young James V, her half-brother, had had brought from Dunbar.

She must not think of that, or of having to leave, or of any of the things which had happened since at last they gave up the Douglas stronghold. She recalled the Earl's first saying "This is England, and we are safe." He had said it since so often, riding back and forth over Tweed, that its early impact was a little dulled. But it was true enough; this was England, and they were safe, though the Earl had gone.

24

"We are safe," she made herself say again in her mind. And they were dry and fed, or would be tonight. It had always dripped with damp at Norham, with its leaking roof and part-breached walls; here both roof and walls were dry and well-tended. It would be pleasant, even for a little while, to accustom oneself to feel warm again, not to have to be roused from ex-hausted sleep after a day in the saddle, and once more have to take to horse by night for some alarm of the Scots King's men nearing which might be false after all. But it had been happening like that now for over a year, and her royal half-brother's heart – *had* James a heart? Madge recalled him as cold-eyed; he hadn't liked her, no doubt because she was a Douglas and the Douglases at that time held him in thrall – hadn't grown softer towards her father or, for that same reason, herself; for in the nature of things she had gone in the end with the Earl, though they said James had offered a reward to anyone now who would find her and bring her back to their mother.

"I will never go back," Madge said to herself.

It was that, not the outlawry, she feared; no Douglas feared death, or the fact that any man might not only kill but rob, ravish, maim or yield them up at will. That state of affairs had come about by the Earl's obstinacy, because at first, after the King escaped from his wardship disguised as a groom, riding hard to Stirling – at first, James had merely bidden the Earl betake himself north of Spey, but Angus refused to go. Instead, he had invested Tantallon and held out against all the King's men and his siege-engines and diggings of fortifications, so that James had in the end had to get a better commander, the Earl of Argyll, to take charge. And still Angus held out, for Tantallon on its rock above the sea was said to be impregnable, and if there had only been the men to think of he would no doubt still be there. But there was herself, his half-royal daughter that he might somehow bargain with, trapped amid the sounds of cannon-fire and crashing of stones against the walls, and if she were hurt or killed there would never be another to replace her; the Queen had sworn she would never live with Angus again as her husband, she had taken out a writing of divorce, as he himself said, to be rid of him after her son the King of Scots was safe and free. "But never fear, lass, ye have Tudor blood and Douglas both, and were born in wedlock," the Earl told

25

Madge, with the gleam in his eyes that he also had when he looked at rose-red Tantallon, his ancestors' stronghold since the Red Douglas inherited the legend of the Black and first wore the Crowned Heart on his banners. The Heart was Bruce's and had been taken after his death as he had asked to the Crusades by Sir James Douglas, who had been by Bruce's side in his wanderings and had helped him win Bannockburn. But Sir James had been killed in battle against the infidel in Spain instead, flinging the Heart before him as he cut his way through the ranks of the enemy. And ever since the Douglases had borne the Heart, and, as a motto, *Jamais Arrière*.

"But we are somewhat in the way of being *arrière* here," Madge thought drily. The Earl might not come to fetch her so quickly here as he had always done from Norham, as soon as there might be safety. Madge did not know when she would see him again. He had said nothing, but she had known from the hard pressure of his arms about her today and the rough caress of his beard against her cheek. Being Scots, he and she, they were sparing of caresses. Her English mother on the other hand had used to load her and James with kisses which meant nothing. "But I am part English also," she thought, "for my mother bore me in England when she fled south after her second marriage."

She turned her thoughts away. She would not often let the memory of the Queen dwell there. Nan Douglas in any case had been put in charge of her after – after –

But it wasn't Nan, tall, dutiful, and mindful of her half-royalty that Madge wanted now, but the Earl her father, he with whom she had chosen to ride out and forsake all she knew, ungrudgingly. She hadn't minded any of the hardship, as long as he always came back to her.

But things had grown worse, especially in winter, and the castellans who had at first received them in bad weather dared no longer do so for fear of the implacable anger of the King of Scots. James was not hotly angry, but cold with the hard unforgiving coldness of the Tudor blood he had in him from their mother. The longer Douglas of Angus stayed an unrepentant fugitive, the harder grew James's enmity, and the more troops he posted along the Border from west to east, and the oftener they must ford Tweed again and again when the water ran high and could drown a man quickly.

So the Earl had at last told her they must come here, to Berwick. He himself would have to leave her awhile. "Bide snug with Strangeways, lass, till I send word of a turn of fortune." A turn of fortune? Nothing could change the Scots King's hard heart now, when they had been put to the horn and even Aunt Janet Glamis, the Earl's sister in the north, was being watched because she sent supplies to them by messenger.

A turn of fortune. She had known from the shifty side-glance of Angus's eyes that he had plans of some sort, plans which did not include the burden of a young daughter and her women alongside in all weathers. That was why she couldn't turn round yet and face the women; her eyes still pricked with tears. She would not let them fall; a Douglas must never cry, as Nan would certainly say to her in the voice she had lately used to reprove her for lack of polite exchanges with the castellan's wife. To gaze out at the river and the sea was some balm to a sore spirit; that same sea that bounded forever below Tantallon, the home Madge had left at last secretly by night, wrapped warmly in a cloak against the snell wind and lowered into a waiting boat by the strong arms of a Douglas serving-man. The cannon were silent at last and there was only the sound of the lapping waves about the boat.

Would she ever see Tantallon again, with its rose-red towers and the three-sided defences, with the fourth a strong sea-girt rock? Or would she be forever a wanderer on the face of the earth?

"Fool," she thought fiercely of herself. The Earl would not abandon her, if only for her royal blood. The bleakness of the thought that it might be that only, and not because he loved her, rose in Madge, and was downed at once; a Douglas woman must not pity herself.

Her soft mouth firmed, and the tears in the blue eyes lessened. Like her hair the girl's eyes seemed lighter than they were, against the almost black colour of a skin burned with sun and roughened with weather. The clear fine arches of her brows still showed darker than the hair, and her lashes were long and thick. It was the face neither of child nor woman, somehow at a loss yet for any certain expression, as though she had already learnt to guard her thoughts against watchers outside.

27

Yet why be guarded against her own Douglas kin, who treated her as she indeed was, half-royal? At Tantallon she had kept full state, and even at the Court of France, where they had all gone briefly while the Earl was under the Scots Regent Albany's displeasure, Madge had been used to be acclaimed as a little princess, though King François, who resembled a fox, had only once briefly pinched her cheek and said not much to her. That was because, as Lady Archibald had explained, the Earl was out of favour at the French Court, the King being the staunch ally of Albany. "It was folly to have come over at all," had said that much-tried lady, sighing a little. "We would have done better to bide where we were; the tide will turn in Scotland."

The tide had turned indeed. Madge could remember, in snippets of recollection that covered the years like patchwork, episodes, changes, importance, power. Suddenly, or so it seemed, her father the Earl was no longer a suppliant for the French King's bounty or anyone else's, but on the contrary the highest nobleman in the land. His handsome head, set on his neck in a way Madge knew instinctively to be confident, seldom doffed its plumed bonnet now to anyone except the red-haired boy, with eyes of cold grey steel, who was Madge's half-brother the King. And even to the King the Earl did not bow over low, for had he not the boy now in ward, with the strength of the Scottish Crown his own in consequence?

Perhaps that was the real reason why her half-brother James had had no liking for her, Angus's daughter. Madge knew this was so, no matter how much the King might noise abroad that she was his beloved sister and he wanted her back. James was almost five years older than she was, and when they had first met at Stirling the Earl had bidden them kiss and be merry. But James had been off-hand on that and other occasions and had even been unwilling to show her his talking parrot, which was killed soon afterwards by the wild birds in Stirling woods. Madge learned later that the King had small use for girls till they were old enough to be made love to, and a sister was of course for this purpose quite useless. Lady George Douglas, never one to hold her tongue, had told Madge the Earl permitted the King to tumble young women from the time he was fifteen, chiefly to occupy his mind and his time so that he would have the less to spare for brooding on the great matters which Madge's father had by now under his own control. She had herself seen Angus hold, in his long jewelled fingers, a large flat round object on which was carved out the figure of a lion in reverse.

"Mark the Great Seal well, my lass," he had said, laughing at the round wondering eyes in her child's face, while her uncle George Douglas, who was always there at the Earl's elbow, laughed also. "Even the King cannot take it from my hand; the grasp's too firm." And they had smiled together in the way they often did, whether here or at Tantallon.

Tantallon was the meeting-place for all the Douglases and their women, who would stay while the men wrought at politics or war. There was Aunt Alison Hume who had a new gown every visit, and Kilspindie's masterful city-bred wife whom he had married for her tocher*, and old Kilspindie himself who was Madge's great-uncle but had little time to spare, for he was close in attendance about the King. And once, memorably, there had come riding down from Forfar the most beautiful woman Madge had ever seen, who was Aunt Janet Glamis with her unpleasant husband, who quarrelled with everyone so that swords were almost drawn. Their daughter was there, and had said to Madge, in a queer northern accent which made the other smile, "Never heed my father; he is aye at it; folk call him Clang-Causey for he will never keep the peace." But Madge had been so greatly struck with the beauty of Aunt Janet that she scarcely took heed of Clang-Causey or the din he made. Afterwards she had looked in a mirror and wondered if she would ever have that flawless profile and smooth golden hair, and the eyes – no, her own eyes were different, without the strange power that glowed in Lady Glamis'. They had gone away in a few days and Madge had not seen them again, but often in the later exile Aunt Janet sent food and clothes and letters, brought by a serving-man clad plainly and without the Glamis livery, for fear of the King.

News from England had come often to Tantallon, either by land or by sea. Madge was taught to pay heed to this and to know who had sent it; as the Douglas women made haste to point out to her, she was, in addition to being a Douglas, an English princess, which was almost as good, having been born in England, though nobody explained why. But soon after her birth,

* dowry

she was told, she and her mother had ridden down to see King Henry and his Court and they had come upon him with all his train a-maying, and he had kissed Madge and sworn that she was the fairest royal babe he had ever seen, as fair as his own daughter Mary who was known as the Pearl of the World. Madge had met Mary, but of course could not remember it, and neither could she recall having met another great personage, her own godfather, Cardinal Wolsey, Archbishop of York. "So you need never be forsaken," said Nan Douglas, adding that everyone knew the Cardinal was as powerful as the English King. Yet at that time, there had seemed no prospect of his being needed.

From her place, Lady Archibald Douglas watched her charge, who was dearer to her than her own many daughters by her constantly ailing spouse. It was perhaps true that a part of her affection for the young Lady Margaret sprang from the pride they had all felt at first news of the marriage of young Angus to the widowed Queen of Scots after Flodden had killed not only James IV, but most of his lords beside him. But it had not taken long for the glory of that second marriage to wear thin; the Queen never rested till she won free of Tantallon, where she complained that the sea sounded in one's ears night and day and the crying of gulls never ceased about the earthworks her first husband, the late King, had dug when he besieged the Douglas of his youth, old Angus Bell-the-Cat. But little Madge, who was returned to them after the Queen had fled into England to give her birth and then gone south to visit her royal brother and been sent back, like an unwelcome package, to take up residence in Scotland again – Madge was a quiet, biddable enough child unless one came up against her royal and Douglas pride, which must be fostered suitably now that Angus ruled the kingdom for the King. She also had a natural love of needle-work, which whiled away many a pleasant hour for them all; she learned her prayers in docile fashion from the priest who served Tantallon; and nothing need have gone amiss had not the young King chosen at last to elude his guardians and make his escape, attired as a groom, to Stirling, where he lowered the portcullis and admitted only those who would help him regain his kingdom from the Douglas faction.

30

The faction had rapidly melted away. It was to Tantallon that the news had come which would change all their lives.

It had been a day like many others. Madge had been sitting with her ladies stitching at an altarpiece for the Priory of Coldinghame, where the Earl's brother, William Douglas, who was also the Abbot of Holyrood, held office. Alice Douglas, one of Lady George's daughters who had a pleasant voice, had been singing a French lay to them. Suddenly she had stopped and said "Is that not a rider in the courtyard?" and shortly the curtain by the doorway had been wrenched aside and there stood old Kilspindie, looking twice his age; Kilspindie whom the King loved and jested with and called Greysteel, after a ballad they knew. Greysteel's face was working in a queer way and his lips were blue with the ride, for he was not used to swift journeying at his age. He blurted out something and Lady George Douglas cried out harshly, so that her voice cut through the stillness, "Speak up, Kilspindie, for we cannot hear! What has befallen?" And so Kilspindie spoke again, spreading out his hands and weeping like a child who sees a favourite toy broken.

"The King has won alone to Stirling, and his lords have joined him there. My lord of Angus is ordered north of Spey, and George and I are to stand surety for him in ward in Edinburgh Castle. But I rode here to warn ye all."

"Warn us?" screamed Lady George. "Will my lord then go north?"

"Not he."

She put her needle in the silk calmly and set it aside, her dark face cold and inscrutable, for she was a Douglas born as well as by her marriage. She spoke then into the silent room. "Our forebears fought, the banner of the Crowned Heart fought, for the King of Scots before the name of Stewart was royal. If my lord of Angus resist the King's will, we go with him. If the King invest Tantallon we will defend it. What if we are only women? *He's* a boy, and no commander."

"Ye ken not yet in what wise the King may command. Take heed of me, and be circumspect while there is yet time." That was the croak of old Lady Kilspindie, but she was a townswoman and no true Douglas, and the rest ignored her. She turned to her husband. "Get yourself food from the servants, then ride back

31

to Edinburgh and let the King do as he will," she said. "He'll have mercy on ye, Kilspindie, because ye are auld, and his minion."

"Minion? I?" roared Kilspindie suddenly. It caused a silence among the first rustlings of indecision, for never before had the old man been known to gainsay his wife. "I will go where my lord of Angus goes, and do as he bids me," he said, "and if I must fall by his side I must."

"It will not come to that," said someone. They had all of them forgotten Madge, who sat with the heavy altarcloth still across her knees, its weight of gold threads dragging at her. Suddenly everything she had lately known as secure was being swept away; it was like that other time when she had been snatched from one warring parent to the other and lifted into the saddle and brought here, to Tantallon which should be safe. Only now it seemed as if the rose-red rock itself was built on shifting sand. What would happen? Where was she to go, and to whom?

In the end the Earl came, and behind him the King's guns. The women shut themselves in the seaward side of the castle and heard the thunder of the cannon and eked out the supplies of food which no one had had time to replenish before the siege, and at times during the day would see the King's red hair, which he still wore long, lifted by the wind beneath his helmet where he rode beyond the double earthwork he was making which surrounded his father's.

Then there had come word that the King was wroth because of the death of his gunner, and the Earl of Argyll was to replace the King as commander of the siege and at that it was decided privately to get the women away. So they had taken what they could and fled by sea, then later, before the end and after the King had put them to the horn, lived in the open and in caves and hayricks and empty churches and byres of farms, never knowing when those nearby were King's men, for the lords who had rallied to him were Maxwell and Montrose and Rothes and Nan's own kinsman, the Earl Marischal, and Bothwell and Arran and James IV's bastard son, the Earl of Moray. There was soon nowhere to go. There was no safe hiding-place in all the Borders, and so there began the riding and wading and walking across fords between Scotland and England where they had as

yet no right to be either, lacking a safe-conduct from the
English King; but somehow by this means evading the chain
of guards the Scots King had set across the land to arrest the
Earl of Angus and bring back the Earl's daughter Madge, "our
own dearest sister," to restore her to the loving arms of her
mother the Queen.

Madge had shuddered when she heard that. She would as
soon have died as go back.

She had a talisman. Almost the last thing she had done before
leaving Tantallon was to unpin the little gold images of the
saints – which had belonged to Bess Douglas her great-grandmother, Bell-the-Cat's wife – from the bed-curtains, and thread
them on a piece of silk and hide them inside her bodice. They
would stay always with her, she swore. At times she would put
her small fine weather-roughened hand against her child's breast,
as now, and feel the hardness of the images, which comforted
her. At Norham, when she had been sometimes alone, she would
bring them out and let the dying sun gleam on their gold while
she said her nightly prayers. They had their separate identities.
There was St Christopher bearing the Christ-child over a flood
higher than Tweed, and St Sebastian pierced with arrows, and
St Catharine holding her wheel, and St Lawrence with his
gridiron, St Polycarp who died of burning when he refused to
curse the name of Christ, St Joseph with his flowering rod, the
Blessed Virgin with her baby, the others whom Madge knew all
by name and history, for she had listened carefully to the priest.
Other things might change, but these were always with her;
not because they were of gold, but because in their lives they
had suffered, and if she too must suffer it would help to remember them and to ask them to intercede for her father, who
had ridden away.

Lady Strangeways had finished her tasks downstairs. When the
birds for dinner were plucked, drawn, and turning on the spits,
and enough platters of different kinds had been found to suffice
the guests, she sought out her husband. She was still ruffled
over the behaviour of the Douglas women and that girl, and
would let him know it.

"That young lady should be taught her manners, Tom. No

daughter of mine would speak or act so without a rod to her back. Is it true, as they say, that her mother is the Queen of Scotland? A sorry state she's in, more like a beggar than a princess."

"Ay, Queen Margaret gave her birth." Tom Strangeways scratched his neck where the armour chafed it. He hoped soon to be out of that and to have leisure to eat his dinner in a stuff surcoat, but he had received the Earl of Angus today, fugitive though he might be, in a state befitting His Grace of England's representative. Angus on the other hand had been as threadbare as his daughter; his armour was rusty and his beard showed threads of grey. He had not stayed to dine. "Poor lass," said Strangeways aloud, "she'd be hard put to it at parting from her father. They say she followed him through muck and mire, cheerful as a man."

"I'd not wish any girl of mine to know such necessity. Queen Margaret indeed! A pity she ever made that second marriage; it was nothing like her first. I mind when I was a young girl when she came to Durham Abbey, on her way north to be married to James IV. The marriage of the Thistle and the Rose, they called it. Her hair was hanging down her back, red-gold, and she had a fine complexion. They say she lost it after she took the smallpox, five or six years since that must be."

"Her marriage to that King brought great hopes of peace between Scotland and England," said Strangeways thoughtfully. "But they were shattered at Flodden, in the end, with the King left dead on the field. The Queen was left like a rudderless craft, no doubt; taken prize by the first man to board her."

"You men don't understand what a poor woman has to put up with, and no husband to shield her; and in a country like Scotland – "

"Berwick town was Scots once. And if Queen Margaret thought Angus would prove a trusty shield, she was mistaken in him. When she was with child by him he abandoned her on their flight to England, and went back to try to make his own peace with the Regent Albany. Lord Dacre, who was Warden of the Marches then, told me the Queen of Scots rode into Harbottle already in labour, almost alone and soaked with the rain and mist."

"That's a bleak place, hardly more than a peel-tower, poor

soul."

"Ay. He had them put her in a room abovestairs, and the girl was born there. Angus came skulking back again then, but Her Grace was none too pleased with him. He left her again to ride south to her brother alone, taking the child with her."

"She'd have been better to leave the little creature at the English Court to be brought up." Lady Strangeways stared at the wall-hangings, which she herself had woven and embroidered here in Berwick, which in old men's memories was still a Scottish town. Still, these fugitives were on King Henry's land now, and must obey his laws. Whatever might happen to young Margaret Douglas was not her concern. Yet already she felt a lessening of her resentment at the girl's abrupt manner. To be half-royal, and yet an outcast . . . born in a damp Border fortress to the sound of rain, and then harried hither and yon . . .

"King Henry wouldn't keep his sister the Queen of Scots at his Court for long," Strangeways said. "They say she was forever pestering him for money. He sent her back to Scotland, to her lord, in the end. But they never dealt well together after that, the Queen and the Earl. I hear only such trickles of talk as reach me here, but I believe this young girl will know a deal more of her father than her mother. Angus wouldn't let go of a Douglas with royal blood in her veins."

"Poor child," said my lady.

"Oh, she's fond enough of him; chose to follow him, after the Scots King had put them to the horn, rather than return to safety with her mother and half-brother."

"Angus has let go of her now."

"I believe he was at his wits' end. They have spent the year without a roof to call their own, and their lives at the whim of every informer. No young girl can lead such a life for ever."

Lady Strangeways said suddenly, "She would be a beautiful child if she were washed and suitably gowned, and her hair combed out. I have never seen such fine hair, but its state – "

The captain of Berwick smiled. 'Do what you may for her in such ways. Maybe our girls have gowns they no longer need, or have outgrown?"

"But the King's niece – and all those Douglas women about her – "

"The Douglases may not stay long. Our King may not grant

them all asylum in his own country. The young King of Scots is his nephew, and so far they seem to remain on terms. But the girl herself, being King Harry's own niece, as you say, he will surely provide for her. Also, the Earl tells me, the Cardinal himself is her godfather."

"The Cardinal?" My lady was suitably impressed. It would not perhaps matter so greatly if the winter's beef were depleted, or even if the Earl of Angus did not pay his promised debt. If the great Cardinal Wolsey were indeed this girl's godfather, then surely he would not see her lack.

"Tomorrow I will speak with her," said Strangeways, "and find out her mind on the matter."

The following day he sent for his young guest, using diplomacy in the way he asked if the Lady Margaret might spare leisure for a word with him. He had half expected her to be accompanied by her formidable Douglas women, but she came alone; young, slight, and arousing sympathy in Strangeways as indeed she had done since her arrival. But as he had foreseen, a night's sleep under a dry roof had relieved the strain in her eyes and manner, and her gown had been brushed and neatly mended where there had been a rent in it.

He bade her be seated on a high-backed chair behind which his lady's needlework adorned the wall, and she did so quietly, arranging her skirts as though they were fashioned of satin and, thereafter, folding her small hands restfully in her lap. Strangeways was amazed at the delicacy of the roughened hands, used as he was to raw-boned Border women. From what royal ancestor had Margaret Douglas inherited such hands? He could not know that a century back, her great-grandmother Elizabeth Woodville had beguiled Edward IV with just such delicacy of bone and such silver-fair hair.

"You desired to speak with me, Captain Strangeways." It might have been, he thought with amusement, a queen with whom he spoke; where had this waif got her assurance? Douglas pride, maybe, instilled into her at Tantallon, over the years when Angus had held the Scots King prisoner and ruled the land. But the Lady Margaret's situation was very different now, and Strangeways sought to warn her as a part of his self-imposed duty. "My lady, I did so desire," he said bluntly. "It has exercised my mind much over the past twenty-four hours as to what form your visit should take."

"You mean whether or not I am to be treated as a prisoner?" He was surprised both at her quick understanding and her acceptance of the situation. She smiled suddenly, the gesture transforming her whole face and reminding him that she was still a child. "I would welcome close guard, sir. You may not know that I – that we, for the past year, have lived often as beasts do, under the open sky. It is possible to be weary of open spaces, especially if an enemy may hide behind a bush. Keep me as close as you will: I'm happy with stitchery if some can be found for me, and – and if news may come now and again of my father. He promised to send word."

Angus promised also to send money, thought Strangeways wryly; but he would believe that when it came. At present the Earl would, he doubted not, go south to try his luck with King Henry. Meantime it might not suit the English King ill if his niece were well treated at Berwick. "You would not," said Strangeways kindly, "care to pleasure yourself by visits to the booths here, and to walk about the town a little? As you will know, this was once a great seaport in the days of your Scottish ancestors, and we still have trays of trinkets to marvel at, ribbons and such things as maids crave. It might divert you and your women to visit the market on a weekday."

A fleeting expression of alarm, like that of a hunted animal, had shown in her eyes. She raised a hand to her bodice, where a thread hung about the neck with some weighty thing, perhaps a crucifix, inside her gown. "Sir, I beg of you do not allow us freedom yet! Not only do we have little to spend, but my half-brother the King of Scots has guards posted across the breadth of the Border, and word will have reached him by now that we are in Berwick. If he knows that we are to be met with easily in the streets and booths, he may well make a raid and capture us even in your own town. I – I feel safe in the castle." Her fingers plucked at the thread.

He noticed that she had referred meticulously to her half-brother, as though to keep James V at a distance even in her thoughts. "You fear the King of England your uncle less, then, than the King of Scots?"

He was trying to draw her out; not only would his lady, as

37

he knew well, question him later as to what had been said, but he himself was curious about the newly independent King James, young as he was, and little known abroad as yet. How would he rule? Would there be peace on the Borders now, as there had been in the time of his dead father James IV, who had governed with a strong hand? But meantime Margaret Douglas's young mouth had hardened, and she took some time to reply.

"I am a Douglas and we do not fear anyone under God. But many may have reason to be wary of my half-brother. When he was a boy at Stirling he stabbed a porter with his knife for refusing to open the castle gates at his command. He has a violent temper, and can be cruel. His usage of my father who was good to him, and of my old great-uncle whom he said he loved, bear witness to that. I would sooner remain a wanderer on the earth's face than return to him; we were reared separately, and have no love for one another."

"But your mother the Queen surely has some affection for Your Grace; she would take your part in such a quarrel." Strangeways knew that he was exceeding his duty in plying the girl with questions; what he had not expected was her sudden withdrawal, like a snail into its shell, at mention of her mother.

"I have no wish to speak further on the matter," she told him coldly. "If you will arrange a guard, you will have my gratitude and, no doubt, that of my uncle the English King and of the Cardinal of York, who is my godfather." A slyness had entered her looks as she spoke of the Cardinal, as though she knew well enough his power in the land and that Strangeways would be impressed by the reference.

He responded. "I had thought of writing to the Cardinal," he said with some weight.

Her lashes were still lowered. "Pray do so." Was she lying? If indeed she had the Cardinal's protection, then he himself need not fear having the guardianship of her. One way or the other, it should be ascertained; he would write tonight.

Margaret Douglas rose to her young height, curtsied formally and left abruptly, leaving Strangeways in the middle of a bow which hid his half-angry flush at the snub. As his wife would say, who did my young lady think she was, kings, queens and cardinals notwithstanding? She had come here in rags and distress, and relied on him, Thomas Strangeways, for the food she ate

and the bed she slept in. It would have been becoming in her
to be more humble. "But ah! poor lass, what is to become of her
in the end?" thought the castellan, who was kindly at heart.
The Queen of Scots had cast off her husband, and was unlikely
to take him back; unless his fortune sped with the King of
England, he was in sore straits, and his daughter with him. It
said something for her that she had chosen to follow her sire,
with all discomfort, rather than remaining in the luxury of
Stirling or Edinburgh.

In any event, he had decided what he must do. Meantime he
would provide Margaret Douglas with the guard she asked for,
and would keep her close, that being what she wanted, until
word came from the Cardinal or from King Henry in the south.

That night Madge had an evil dream. She dreamt she was back
at Holyrood with her mother, in one of the small rooms whose
walls bore swags of flowers all painted on the new-fangled plaster
King James IV had had spread over the chilly stone walls at
the time of his marriage with the Rose of England, twenty years
back. Then Madge's mother had been indeed a rose, and poets
had written of her bright beauty. But now, since the smallpox,
she was disfigured. All that was in the dream; and the Queen
was behaving as she often did, in a noisy wanton way, for there
were men with her in the chamber. One of them, who had come
in without ceremony and tossed his plumed hat on the bed,
went across to Queen Margaret and cast an arm about her
and kissed her, thrusting his free hand down into her bosom.
The Queen laughed, and slapped his face lightly and called him
her handsome wretch, her dear Harry Stewart, but his eye, for
he was two parts drunk in the dream, lighted on Madge where
she stood by the wall. He tried to come to her, but the Queen
detained him with a plump white hand, and clung to him so
that he could not leave her, laughing still out of her pock-marked
face, but with no laughter in her eyes.

"Never that," she cried, "you are for me, Harry, and shall be
my husband; what do you say to your brother the captain of
Doune having my daughter? Will that not be a fair exchange for
all parties?" And swiftly the flower-painted room was filled with
loud drunken laughter, and smelled of perfume and wine and
sweat. Hands seized Madge then, and she saw a face come close

39

to her own; a man's lecherous avid face, the eyes suffused with blood from heavy drinking. He kissed her, and she smelled his breath foul with wine; his hands explored her body briefly, then left her.

"She is but a child still, Your Grace. Maybe come Yule..."

Madge woke, to find herself at Berwick, filled with fear and terror still. Christian and Marjory Douglas, Lady George's young daughters who shared her bed, slept quietly. She listened to their even breathing, still with the remembered loathing of the captain of Doune's fingers pinching, probing. He had winked as he left her. "Be not so proud, my young lady. I warrant when ye have a man in your bed ye will be lusty, like your dam."

There should have been an end to the dream, she knew. She should have run out through the winding dark passages and down the twisting stairs to where the stars shone through the door, crying out "Take me from my mother! Take me from the Queen who means me ill!" And out of the darkness had come her father's voice, warm and reassuring, and he had wrapped his cloak about her and taken her in his strong arms.

"You shall not be left with Her Grace again, Madge, I promise it. We shall be together, the two of us, you and I." But his promises were not always kept, and now again he had left her alone; and the dream was no dream, as she knew, but bitter memory, thrust down in her mind by day. There was no strong father now to run to; she had only her wits to trust. But here at least she was guarded by her own request, and the King of Scots might seek for his "dearest sister" in vain. She would never return to him and to such a mother.

The time passed at Berwick and Strangeways began to have a grim look about the mouth. He had received a letter from the Cardinal, begging him to guard his god-daughter, so that part was true enough; but no money had come with the letter. Neither, despite his promises, was there any from the outlawed Earl. Perhaps he need not have expected that. But the young lady and her train were costly to keep, and he would be glad when he heard from the King of England that he might hope for recompense.

To Madge's Great Joy, the Earl of Angus returned to Berwick within the month. He was jaunty though still shabby, with an air of secret elation which she knew by now meant that he had met with success in some manner, somewhere. Dared she ask him if her half-brother had relented a little, perhaps enough to allow them all to return to Tantallon?

They walked together about the parapets of the grey castle, with a late-summer wind whipping at the cloak the Earl wore and at his daughter's blue petticoats made down from a dress of Lady Strangeways' own. Angus surveyed his daughter with satisfaction. During the stay at Berwick Madge had filled out with the good food and rest and her skin no longer had the colour of a vagrant gypsy's. She was fair as a rose, Angus thought, with the shining hair washed and combed becomingly, enclosed by a small round hood against the wind: more beautiful than her mother had ever been. Angus had no love for the Queen's Grace and any feeling he had ever known for her had been prompted by ambition. It pleased him that he could feel affection for the daughter she had borne him. He hid a smile behind his hand as they walked. Nothing must be said here about that other love of his, wild strange Janet of Traquair with whom, very often, he had rested awhile from his wanderings, refreshing the love they had felt for one another ever since he'd ridden home alive from Flodden to find his first wife dead. He had cared nothing for *her* either, a puling Hepburn girl who had died in childbirth

41

when she was scarce more than a child herself. He had gone
to Janet and found her spinning at her window, and in the gape
of surprise she had shown at seeing him safe back when so many
lords were dead he had taken her hand from the wheel, and her
body to her bed, and they had lain there a long while making
love and murmuring. It had not been possible then to acknowledge Janet or the child she later bore him, for he was already in
pursuit of the widowed Queen by the advice of his ambitious
old grandfather, Lord Drummond, and that equally ambitious
prelate, his uncle Gavin Douglas, Bishop of Dunkeld. It had been
like plucking a full-blown blossom from the stem to wed the
Queen, and soon afterwards, when the petals were fallen – Angus
smiled again at the analogy – Queen Margaret began to repent,
but the marriage was made, to the scandal of Scotland. They had
borne with one another for a while, but her crazy schemes to
kidnap the young King into England warned Angus away from
her, and he had returned to Janet then, in time to hear of the
birth of this half-English lass of his, by the Queen, at Harbottle.
Thereafter it had been a matter of gaining possession of the
girl from her masterful mother. By now he had weaned Madge
away; but what use of it all when they were fugitives? However
he had a plan –

Madge had brought herself to ask, in the meantime, if they
were to be permitted to go back to Tantallon. "Will it ever
happen?" she asked, blue eyes on his face. "I – I loved it well."
Above all other places, the great red castle had been her home;
she had had to be beholden there to nobody, not to the wife of
Strangeways who was beginning to cast sour glances at the food
they all ate and to make remarks concerning the coming winter;
nor to Strangeways himself, who had been very civil for a while
after the Cardinal of York had answered his letter bidding the
captain give her, his godchild, every comfort. He had certainly
done so, but lately some matter was amiss; Strangeways no longer
smiled when the Cardinal was mentioned, and Madge knew that
they were less welcome at Berwick than they had been. But
how to explain all that to her father, striding along here against
the wind looking as if he were king of the world? How handsome
he was, the grey in his beard not spoiling the smooth, agreeable
cast of his features or his shrewd knowing eyes! Aunt Alison
Hume, the only one of all his sisters at home who would speak

her mind about him, said the Earl was a rogue. It was maybe true, but how much better than to be a dull and prosy man like her uncle William, the erstwhile Abbot of Holyrood, who had lost his benefice!

"No, Madge, lass, it may be we will not see Tantallon again till both King and Queen are dead."

"But that will be – " She put a hand to her throat. How could a young man like the King die, except by murder? And as for her mother – "Do they think to kill the King?" she asked fearfully.

"I didna kill the lad when he was three years under my ward, and it's not like I'd do so now. Your Aunt Janet breathes vengeance at Glamis, but the King has ta'en all her goods from her in the north, for aiding us. There is not one of our clan but is persecuted in whatever way he can devise: when James hates, it is forever." He forebore to add that that was the Tudor blood in the King; for had not his daughter Tudor blood as well?

"Why does he hate you so?" she said. "You guarded him, and he won free. Is that a reason for hating a man for life and hounding all his family?"

Angus looked away. "There is another reason," he said in a low voice. "Madge, ye are near a woman now and I may speak of things I could not before, when ye were a child. Ye spoke of murder. There was murder done, not to the King, but to his dear friend, the Earl of Lennox, who had twice tried to wrest the King from me. Lennox was killed before James's eyes at a fray we had outside Linlithgow."

"By your hand?" she said fearfully.

"Nay, by Hamilton of Finnart's. But Lennox – he was a big fine man, and kindly – had surrendered himself, and Finnart did him to death thereafter. That was a dishonourable thing, but I was not by to hinder it; and on the way your uncle George Douglas had told the King, who was trying to aid Lennox by delaying, that we would let his body be torn in pieces if they tried to take him from us. Those are words James will not forget, nor would any man."

"So the King hates us," she said, "and will not have us return to Scotland. What is to become of us, my father?" She looked at the English bastions, the glittering Tweed and the sea; they could not stay here forever. Would it be France again, with

43

the long-nosed king less ready than ever with his welcome? But Angus was laughing, showing his teeth in his beard.

"Fear not, my lass; there are friends in England, in the south, where our thoughts must turn."

"The Cardinal?" For long her mind had dwelt on the great Cardinal Wolsey, her godfather, and whether he would soon send money to take the sour look off the face of the captain's lady. He was very rich, they said. Within herself she realised, wryly, that she had got into the way of accepting aid; there was nothing else to be done. But Angus was frowning, and she thought also of Strangeways' frown at mention of the Cardinal. Her quick mind encompassed it; something had occurred to weaken the great churchman's power, but what could it be? He was the King of England's minister, she had heard, entrusted with matters of great import abroad. Had he managed them badly? Could so great a man be brought low? It was possible; they themselves, the Douglases, the greatest in the land, had so fallen. The sound grey stone of Berwick seemed to shift beneath her feet, as Tantallon had done. Was there any safety in all the world?

Angus had taken his time to speak. Whether to tell the girl all of what he had heard rumoured, or not, he was uncertain. In the end he decided to keep his counsel. King Harry fancied a wench, and wished to wed her, but he had a wife already. It was a situation which had happened before and would again. It might pass over. Meantime, if Madge were to go south to her kin as he hoped, it might be better were she to know nothing, as the other young folk there would know nothing, yet. He let his brow clear, and turned to her.

"The Cardinal is old and ill, and has lost the King's favour for the time. He could not help you greatly even if he would. There is another, and a greater, source of help, which I must sound carefully. A wrong step could put us in great jeopardy."

"You mean the English King, my uncle?"

"Ay . . . and his wife, Queen Katharine, and your own aunt, the Duchess of Suffolk. There are still kind hearts in high places, Madge. I do not think ye will spend Yule at Berwick, lass."

Yule. *I warrant when ye have a man in your bed* . . . she was still near enough that danger.

"I shall go south gladly," she said, and suppressed a shiver of fear at the unknown. All these folk her father named meant

44

nothing to her, except that she had heard that her uncle the King of England was handsome, and played tennis and the lute. The Duchess of Suffolk would be her mother's sister. "Pray God she is not like my mother," thought Madge, "or I shall have exchanged one state for another like it, after travelling far."

"The wind grows cold," said Angus kindly, and wrapped his cloak about her as he had done that time at Holyrood. "Fear not that we shall be long parted, daughter. I am constantly about your business that it may fare well."

IN AN INN in the town of Berwick, later, the Earl joined another traveller who sat at a bench alone; his brother, George Douglas, whose fierce lady had lately journeyed back, despite the danger, to Scotland to their two young sons. George raised his head as his brother came in. He was less handsome than the Earl, with a narrow, shrewd face and a beard less jauntily set. He was beginning to savour all things English. He beckoned the serving-maid to bring the pair of them flagons brimming over with English ale. Angus sipped and grimaced at the wry taste.

"A watery sour drink," he said, staring out beyond the inn-door where all manner of folk jostled one another in the street which had once belonged to Scotland's finest seaport in old time. It was market-day, and they might not long have this corner to themselves; but he had grown as weary of the hospitality of the castellan of Berwick as that knight had of him, and he had chosen to meet with his brother here, watching the short-legged ponies of the Borderers go by, and the pedlars with their orange-apples and marchpane and gingerbread, and sometimes even those dark folk who had come to Scotland in his grandfather's time and been treated with honour, for they called themselves the Kings of Little Egypt. One of them, a woman, had pressed him for silver today on the way in and said she would read his hand. Angus had refused her. He would make his own fate, whatever it was.

George stared down into his ale. "I have drunk worse," he said, "and stayed in worse places. They tell me, in word sent by

46

Janet's man of Glamis, that my lady has won home to Pittendriech, where the King's wrath will surely not follow her." Janet, Lady Glamis, that most beautiful of all the sisters, solitary now that her quarrelsome husband Clang-Causey was dead, sent them aid and news whenever she could.

"And the boys?" asked Angus, who had not been sorry to lose his squinting, coarse-visaged nephew, young James Douglas, though he liked the elder boy well enough, who was delicate.

"Davie coughs his soul out, as always, and James has disguised himself as a farm-labourer, and goes where he will."

Angus threw his head back and laughed. "I doubt James Douglas will carve his own way without aid from any man."

"Ay. What of yourself, Archie?" The two brothers were on close enough terms for Christian names; from as early as he could recall George had been Angus's henchman, and whoever was his brother's foe was also his own.

"I ride to Traquair."

"Again, so soon?"

"Again, so soon."

"Yon woman has laid a spell on ye."

"Maybe."

George Douglas began to remonstrate. "My lord, are ye daft? The news of the Queen's divorce of ye can but harm your interests with the English King; best go there and obtain a hearing of him. Did ye tell the lass?"

"That her mother has taken the notion to divorce me at a time when our fortunes are lowest? No, for I shall see to it that no harm comes to Madge, to disinherit her."

"If the English King owns her bastard, there is little ye can contrive, Archie."

"Except to refuse to marry again, to refuse to accept the divorce as on both sides. The marriage, God knows, was made in holy kirk, and our uncle Gavin himself married me to the Queen that day. Such things cannot be undone for such reasons as she has given."

He brooded over the reasons. The most preposterous of them was that James IV was not dead, but had gone, unbeknownst to the Queen herself, as a pilgrim to the Holy Land after Flodden to make reparation for his sins. Another reason was that Angus had kept the Queen's daughter from her. His mouth tightened. That last she should have good reason to hold to.

"I doubt if King Harry will take the news of his sister's divorce kindly. She is thought highly of by no one since she took young Harry Stewart of Avandale to her bed. I think it may be a sign in our favour when we win to His Grace – His Majesty." Angus smiled in his beard, recalling how lately the English King had adopted the more glorious title by contrast with that which was used also for prelates and dukes of the realm. He had heard that James of Scotland now also demanded the title of Majesty. A twinge of regret crossed his mind at the loss of that wilful yet charming red-haired boy. He had kept him under close guard, it was true, but had felt as if he were the lad's own father, and now –

George answered his thoughts, as often happened between them. "My lord, would ye not desire to remarry and beget sons of your own body? It is an ancient earldom, and all to go to a lass."

"She shall not have more taken from her than has been done," said Angus shortly. Guilt gnawed at him for the way Madge was obliged to live on charity, but he dared not take her back into Scotland for the present. She was the only card left in his hand; he would get her south to King Henry, once he had made certain the latter monarch would not return her to her mother. For that, caution would be necessary; best wait on events, which changed at present from day to day. Bitter laughter beset him. The Tudors shifted like sand in their marriages! They said the young woman, Nan Bullen, who had bewitched the King had long black tresses, like Janet of Traquair . . .

"What has befallen Lennox's sons?" said Sir George à propos of nothing. He was fingering the dagger with which he had helped dispatch the Earl of Lennox after Linlithgow. The two brooding Scots faces made folk coming into the inn avoid their table, though they did not know who the cloaked and armoured travellers were. Angus looked up, surprise in his eyes.

'Why do ye ask of them? They were taken, I believe, to France. Maybe James will send for them when his kingdom is in order again."

"That will take a while, and the Lennox boys are younger than he."

Sir George called for another round of ale. Presently they both went out and on their separate ways; the one to the south, the other north to Traquair.

MADGE RODE DOWN into King Henry's England by the same ways her mother had taken to come north as a bride; by Alnwick, Morpeth, Newcastle, the Austin Friars at Durham, and Branforth where she stayed a night. This was reported in a letter sent secretly south, to that most confidential of creatures, the King's man Thomas Cromwell; his greyish, swinish face bent over the news that the King's niece travelled south, assimilating it with other information. By Hexham and Allerton she had come, Newburgh and York at last, with its Minster pointing to the sky as it had done the day her young mother had gone to Mass there long ago in cloth of gold, a belt of gems, and a necklace all studded with stones of the Orient. But the Archbishop's palace, where Queen Margaret had then held court, had no host now and no word for them. What ailed the Cardinal?

It was cold, wintry weather. No echo of Her Grace of Scotland's still unforgotten singing minstrels, trumpets and sackbuts playing with "high woods sounding" and horsemen curvetting to the sounds of their own bridle-bells, rang as the Queen's daughter went by. There was only the sharp wind singing in the streets, from which folk hurried indoors whenever they could; and Madge drew closer the coney-lined hood which Lady Strangeways, to her surprise, had given her on parting with the escort which Sir Thomas himself was to lead south.

"It is scarce worn, my lady, and will keep your ears from the cold."

Madge, spurring her mount between the silent captain of
Berwick and his men-at-arms, wondered whether her father had
ever paid the captain what he owed for her three months' stay,
with all her train. It was perhaps better not to ask. Lady George
and her daughters had departed back into Scotland, trusting the
King there would not make war on women: but Lady Archibald,
with all of hers, still rode behind. It was uncertain what would
become of so large a family of aliens in London. "Will my aunt
of Suffolk agree to house them as well as myself?" Madge wondered. It did not seem likely, although one was given to understand that Her Grace of Suffolk was both charitable and kind.
"She is my mother's younger sister," the girl thought again, "and
was once Queen of France."

Her mouth set. It was to be hoped the Queen-Duchess would
be different from the Scots Queen. Now, with every beat of the
horses' hooves, Scotland itself was left further behind, and the
hunt for her own person lessened and with it the dreaded forced
return to her mother. Perhaps aunt Suffolk would be merciful.
Madge raised her hooded head and sniffed the air. It was good,
although she had herself requested the guard at Berwick, to be
free again. Freedom was a thing one did not miss till it was
taken away. "I hope I may always be free hereafter," she thought.
Whatever lay ahead must be faced, nevertheless, as the past had
been.

South of York they overtook a procession; men-at-arms wearing
the Percy livery and plodding with unwonted slowness through
the mud. Strangeways' mouth took on its grim look: he opened it
to speak and then closed it again. Presently Madge saw the
reason. In the midst of the men-at-arms was a stout heavy-
browed old man, placed on a mule, their prisoner. His ankles were
strapped to the stirrups; he must be a malefactor. Yet –

Strangeways was murmuring something in a low voice to his
second-in-command. Both men stared ahead of them, and did
not acknowledge the jolted figure on the mule. Madge stared at
him for moments, then turned her own eyes away, seeing with
pity that he was a sick man. The heavy eyebrows were drawn
together with pain, and his skin had a greyish tinge. "Who can
he be, sir?" she asked Strangeways, when they were past. Such
escort argued a person of importance, and yet the old man himself seemed of little enough consequence by the way he rode.

The captain laughed heartlessly, the sound being borne back on the wind.

'That is his Grace, the Cardinal Archbishop of York, riding back to his earthly reckoning; as for the other, it is a matter for his conscience, I doubt not." But Madge halted her horse, and would have turned back to wait for the escort to make up on them. Strangeways laid a hand on her bridle.

"Do not turn," he said sternly. "In the name of God, my lady, ride on!" But she reasoned with him.

"Cardinal Wolsey is my godfather, and has been kind to me; he wrote to you at Berwick on my behalf. Permit me to go and ask his blessing." But he only dragged the harder at the bridle, his face flushed with sudden anger as well as with the wind.

"Hear me, madam, ye are suppliant to the King's Majesty, and whether ye eat off silver plate, or maybe eat at all, depends on his whim. The first thing to learn is that the King must not be displeased – God's blood, before we even reach him, to have a Percy man report that the Lady Margaret Douglas knelt before a felon, under the King's displeasure and on the way to death! It is for your good I say it."

"I fear he may die before he reaches the King," she said sadly. It was true; there had been death in the old man's face. What could the Cardinal have done to fall so swiftly, and from so high a place? She ventured to ask Strangeways but he growled at her to hold her peace; he was not often discourteous, and between her concern at this, and her shame at having to disown the Cardinal whom in the days of his power, she knew, had been courted, even pestered by her mother on her behalf, Madge asked no more. Nor did any come to her later to tell her, in the privacy of the Carmelite cell where she lodged at Doncaster, for they had all of them ridden straight through Pontefract. The captain and his men slept at an inn; within a few days now, they would be within sight of London.

Madge found that she could not sleep, despite the day's weary ride. She stared at the whitewashed walls of the cell, which the moonlight showed silver with blackest shadows where the crucifix and the Flemish wash-basin stood. She could not forget the face of Wolsey and the change in his state; such power kings wielded, and if they were pleased one was raised to the heights of possession and influence, and if they were angered, it all fell down like a house of cards. She prayed for the Cardinal, her father, and herself; might she never anger the English King by anything ... They had told her, often for he was much spoken of in Scotland, that he was a generous prince, and liked merry faces about him, especially in women. She must learn, accordingly, to smile, and laugh. It should not be so difficult, provided her father might come to see her at times, and she was made safe from a forced return to the Queen her mother. If King Henry took a liking to her, if she was merry enough, he might bid her stay nearby him, perhaps with his daughter, the Princess Mary, who after all was her own age and had, Madge's father had told her, an establishment at Beaulieu in Essex. How many new places there were to know and see, and how different the rich flat lands through which she had ridden today and yesterday were from the barren, troubled north! Yet something in her blood would always cry out to be north of here, within sound of the sea. Perhaps one day, when the Queen no longer desired to make sport of her, and the Scots King's anger was appeased, she could return ...

She drowsed, and before she slept it seemed as though trumpets sounded. A litter surrounded by men in green and white livery with the entwined arms of Scotland, a rose and a portcullis passed by, and a girl in a rich gown looked out from among the litter-cushions: her mother, long ago. The two countries had almost been one then, thought Madge: and turned to sleep.

They came within sight of London at last, and at the same time as a thickening and darkening of the air, like a distant threat of storm, there arose distant spires and towers against the dull sky. Likewise there was a bustle of traffic upon the road, both going and coming. Country carts, voided of the produce they had taken in laden at dawn, were making homeward, with the flat-capped drivers nodding over their mules, sometimes with their wives seated beside them with purchases made in Cheapside and Friday-street. Into the city hastened parties of riders such as that among which Madge was travelling: some showed livery, so that one could tell who they were and whence they came, but not their reasons for coming into London. Everyone was intent on his own affairs; a party of friars rode together, the great cross sewn on their grey tunics proclaiming that they came from the City, as Strangeways told her. The castellan seemed familiar both with the traffic and the place, and it was possible to be aware that before he had been posted to the charge of Berwick he had ridden, perhaps many times, back and forth to the capital to the King. But after their sight of Wolsey and his curt words then, Madge did not care to ask him further questions. She would be given an answer in due time, no doubt, if she held her peace.

Soon the mired, rutted roads gave thankful place to cobbles, and by now on either side there were houses pressed so close that women, wrapped in shawls and cloaks against the cold, could lean out of upper windows almost to give a hand to a neighbour opposite; gossip was exchanged or washing hung out on a hempen line stretched between the houses, so that it festooned the street like tapestry hung out on a feast-day. Below, braziers with burning coals made thick smoke, and vendors sold hot muffins or roast chestnuts from Spain. Their raucous cries vied with a tune a lame fiddler had struck up, the antics of a tame bear held by a leader, and the screams of scampering barefoot children. The riders jostled those on foot, sometimes flinging a coin to make amends: in places there were long middens, giving off an evil smell even in this cold weather. Once they passed a lady's litter, but the plump hooded face that looked out between the curtains was that of a merchant's wife; she clutched a little dog to her. There was nobody of note in the streets. Madge found tongue to ask Strangeways concerning it, it was so different from Edinburgh; was the Court gone out of town?

"Not at this time of year," he replied, "but great folk travel by water. Wait a little and you shall see the Thames."

They came on it at last, and with it the jumble of houses built on London Bridge, so heavy with them that it was a wonder it stood the weight despite its mighty stanchions. Above, on the bearings of the bridge itself, were shrunken heads of criminals, borne on long poles. Folk came and went across the bridge as if it were a common bridle-path, not heeding the wide grey water beneath which could swallow them with their mounts and bear them away, except that it also was filled with craft and barges going to and fro. Madge looked down fascinated at the world-famous river. She had the feeling that all of life was centred here, in London. "It is surely the heart of the world," she thought. How could her mother have borne to leave it? For the first time she herself had forgotten Tantallon and the childhood she had left behind. Excitement surged in her veins like wine: she felt her cheeks flush with it.

London, thou flower of cities all per se. The poet Dunbar had written that when he had come south for her mother's betrothal. Had his weary journey, like her own, seemed worthwhile as soon as he glimpsed the spires and barges?

There was a small crowd nearby the water-steps. Without thinking what she did she reined her horse in, to gape like them, she told herself. A great barge was coming at speed down the Thames, with the long wooden poles of its oars moving swift and evenly; Madge marvelled at their rhythm, so many men pulling as one. The barge was covered with rich gilding, and the sound of music came over; in the centre, beneath an awning, sat two figures, a big handsome man in a plumed hat and a woman wrapped in furs, her dark hair showing plainly beneath a black hood set with gleaming pearls. So much had Madge time to see, and to note the woman's face, which was thin and sallow with great dark eyes. The man in the plumed hat inclined his head to her as they passed, and made some remark in her ear; she smiled, and the folk on the bridge set up a roar.

"It is the King himself," said Strangeways' voice at Madge's elbow. "You have lost no time in obtaining a sight of him." But she had taken no leisure to look at the big richly-clad figure of the man, being too intent on the woman who bore him company.

"Was that the Queen with him?" she asked the captain. He gave a wry smile, and edged the horses on their way.

"No. You shall see the Queen in time, I doubt not, and the Princess Mary their daughter. But now we go to wait upon your aunt the Duchess of Suffolk, who was also a Queen; see that you use all courtesy to her, for should she befriend you she will give you a home." He spoke as he might have done to his own daughter, for so he had come to think of her in these past months. He moved on, and Madge was perforce obliged to follow lest their train crowd the way too greatly; but she did not forget the strange dark woman who sat by the King, especially as she heard some folk in the crowd murmur after the royal barge had gone by.

"Nan Bullen was with him. The goggle-eyed whore. What can have bewitched him in her when he has so good a wife? But all men are so."

Madge lowered her eyelids and rode on. She had her answer.

54

Already she had become discreet enough to say nothing of what she had heard. It seemed a long time since she had been an impulsive child who was hurt because the Scots King would hardly show her his talking parrot. The world was a strange place, and perhaps one could not walk in it without danger. What had become of the Cardinal by now, who had been so great in the land, and now was nothing? Perhaps she would hear at the Duchess of Suffolk's house, if she kept her ears open.

There was much coming and going about the palace of Stepney, where the Princess Mary Tudor, younger sister of King Henry, ex-Queen of France and present wife of Charles Brandon, Duke of Suffolk, stayed when she was in town. Straw blew in the court-yard from the horses' stablings, with two grooms in the Suffolk colours sweeping it up; a great destrier which had belonged to Suffolk himself in the days when he rode in the tourney, and which was still cherished by him, was led past as they rode in, its nostrils flaring, eyes glinting red at the sight and smell of strangers. There was orderliness about the place, for the Queen-Duchess and her husband kept few servants for the size of their household and those who were here must work. Madge was helped out of the saddle by a groom who laid aside his brush, and then everything seemed to merge into a blaze of light and welcome, and the embrace of a fairylike little lady whose dulled gold hair was held in place by a plain coif, like any housewife, and her gown was not of the first fashion, and much worn.

"My own sister Margaret's girl! How tall you are grown, taller already than I!" She held Madge back, assessing her young height with kind blue eyes whose depths held a hint of sadness. Madge had made her curtsy, knowing that this was not only a Duchess and royal princess but an anointed queen. Mary Tudor had been married against her will to old Louis XII of France when his wife Anne of Brittany died, and everyone said she had danced Louis into his grave within weeks, thereafter marrying her true love Charles Brandon, whom the King of England had unwillingly, for he was much angered at the marriage, created Duke of Suffolk. At the clasp of the small, eager hands which drew her inside the palace Madge knew a sensation of tears at the back of her throat; this was the first of humankind since leaving Tantallon who had made her feel that she was welcome for her own sake, not grudgingly admitted as a fugitive. Already she loved her aunt the Queen-Duchess. The awareness remained with her all through the meetings with strange new folk assembled inside the hall; a big narrow-eyed bear of a man in a fur-lined robe who turned out, surprisingly, to be the same Charles Brandon Mary loved and had married in defiance of the might of both England and France. He bowed over Madge's hand punctiliously enough, but Madge could not like him. Then there was a girl with hard grey eyes of about Madge's own age, who was Frances Brandon, the Suffolks' elder daughter; and another little slender figure in a brocade gown with huge dark eyes in a heart-shaped face, who was Katharine Willoughby, godchild to the Queen and daughter of the latter's Spanish lady-in-waiting, Maria de Salinas. She was being brought up in the Brandon household. There were others in the hall, assembled about the trestles which had been put up already in preparation for the meal; after she had washed off the stains of travel Madge was conducted to the high table between Suffolk and his Duchess beneath her cloth of estate, and she glimpsed the captain of Berwick being entertained with his men in the hall below. Already it seemed a long time since the day Strangeways had chided her for wanting to turn back for Wolsey's blessing on the road. Imperceptibly she felt herself to have become, in this kindly place, as she was by right, a princess among others of her blood, eating daintily from the platters served by Suffolk's pages at the board. The state they kept did not awe her unduly; it was plainer than that she had been used to at Tantallon, and the meat and game were less fresh, many of the dishes being highly spiced to disguise their staleness. But Madge was hungry from the ride, and ate her fill. Suffolk himself on her left said little, grunting the occasional remark as he stuffed food into his mouth; her aunt on Madge's other side talked gently through the meal, addressing a word now and again to little Katharine Willoughby as well as to her own daughter, who did not always reply and appeared sullen. No doubt she had inherited a certain unpleasantness of manner from her father, Madge decided, and herself tried to atone by speaking whenever she might with the charming little Queen-Duchess, telling her of incidents on the ride, of her stay at Branforth and with the Carmelites. Mary Tudor listened, the great sad eyes fixed always on the girl's face as though she ached to

56

hear more and more; there was a look about her which Madge recognised, fearfully, as ill-health of the kind she had already seen in her kinsman Archibald Douglas of Glenbervie, who was forever ailing, and her uncle George's eldest son David Douglas, who coughed always. They all of them, and her aunt also, had a fragility of flesh which made them seem almost flowerlike, as swift to die as a flower when it is pulled from the stem. Madge thrust fear away from her. She had only this night reached Stepney, and it seemed as if they were glad to have her stay; why bring in thoughts of sickness and of death? But she knew one could die of consumption, especially if one was young: and her aunt Mary was younger, by far, than her mother and their brother the King of England. Perhaps it was no more than a passing rheum with the cold and fog in the streets. She put the thought from her as the talk passed round the board with the food and ale and they were all gay.

Afterwards Madge was told she must share a bed with Frances Brandon. "You have little gear," said her aunt, surveying the smallness of the baggage Madge had brought from Berwick. "We must furbish you with some of Frances's gowns meantime, for you are of a size; and you shall have a bed-gown lined with budge against the cold tonight, for she can spare it. I hope you will sleep well, child; do you say your prayers?" She smiled, half teasingly. Madge replied gravely that she never failed to pray for her father and to ask the saints for his protection.

"Pray too for me," said the Queen-Duchess lightly.

"I will pray for your grace with a glad heart. It is kind of you to let me stay here." Madge, already in the budge bedgown, with the hardness of the golden saints against her breast, wondered if Frances Brandon would mock at her afterwards for praying so diligently as she did; but she would not let such a creature stop her. After the Queen-Duchess had gone out Frances turned to her, shaking the loose brown hair back from her shoulders.

"You need be in no awe of my mother because she was crowned and anointed in Notre Dame," she said disagreeably. "She demeaned herself afterwards by marrying my father for love, it is said. Love! That is not for princesses. My parents are not well received at Court when they go together, I can tell you; my father as a rule goes alone; we only accompany him at Christmas and Twelfth-night, when all the world goes. If you came here hoping to see the King by my mother's means, you will be disappointed. She has no influence." She spoke as she must have heard her adults speak, with certainty and without compassion. Madge lowered her lashes to hide her growing dislike of this cousin.

"I hope for nothing from anyone,' she replied. "I am grateful to my aunt for receiving me, as I said.' She climbed into bed, determined to face away from Frances while she told her beads, not kneeling as she did by custom because of the other's mocking presence. Frances Brandon shrugged, and laughed unpleasantly. She had, as Madge was to find out, a demon sitting on her shoulder because she had been conceived before her parents' marriage was made legal by the King's permission. Her young sister Eleanor was free from such taint.

"You need not make pretence to be so humble, Margaret Douglas," she said now. "I have heard that you are proud enough. Your mother was an anointed queen also, for all she has divorced your father. Such things aren't heard of here."

"They were heard of in France, where Louis XII divorced his first wife.'

"She was a cripple."

Madge flushed, taking up such cudgels as she might: it was the first time the divorce had been mentioned openly to her. "The Douglases are of blood as ancient as any King. They hold themselves as high." Her fingers clutched the golden saints; might she not lose her temper, on her first night under her aunt's roof, to this ungenerous girl!

Frances laughed loudly. "Is that indeed so? Then if they find that you are no uncouth savage, perhaps our uncle will send for you the sooner. You must forgive me if I appeared ungracious; but my lot vexes me. King François would have wed my mother after her old King died, and I would have been a royal princess. He would even have put away his own wife for her. But she'd have none of him, and got herself pregnant by my father, and almost broke the peace England had made with France for the marriage. The people would have stoned her as she passed through Calais with my father, and they had to travel miserably and in hiding till they reached England again, and my uncle's wrath."

"Did the King imprison them for marrying for love?" asked

Madge curiously. She had only once before heard of that emotion in connection with marriage: her mother was said to have married her father "for her plesour", and had angered a great many of the Scottish nobles thereby. Evidently this "plesour" did not last. Such marriages as Madge had known were made by arrangement, the bride and groom often never having met one another before the ceremony. Would she herself ever marry, and would it be for love? She did not understand it, only that her aunt had been brave to risk her royal brother's wrath to wed the Duke of Suffolk, who to everyone else's eyes looked like a bear.

"No, King Henry rated them and cast them from his company, which is why we live from hand to mouth both here and at Westhorpe," said Frances crossly. "Must you talk on, or shall I get my sleep?"

Madge fell silent, fingering her rosary until she too slept, not hearing the watch passing by to call out the hours of night.

THE MONTHS Madge spent with the Duchess of Suffolk were unlike any other period of her life. Short though they were, they moulded her; she was always to be influenced by them, both in her manner of living and in her swiftly developing tastes and loves. Never before, at Tantallon or Stirling, had she seen with her own eyes the loving care of a wife to please a lord and husband she adored. None of the Douglas ladies, whose men were forever away at war, would have soiled their hands with the tasks this royal princess was forever at, because she loved it; making wines, making conceits and syllabubs, watching the bread dough rise before it went into the oven; compounding, from herbs picked and dried at their summer-place of Westhorpe, unguents for the skin and for wounds, medicines for sick children and glutted men. Many of these were from receipts culled from Mary Suffolk's own grandmother, the wise, tiny Countess of Richmond, mother of Henry VII. Madge copied them carefully into a book she kept: she delighted her aunt with her aptitude and thirst to learn, for the Duchess's own daughter Frances scorned all such tasks as fit only for servants, never thinking of the time when she might have to use them in her own household. But Madge's small hands seemed to have a natural facility in fashioning the remedies and possets, and it gave her a joy she had hitherto known only in stitchery when the stuffs beaten in the pestle ran of a sudden into a cream beneath the mortar, and later were put into jars carefully labelled and dated. She would

60

make a good housewife, her aunt said; and for the first time Madge could see herself one day as having a house to keep and a lord she wished to please, and children about her skirts. That was what she wanted, and knew it now; there was plenty of time still to learn as much as she might. If only her children might not be as ungracious as Aunt Mary Suffolk's! "I think if Frances spoke so to me, were I her mother I would slap her," she said one day to Jane Dormer, who was also with the household. Jane smiled her quiet smile, and small Katharine Willoughby, who was with them also, giggled. All three girls disliked Frances Brandon, though they did not quarrel openly with her. She should have been a boy, they agreed; then she could have used up some of her bad temper in horseplay and sword-play with the pages.

On one matter all of the girls did not agree. Jane Dormer and Madge were devout in their religion, Frances and Katharine sceptical and given to argument about things which had hitherto been accepted without question. This disturbed Madge vaguely, for she did not yet know that it was a sign of the times, and that beyond Stepney and Westhorpe differences of opinion raged, from the King down, since before the Cardinal's fall.

The Cardinal was dead. Madge had heard the news with less regret than she knew she should feel, for he had been good enough to write to Strangeways at Berwick to bid him care for her. But her life was so full that she had scant time to remember an old man carried dying to Leicester on a litter. She wished repose to his soul, as would have been done at Tantallon. The girls were alone in the solar when she said it, and Frances laughed.

"You won't be long in favour at Court if you don't mind your tongue. The Cardinal did a disservice to the King and Mistress Nan. *That* wasn't forgiven him, whatever may befall his soul. In his day he had too much pride for a butcher's son," stated the daughter of Charles Brandon. "They say it gave young Percy much pleasure to ride north and arrest him by the King's order; they say too that *he* in his day wanted to marry Nan Bullen, but that the King prevented it and made Percy marry Mary Talbot, with whom he is miserable enough."

Madge bent to her sewing, with an eloquent glance to Jane who sat opposite. How did Frances hear such things? The name of Nan Bullen recurred through all her spiteful talk, never the name of the Queen. Yet the Duchess had promised, only yesterday, that they should all of them go to Court in the new year; at last she would see again, for she had of course no remembrance of meeting him as an infant, the fabled King himself, whom she had forgotten to look at that day in the barge because of . . . Nan Bullen.

Nan Bullen. Madge pricked her finger and sucked the blood. Why was it that that name had the sound of a knell? Perhaps it was by reason of the Cardinal's fall and death by her cause. "I *will* pray for the repose of his soul, whatever they may say," thought Madge, and began to say the prayer for the dead and that eternal light might shine on the soul of the man who had once been the King's greatest minister. Wolsey had shown her nothing but kindness, and she could repay him now in no other way.

Further change came soon. As Frances had scornfully put it, all the world kept the King's Christmas and Yule. There came a time when the Duchess of Suffolk's party, shivering as they ascended the water-stairs, drew their hoods closer against the few flakes of early snow which had begun to fall. It grew thicker as they approached the King's palace, obliterating the marks of other folk who hurried there on foot or were borne, in the common way, by litter. The whole world seemed buried under snow at last, and very cold. Madge clutched her furred sleeve-linings to warm her icy hands. She had forgotten her appearance, with which the Duchess had been pleased, and her gown of black velvet made over from old, very frail stuff which Her Grace had taken with her long ago as part of her royal trousseau to France. It was so delicate it would surely tear with the least strain, but meantime it set off Madge's fair hair, fair skin and blue eyes. But now it did not matter what she looked like, if only she could cease to be cold. Then suddenly, everything was warm; a medley of sensations overcame her, mingled remembrances of gorgeous ushers in red-and-gold livery, bearing staves; the entwined initials HK everywhere on pillars, ceilings, gateways; throngs of courtiers, apple-cheeked with drinking the maids' allowance of two gallons a day of small-ale and more, and giggling with that and the warmth and the promise of merriment to come. Richly clad they seemed, the women in square-necked gowns and jewelled hoods either shaped like a heart or pointed, in the way Nan Bullen had made fashionable, by pinning up the lappets of the long old-fashioned headdress such as the Queen still wore, and giving it an air of gaiety: and the men in great padded shoulders and furred collars and chains, to try and emulate the enormous height and breadth of the King himself who would shortly be seen ... Madge felt, as she had never done before even watching at Norham above the lonely Tweed, the loss of her own identity, that she was no one now, only one more hurrying guest in the throng, not heeded even for a moment among the rest. It came to her that always formerly, all of her life, she had been the centre of attention, some of it unwelcome; now there was none. Loneliness beset her, then the awareness of a strong overpowering personality governing and drawing together all this coloured moving glittering medley of souls, which made her own spirit shrink and become infinitesimal; she cowered inwardly, feeling her limbs already tremble with new fear. Yet what had she to be afraid of, except further change of fortune? And surely, surely now that she was placed with her kind aunt of Suffolk, fortune would spin its wheel for others and leave her be, to go to Westhorpe in the summer and continue her lessons in the apothecary's craft and in cookery, and the way to dry rose petals so that the scent persisted and they did not turn mouldy, and gave sweetness all year.

Then she saw him. She saw the King, and this time was unaware of the others by him, the stout ageing woman with a high forehead and sad, kindly eyes and, near her, a little pale-faced girl. Afterwards Madge would meet those others, afterwards they would come to mean more to her than most, but now ... now there was the King, her glorious royal uncle who towered head and shoulders above everyone here, and whose boisterous laugh rang out like that of Jove, so that his bright curling hair and short beard gleamed and shook with the great laughter and his skin flushed rose as it had been wont to do in the days when, as a young man, foreign ambassadors had written home in marvellous terms of his beauty, his athletic prowess, his clothes covered from head to foot with jewels, his skill on the lute and at rhyming, his learning and wit, the love the very sight of him roused in his people.

That had been in youth. But now Madge loved him instantly and was received into his bear-like embrace like a small piece of flotsam which is taken by a giant wave and borne to shore. She laughed with joy as he tossed her up almost to the painted ceiling and caught her again, and roared, so that everyone in the hall could hear.

"Why, can it be my own niece Marg'et, that I have not seen since she was a babe in a lawn hood? Welcome this Yule, sweetheart, and may it be many more before we lose sight of so pretty a face. A Douglas, eh? But a good Englishwoman now, and no Scot, I swear. See, Kate, here's my sister's girl; no time at all's gone by since we all of us sat beneath a canopy of twined roses after they rode south, and now see how she has grown and how fair she bids to be!"

And he swept Madge round to make her curtsy to his Queen and to their only daughter, the Princess Mary, as though there were no wrong between them in all the world.

II

White Lion

MADGE KNELT in her place at the prie-dieu to which she had been shown, trying to pay heed to the prayers for the nuptial mass which was at this moment proceeding for Henry Howard, Earl of Surrey, and Frances de Vere. She could see their bent necks, the bride's covered by loose hair beneath her rich coif, the bridegroom's startlingly handsome above his padded satin coat. Behind, the relatives knelt, with their foxy Howard faces intent on whatever they were separately thinking; chief among them was the Duke of Norfolk, who had slain Madge's mother's first husband, the Scots King James IV, at Flodden. No one remembered that now, except that Norfolk had got his dukedom because of it. Madge recalled Scotland only as a passing thought, aided by the joyous remembrance that her uncle the King, very lately, had granted her request that her father be permitted to reside at the English Court: he would come soon. Madge slid her fingers through her beads in gratitude. There was, it appeared, very little her royal uncle would not do for her, or give her, to bring her comfort. He had made her very happy. She was happy now, with a certainty that brightened the already brilliant colours spilling from the stained-glass window across the stone of the aisle; red, green and blue, the colours of jewels. And all jewelled, as was customary, was the Court assembled here today; and not the least among them was herself.

She tried to down her satisfaction at her jewels and her gown, which was rich with embroidery, only one of the many the King's allowance gave her and Peter, the embroiderer allotted to her, decked out in dazzling fashion, with much gold and silver and azure thread, velvets and brocades and furs. She had never had so many gowns, or so frequent occasion to wear them. She was becoming, Lady Salisbury the royal governess feared, a peacock in her own estimation; but that had been so kindly said that one took no umbrage against that lady.

Madge bowed her head, aware that the Lady Governess herself knelt two paces away and could easily have an eye to her. If one turned one's head one could see her; black hood, of the older generation, falling forward as she prayed, half hiding the long Plantagenet face. Lady Salisbury had grown thin with fasting and prayer, but she never aired her piety; so long as one was near her, however, a little of it shone on oneself, making one remember to heed the priest as he chanted the *Kyrie,* and join in the orisons as the Queen and the Princess were doing whole-heartedly. But pleasure today made Madge inattentive, and presently she became aware again of those two figures, that of the Princess tiny and erect as she knelt, that of the mother thickened with long and fruitless childbearing so that the Queen was now a dumpy little woman, but with kindness and dignity in her every movement and word. "She has been as good to me as she is to her own daughter," Madge thought, re-membering however that Queen Katharine's chief love of the mind, the speaking and writing of Latin, was a closed book to herself; she could neither write nor speak it as could the Princess Mary, who had been brought up to use it as a second language from her cradle. The Princess could play the virginals, too, as well as anyone. Madge stared at the small intent figure without envy. She loved the Princess Mary, as she had come to love all the royal family, but the Princess and she were near of an age. Their friendship had begun the day Madge came to Court, when the King had greeted her and the Princess had come over after-wards saying, in her gruff friendly voice, "Come, my father has given us money to spend at the play; let's go and spend it," and so they had, and Madge had taken pleasure in the new-fangled pictures the cards bore, with likenesses of the King and Queen, crowned and hooded, on them; it did not take long to accustom oneself to the new style, different as it was from the bells, leaves and acorns she remembered playing with at home. She had won,

and then had lost; the Princess Mary had lost and then won; then
there had been a basse-dance, and they had all of them danced
and laughed and enjoyed the season, and Madge's ancient black
velvet gown had been ripped at the seam, which made them
laugh too. It did not matter now; the King had taken her into his
daughter's household, and she need not stint herself of goods or
gowns any more. How glad she was that she had journeyed into
England! And soon her father himself would be here, living on
the King's bounty also. What more was there to wish for? Madge's
cup was full.

She spared a glance for the Howards again. The bridegroom,
his handsome head erect again now that the prayers were over,
was among the finest; rivalling him in richness of dress was young
Henry Fitzroy, the King's bastard by Bess Blount. Both young
men were poets, and played tennis well. There was a third, with
burning dark eyes, whom she did not know; his gaze was fixed
on herself. Madge almost giggled, so intent was he; who *was*
he? He must be a Howard. There was only one thing to do, and
she did it; lowering her lashes, and affecting to return to her
prayers. Lady Salisbury would surely rate her – no, rate was too
strong a word for that gentle, stately lady – in any event, be
sorrowful that she had so demeaned herself as to exchange glances
with an unknown young man in church. "In fact," she thought,
"it is the first time I have ever been noticed by a young man."
One did not count the sunburnt, grimy Douglas brood, her cousin
James and half-brother George the Bastard, and the rest in the
half-forgotten days along the Borders, when she had been as grimy
as they.

Curiosity stayed with her regarding the young man with dark
eyes; he was hardly more than a boy. Later, after the marriage-
feast, there would be dancing, for which she was to be permitted
to stay. Would she encounter him again then? What a beseeching
glance it had been from someone she did not even know! The
sunlight, Madge was well aware, shone on her hair as it filtered
through the stained glass, and would make her conspicuous, perhaps pretty. These new round hoods showed off one's hair above
the forehead in the way the old French ones had not done. Peter
had trimmed her present hood with pearls, like the one Nan
Bullen had worn that day she had seen her with the King on the
barge on the Thames. Why must she think of that now? Nan

Bullen was a shadow on everyone's happiness. Frances Brandon's spiteful tongue had said something, last time Madge had seen her at Stepney; what had it been?

"The King means to divorce the Queen and marry Nan Bullen. All the world buzzes with it, though it's supposed to be a secret. Nan hasn't let him make her his mistress in all these years, and that is why he's so hot for her. They say she won't give way for less than marriage; her mind is set on being Queen of England."

The sun had gone in and the colours faded. Madge lowered her head and returned fervently to her prayers. The saints no longer reposed inside her bodice, but pinned up in their due places about her bed-curtain. Lady Salisbury had said she was to put them there to watch over her while she slept. It was pleasant to see their bright watchful shapes again, as she had been used to do at Tantallon.

Behind her, the Countess of Salisbury prayed, as she always did, for the Queen and the Lady Mary's grace, that trouble might not come to them. Then she prayed, as was also her wont, for the soul of her murdered brother, Warwick, the last Plantagenet heir to the throne. It was so many years since his blood had stained the scaffold that perhaps no one remembered now except herself. Lady Salisbury cast an affectionate glance at the Queen's stocky, kneeling figure. It should have been in the nature of things that she hate the Spanish bride for whose sake Warwick had been done to death, for the marriage had been forbidden as long as he might live; but she did not hate the Queen, there was much love between them, and she had served the Lady Mary, at the Queen's instance, with all her heart. She would always be loyal. Change came, and God knew some of the changes seemed at first to be evil; but one must accept them as Margaret Salisbury had accepted so many things in her life.

"May light eternal shine on him," she thought of her brother. He had been weak of wit, and had not known, when they brought him to the scaffold, what it was or why he was there. "Life ends for us all, soon or late," thought my lady. Suffering meantime must be offered to God. The Lady Margaret Douglas, in front, seemed assiduous in her prayers. She was a pleasant child, if a thought too eager for grandeur. My lady smiled. That was understandable, when the girl had spent the past two years from hand to mouth living as an Egyptian. One had to make allowances. Even the Princess Mary, whose education had been carefully watched over and tended, loved grand gear.

"I must put in a word for my uncle Tom: he is sore smitten with you."

"Your uncle Tom?"

"He is younger than I and says that you are lily, rose and pure gold; that he has never seen anyone as beautiful in his life; that he is sure such sweetness and gentleness of feature cannot mask a nature that is otherwise. All this he says, and dares not ask that you regard him with kindness – "

They were dancing, among the wedding-guests, a stately pavon, she in her turn with the bridegroom, the young Earl of Surrey; his madcap eyes danced also, and she could not tell whether half he said arose from his poet's imagination or had, in truth, come from the other young man on whose behalf he spoke, his kinsman Thomas Howard, whose burning eyes had devoured her today in church and who was now nowhere to be seen. Madge was used to the company and talk of men; she showed no shyness, if no boldness either, in her reply to Surrey, who besides being a poet, and always sighing after some lady-love or other, was a rapscallion who was often in trouble with the watch, for breaking townsfolk's windows and the like, for his own and his fellows' diversion. Madge smiled; the courtly rhythm of the dance gave her leisure for a thoughtful answer, not as though he had been lifting her up by the waist in a high-dance such as the boisterous King loved. Surrey had long legs; he made her an adequate partner, and she would take note of his spare frame, amusing face and cocksure nobleman's air before dismissing him from her mind, with that other. She smiled; she had a place at Court and an embroiderer and two women in waiting and a half-dozen new gowns, and now it appeared she had a swain also, if this Lord Thomas Howard ever came in person to speak up for himself. "Tell me, my lord," she said, looking up at Surrey, "why if all these conceits came to your kinsman as readily, he had not the address to present himself? I do believe that half of it is in your own mind, to be formed into verse."

"Tom is shy; he is newly come to Court from the country – "

"So am I."

71

" – and he knows that I can frame words more readily than he, but his heart is the more constant in that he does not speak with ease. Be merciful to him, Lady Margaret, I beg you; spare him a word, a token – "

"If I spare words and tokens for young men I shall not long keep my place about the Princess Mary at Beaulieu. Lady Salisbury would look with ill favour on – on such things." The laughter brimmed up in her; she thought for instants of that worthy lady's long face if it were proved that she, Madge Douglas, had a young nobleman already in love with her, who sent her letters and tokens by the mouth of his turbulent, if poetic, kinsman. "Tell me," she essayed, to turn the subject from Lord Tom, who she dared say would embarrass her now if they met, "how it is you frame your verse so readily? I know little of such matters, but – "

"But you had a great-uncle, Gavin Douglas, who wrote some of the fairest verses these hundred years, and he lies buried here in London, where he died of the plague."

"My father comes here also shortly," she said, turning in the dance; her eyes saw her own gleaming kirtle, rich with Peter's embroidery, swing bell-like and then, again, hang still. How glorious it was to dance and be gay! She knew little of poetry, though she had heard of her great-uncle Gavin, the Bishop, who had once written of her mother as bright-haired Venus drawn in her chariot among flowers. Their hands met again, her own and Surrey's, in the returning figure; she curtsied, he bowed to the sound of the rebecks and fifes. "Then Tom will assuredly speak to your sire, for as I say he is sore smitten," said the Earl. The laughter welled up in her; she flung back her hair, which had worked loose from its hood in a spiral of fair gold. "If he cannot speak up for himself, how can he speak to my father?" she said, and left Surrey secretly smiling, in the way of the Howards. Someone else bespoke her for the next dance, and she forgot about Tom Howard and his tongue-tied love. Later she remembered, and marvelled for moments that he should find himself so bold as to address the King's niece, even by proxy. But it was true that the Howards regarded themselves as half-royal, for Norfolk's first wife had been a Plantagenet princess, a sister of the King's dead mother Elizabeth of York. They were grown the more proud since Flodden; at that battle, Norfolk, as he was now, had stood near the Howard standard of a white lion while the Scots King fought his way up the slope to within a lance's length of old Surrey, Norfolk's father, the commander. *We disappointed them of their long spears in which they put their greatest trust.* Where had she read that, or heard of it? And after the battle was over, her own father had ridden home . . .

SHE SAW THE EARL SOON. He came riding down to the Princess's establishment of Beaulieu, high-ruffed in the latest fashion and with his cap set at an angle on his head. Lord George rode by him as always. They made their obedience to the young Princess and to Lady Salisbury, then the Earl requested leave to take his daughter apart. He and Madge walked together up and down the pleasance, for·the delights of Beaulieu did not include stabled horses for the Princess or her ladies to ride out across the flat Essex countryside, and this garden was as near privacy as they might attain. They stared smiling at one another, both aware of changes; unseeing of the tame English flowers which were beginning to open under the gardener's care, the young buds turning a frilled yellow-green, the new grass springing. The Earl was pleased with the changes in his daughter, no longer a brown ragged waif as he had left her, but a serene young woman whose complexion bloomed like the flowers, whose small hands were white and well-tended with rosewater, whose shapely slim body was set off by the heavy dress all the Court wore, with the great turned-back sleeves known as rebas that Nan Bullen, they said, favoured because they gave a diversion which drew folk's eyes away from her secret sixth finger, the devil's mark. But Madge had no such disfigurement to hide. Angus's smile widened; he was proud of his daughter, and of the good words she had put in for him to the King. That monarch had yesterday embraced him, and called him brother-in-law; it was evident that, largely

74

perhaps due to Henry's fondness for Madge, he would not allow
that bedding of her royal mother with Harry Stewart of Avandale
to be spoken of as marriage here, whatever the young Scots King
might say. Affairs in Scotland were against the Douglases where-
ever they might be found, still . . . Angus's smile faded, remembering what he had had in his mind as he rode south. His
daughter's candid eyes searched his face, then she said outright
"Why do you frown, sir? You were gay a moment since, and said
the King received you gladly." Triumph dwelt in her regarding
this; one day some weeks ago, when the King rode to Beaulieu,
he had asked her what he might do for her, and she had said
"Bring my father the Earl, I pray, your Grace, to Court," and
here he was. It completed her joy, which she had thought already
was complete. How much more could God send her? But Angus
was already giving her her answer, and at what he said fear crept
again into Madge's heart, only for moments; the matter now, the
Earl said, was done with; but for how long?

"Your aunt Janet Glamis was accused of poisoning her husband,
who as you know lately died. The jury refused to serve, and they
had to get another; and they found her innocent."

"My aunt Janet . . .' Memories of the beautiful woman who had
come riding once to Tantallon assailed Madge now; she could
remember the long beguiling eyes, the golden hair like her own.
Aunt Janet might be as fair as the Queen of Elfland, but she
had the spirit of a man. Madge knew, had known from her Border
days, that Lady Glamis had often sent money and clothes, and
messages of cheer to the outlawed Earl, her brother. That would
not be forgiven by King James, who had put all Douglases to
the horn. He would even make war on their women if he might
devise it.

She said, "I doubt Clang-Causey would not have suffered himself so to be put down by poison. He was a turbulent man, I
recall."

"Ay, and as we are here I may safely say my sister is well
rid of him. But she would never have hastened his death. The
folk who live in those parts know her well, and never a man
would judge her guilty of so foul a thing. It is all because she
has aided me."

"Well, father, maybe you will no longer need such aid now
my uncle regards you with favour. I am very glad of it."

"I have to thank you, daughter, for your offices." How formal they were with each other! How well she had thought she knew him once, when they rode together knee to knee across a black night's moor or ford, or shared caught game cooked over a bonfire! But now he was older, greyer, hard as whipcord leather, and – she must admit it – sly; his eyes no longer met hers, and she could not find it in her readily to ask what he had been at since last they met, and expect to be given an honest answer. Outlawry made knaves of honest men, that was it; she herself, in constant danger, had for a while grown cautious and sullen, but now –

"My lord, I am so content that I wanted you to share my contentment," she said truthfully, and at that Angus turned to her again and laughed, throwing his elegant head back to show the new-trimmed beard.

"Maybe so. What is this matter of a young man, Madge? Never blush, now; you could maybe do worse than mate with a Howard, for they are near the throne and have done good service to the King's Grace. It is strange to think that I myself once bore arms against this lad's father and grandsire at Flodden."

"He – Tom Howard – has spoken to you?" She laughed, hardly crediting it. Tom Howard had once or twice, with Surrey always by his side, come here, and had behaved with enough decorum to satisfy Lady Salisbury; all he had said at first to Madge herself could not have been construed as loverlike, and yet, she knew, it had been honest.

"I – I have a rough tongue," he had stammered, and she had laughed to put him at ease.

"Indeed, my lord, you have no tongue at all, for your nephew makes all your speeches." And at that Tom Howard had taken fire and had said for himself, not looking at her, "Lady Madge, I – I cannot sleep for thinking of you. I love you more than any living creature."

"More than your falcon, my lord, or your horse?" He was but a boy, she thought. But Tom Howard flushed, and tears came into his eyes.

"You torment me," he said. "I can get another horse and falcon. But since I saw you that day in the church, at your orisons, I have never had a moment's peace till I should be brought to you, and now – "

"And now here I am, my lord, but in no wise so great a matter

76

as you would make me out." She delighted to tease him, and as their acquaintance progressed – for it did so, largely with the help of Surrey, who could not bear to see true love run awry – their relation to one another became almost that of mother and child, for Tom was so sensitive and easily hurt that Madge curbed her teasing, yet loved the power she knew she had to rouse him, if need be, again almost to tears. Tom. He was at once above practical things and yet surrounded with possessions; his doting mother the Duchess grudged him nothing, neither money nor servants, a jester for his diversion, two body-men, a whippet. He was always richly clad and yet cared nothing for riches. He cared instead for her, the King's dowerless niece, who lived on the King's bounty, knowing that she was not the greatest match that he could make; yet Tom would never think of that.

Tenderness showed in her face, and she became aware of the Earl's quizzical glance, and blushed again. "What did you answer Tom, my lord?" she said, and felt her heart beat fast. It would be strange if to her, Madge Douglas, should fall at once everything that could be hoped for in this world, happiness, riches, the King's favour, a marriage both of heart and policy, if that last must be considered. Angus's face showed that it must.

"I told him that it depended on the King," he said. "You are in his Grace's ward, and the only daughter of his elder sister."

"That cannot signify. The Princess Mary is heiress to the throne."

"Strange things may happen. Be not too sure of anything, Madge, till it is under hand and seal. I have been in Court lately, and I know what they are saying."

"What is that?"

He turned his head slightly in the little green pleasance, to ensure that they were still alone. No breath or movement stirred; but as he spoke there came a little cold wind.

"That the King will declare the Princess Mary bastard and divorce her mother, despite the lack of sanction from the Pope who is the prisoner of the Emperor, Her Grace's nephew. Then he will marry Anne Boleyn."

"Anne – " Then she understood; Nan Bullen had glorified the spelling of her name, just as she had done her existence since she had bewitched the King and ousted Cardinal Wolsey. Pity claimed Madge for the friendly, scholarly Princess who had done no man any harm, and as for Queen Katharine – "What will become of the Queen's Grace?" she asked fearfully.

"She has already refused a separate and honourable establishment where she may live as the King's sister; she was married first, as you know, to his brother Arthur who died, and later wed Henry himself. He is claiming now that the marriage is against his conscience, and that that is why God has sent him no sons."

"But after all these years he cannot cast his daughter off like an old clout! And if the Pope decrees otherwise –"

"Keep your voice down," said Angus, glancing at the close hedges. "The Pope may not long be heeded in England if he does so. Say nothing of what you have heard to Lady Salisbury or the Princess, if you value your place."

"I will say nothing to anyone. But is it not iniquitous?"

"Learn to keep your opinions to yourself. Remember we depend on His Grace's bounty. If you should ever meet with Mistress Boleyn, use her with courtesy."

He took his leave shortly after, leaving her sorely troubled in mind. The devout plain face of Queen Katharine at her prayers rose before her, and the other face she knew so well – the Princess Mary, although Madge's own age, who seemed no more than a child despite her wisdom, so tiny and meagre of body was she – with its shadowed eyes, for the Princess had great pain with her courses, and its obstinate mouth which promised resistance to change. How would the Princess take this news if it were true, and who would stand friend to her if she were so degraded? Lady Salisbury, no doubt, would stay loyal; and –

"I myself will not leave her, or forget her in my prayers, no matter what it costs me," thought Madge. For the moment she had even forgotten Tom Howard. But this unsavoury matter could in no way concern Tom, although now she recalled it he was related, in some way through the complicated Howard remarriages, with Nan Bullen; or, as one must now call her, Anne Boleyn.

"They Have Taken my mother away," said the Princess Mary. "I do not think that I shall see her again."

They were alone in the room, the two of them; the maids were elsewhere. The large staff the Princess had formerly kept at Beaulieu was depleted, and by this time there were few about her now the King had ceased to ride down. Madge thought fiercely how she herself would never willingly desert the Princess, whom they were trying to force, now, to cease calling herself by that title. She knelt down by the small rigid figure and put her arms about her cousin.

"Take comfort," she said. "The King's Grace is not cruel. He will not keep you and the Queen apart for longer than it takes a fit of anger to die." King Henry was, as everyone knew, enraged by the obstinacy of the Princess, and the obstinacy of the Queen; failing all else he had decided that to separate them would be to halve their strength. Madge knew also, for it was common knowledge, that Anne Boleyn prevented his coming to visit his daughter. "If he were to do so," she thought, "his heart would surely be softened." She could not think of the King as other than she remembered him from happier times; kindly, gigantic, jolly, generous of heart and purse. He could have no part in this persecution which took place in his name. "You are new to sorrow," she said gently to Mary, "and so it bears hard. Hear me in this; you have at least known the love of your mother, and loved her. Is not that a thing to thank God for?" She thought of her own.

"I have known sorrow," said Mary, still staring out of the window. She had not shed a tear at the Queen's going, and now her young face had the quality of a stone, as if all softness had dried up. She spoke in a flat harsh voice, without emotion, as though to talk would relieve her somewhat. "All my life I was brought up to believe that I was to marry the Emperor my cousin, the greatest prince in the world. I was to be reared as a Spanish lady to please him, as my parents would not have me sent so early into Spain. I learned languages, and Latin, hard for many hours each day so that I might converse with him. I practised playing on the lute and the virginals and regals for his diversion. Once he came to England, and my mother led me by the hand to meet him at the top of the water-stairs. He kissed me, and there were great masques and pageants and much merriment."

"Was he handsome?" said Madge, to try to divert her cousin; it was better, she thought, for the Princess to talk, instead of the continued arid silence, the prospect of bleak window-glass shutting out the wind and trees. Once she herself had stood so at a window, but not for any sorrow as deep as this.

Mary laughed a little, with a small dry sound like a sob. "Oh, no; those one loves are not always handsome. He was very tall and shy, with an underlip that thrust out too far. He was pleased with me, I thought. I was very young at that time. After he went away I heard nothing, and in the end I sent an emerald to him in Spain with the hope that he was faithful to me; they say it pales its green if the lover is untrue. He put it on his finger and said he would wear it for my sake; I never heard whether it lost its hue or not. Then – "

She swung about, so that her back was against the light. "Then I heard he had married a Portuguese princess," she said. "I believe she was very beautiful. They say that word had reached him that my father – even then – had it in mind to – to – "

To disown you and cease to regard you as his heir, Madge thought; and Charles V had played for caution. She sought for words to comfort Mary, but what was one to say? Such a sorrow could have been nothing to what she felt now. There was nothing to do or hope for, except pray. But how could one keep harping on the name of God as solace so soon?

Lady Salisbury had come quietly into the room by the further door; they heard her by the hushing of her skirts. They turned, and answered her stately obeisance. The Countess would never permit familiarity or lack of courtesy, even in times of great trouble; she had lived with formal manners so long that they were natural to her, yet her eyes showed pity and understanding. Her long fingers told her beads; all day, when not occupied with embroidery or reading, my lady would say constant aves and paternosters. Her words told the two girls that she had overheard what they were saying, yet she made no comment on that matter.

"Do you remember, Princess, how you translated as a child a prayer of St Thomas Aquin?" she said. " *'That I fail not between prosperity and adversity, but that in prosperous things I may give Thee thanks, and in adversity be patient, so that I be not lift up with the one, nor oppressed with the other?'* We all of us have our testing time; of what use to pen words by one of the greatest saints if one has no faith?"

"I have faith, my lady; but at such times as now my heart fails somewhat."

"You have a strong heart and mind, and you are young. God sends comfort in His own way."

Madge remembered the times Lady Salisbury herself must have needed comfort; from a girl she had been motherless, and they said her mother died of poison. Her father, Clarence, had been murdered, and her brother sent to the block. Yet she was always cheerful and equable, and no one ever brought her any matter which did not receive its deserts, carefully weighed. Madge asked her shyly "Does God also send us suffering, to try us?" As she asked she thought how small her own erstwhile suffering now seemed; it had only been, after all was said, discomfort of the body, perhaps fear of the unknown. For instants Margaret Salisbury's gaze met hers; the old, deep-set, honest eyes held great kindness. "I do not presume to judge the ways of God," said the Countess, "but be sure that even deep in prison, it is never hard to reach Him, for He is there. And if one offers suffering as part of the suffering of Our Lord, then it is lessened strangely. That is all I know, and live by."

The Princess Mary smiled with stiff lips. "You have both of you brought me comfort, I believe through God. I pray that He will be with my mother also." There were tears in her eyes at last; the tension had left her.

"He will not leave her comfortless," said Lady Salisbury.

81

F

"And I pray also that neither of you are ever taken from me. While you are here I have strength. If I am ever alone – "

"Child, the Lady Margaret hath not her own disposal; she must obey the King, as must we all, and her father. As for myself . . . why, we must every one be alone in the end, as God's Son in Gethsemane. Do not rely on any creature, Your Grace, but only on God."

"But you will not leave me?" said Mary stubbornly.

"Not unless I am commanded; and if I am, remember what I have said, and do not spend that time grieving which is better spent in prayer."

Long years afterwards Madge would wonder if the Countess had a premonition of her own martyrdom. They said it was brought about, at last, failing other evidence against her, by the finding of a piece of embroidery in her house portraying marigolds entwined with pansy-flowers. Pansies were the emblem of Pole; those who accused her were to say the Countess had designed from the beginning that Reginald de la Pole, her son, should marry the Princess Mary. That was all they could prove against the last of the Plantagenets, granddaughter of the Kingmaker; but, in the event, it was enough.

"I HAVE NEVER," stated the Queen-Duchess, lying on her day-bed with one small thin hand in her husband's large one and the other fiercely crumpling a linen kerchief, "willingly disobliged my royal brother since he ordered me as a girl to take part in a court pageant and, being shy, I wore an Ethiop mask for it – but I *would not* go to France in that woman's baggage-train; it was an insult to ask it of me. The French Queen herself has declined to meet her: the whole world knows the wretch for what she is, and has brought about in England." She fell to coughing; the kerchief came away presently with flecks of blood upon it, and Suffolk, who was fond enough of his royal wife even though he could not by temperament echo her lifelong passion for himself, glanced briefly at it and then away.

"You could plead ill-health," he grunted, and because he could not bear to look at his wife's wasted face transferred his glance to where a group of young girls sat at the window, talking in low voices. They were his daughter Frances, her cousin Madge Douglas and little Katharine Willoughby. They did not appear to have heard his Duchess's indiscreet speech; either ill-health made her feverishly garrulous or else the fact that King Henry was at present in Calais, accompanied by the lady whom he had recently created Marchioness of Pembroke, lightened the air of the fear it had held for everyone about Court since the banishment of the Queen. If a good and faithful wife of more than twenty years could be so heartlessly put away, who would be

83

next? But the King had, after all, forgiven Charles Brandon to a certain degree over the years for the offence of marrying his younger sister out of hand when Dowager of France, although they had never quite regained the boisterous friendship which had been theirs in their youth. Suffolk had, in fact, been present to see Anne Boleyn, last month, created marchioness in her gown of crimson velvet and ermine-bordered state robe of the same. By now, the lady would have made her curtsy to King François, if not to his Queen. There could be little doubt, thought Suffolk, that at last Anne Boleyn was King Henry's mistress in truth: that the citadel had fallen was proven by the anguished verses of Tom Wyatt, who had loved Anne since before the day, long ago, when Wyatt and Suffolk and the King had played at bowls, and the first and last had both of them shown tokens Anne Boleyn had given them. "The King was wroth, I remember, and strode away from the game," Suffolk thought. Wyatt's haunting verses stayed in his mind, disturbing him with sensations he was not used to feel, had not done since, perhaps, he had been a young knight in France at the death of Louis XII and had heard that the new King, François, with one wife already, had tried for the sake of the English alliance to compromise Louis' young royal widow when she was keeping her chamber, in the strict white mourning of French widowed queens. Mary had confessed that she loved none but Charles Brandon, and begged François to leave her be and let them marry. And so they had done, and in the end had been happy enough after much adversity.

In adversity.

> Forget not now thine own approved,
> The which so constant hath thee loved,
> Whose steadfast faith hath never moved,
> Forget not yet.

Wyatt's lines were still with him, beating in his head. To banish them he said aloud, fondling his sick wife's hand, "We've had enough of France already, the pair of us, eh?" and then beckoned to young Madge Douglas to come over. She rose at once; she had not been joining in the talk of the other two. He watched her cross the room, fashionably clad in her pointed hood and square-necked travelling-gown; a lovely wench, he thought she was becoming, with a look about her of his wife herself when young, the same brilliant complexion and fair hair. Mary was fond of her, he knew, and her father had brought her over to spend two days with them at Stepney while he himself went on to York Place: best let the girl talk to her aunt, and cheer her. Suffolk rose from the bedside, heaving his bulk easily enough for although he had put on flesh as ageing athletes will, he was still active; bowed his niece by marriage into the chair he had left, and went out.

Madge sat in the still-warm chair and looked out at the October day. She was at a loss for news to give her aunt; the Princess Mary was laid on her back in bed at Beaulieu with one of her cruel migraines, and could see no one, and Madge herself had idled for a time and then sought permission to ask her father to take her to visit the Suffolks, as her aunt was unwell. How ill the Duchess was she had not known till now. The sweet face she remembered was almost fleshless, with a hectic flush on the cheekbones echoing, sadly, the rose-and-lily complexion of the Queen-Duchess's youth. The feverish talk went on as though Mary Tudor knew there was not enough time left to say all that should be said; she prattled for a while, then fell silent, smiling and coughing.

"Sweet Madge," she said, "what of your swain? I am glad to hear that you are to marry for love." Her eyes sought the door out of which Suffolk had lately gone. "Say what they will, it is our nature's way; I was fortunate after the first, though," she added, as if propitiating some ghost, "King Louis was kind to me. I tried to be grateful. But I loved Charles always. There was great anger through two countries because of that. But had I to endure it all over again, I'd do the same." She struggled up on her cushions. "But I asked you a question, then did not wait for an answer. How is your Tom?"

Madge studied her fingers. "My father says we are too young yet to wed. I do not know if he has spoken of it to the King. He says we may see one another when we will, which is merciful. Tom is – is in France at present with His Grace." She hesitated before again mentioning that country to the Duchess. She certainly would not tell her what Tom's last letter had described, with Nan Bullen – Madge still could not think of her as other –

queening it in a hall all hung with tissue raised with silver, bordered with precious stones and pearls, at Calais after she had been neglected four days at Boulogne by King Francois' party, which was made up of noblemen only. Tom had added that Nan was not best pleased with this treatment and with her lack of reception by the French Queen. The banquet at Calais, to atone, had been very rich. King Henry had honoured Nan as if she were already his wife, before the French King and all the company. There was talk, Tom added, that King Henry would certainly defy the Pope and marry her. He ended with his dear love, for he was bolder on paper than in fact: when they met, he would kiss Madge's hands often enough, but never her mouth; perhaps, as the Earl said, they were too young.

She smiled, and talked to the Duchess of the gentle things they both loved, receipts for possets, herb medicines and cures; had Her Grace tried horehound and borage for her cough? Yet all the time Madge knew that neither these nor any other herb or concoction would be proof against this dread disease; her aunt had a consumption, and would shortly die. One could not disguise the thing to oneself, but it should still be possible to deceive Her Grace; Madge tried, and talked for half an hour of unimportant matters. How could she do other to this frail, kindly woman she owed all of home she would ever know in youth? The Princess Mary's establishment had been too grand, and now was too shrunken, to warrant that word, despite the devotion of Lady Salisbury and the friendship of the Princess. But here at Stepney Madge had learned of the matters that make up every day in a house where there is a father and mother and young children and much bustling and love. Some day, perhaps, she – she and Tom – would own such a place, would love one another and their children, and she would tell the cook what to make for the meals and dose the children when they fell ill, though not, please God, so ill as this . . .

She kissed the Duchess and left still smiling, but near tears for she knew she might not see her aunt again. Behind her, the wasted face on the bed lost its animation, and faced the growing shadows of the early autumn dusk. Mary Brandon had almost reached the place where one is quite alone. She would say nothing of it to anyone, not even Charles. It would sadden his contentment, and she had still some months to live.

QUEEN ANNE BOLEYN – the King had married her on St Paul's Day, when she was two months pregnant – craned her long neck in its jewelled collar which hid the other of her two devil's marks, and looked, with the fiery dark eyes which were her one true beauty, at a game of cards which proceeded in the lower hall. The great chamber was crowded, and, as if some restraining hand had been lifted, noisier and more familiar than it had been in former days. Dresses were gaudily coloured, sleeves wide and cuffed with velvet or fur in the way Anne had designed them, and nearly all the women wore the saucy pinned-up headdress she had conjured out of the old Court version, like a weather-vane pointing two crazy ways on each head. The decked heads bobbed and busied themselves over the cards, while the warmth and the buzz of voices rose towards where the King and Queen sat on the high dais. Anne had fixed her gaze on one white neck, which she already knew to belong to the Lady Margaret Douglas, the young girl His Grace had rescued from penury in Scotland. Madge made a pretty group with Mary Howard, who was shortly to marry the King's bastard son Fitzroy who was now Duke of Richmond, and two other Howards with Richmond himself, who hung about the table. Four of the heads were intent on the game, but one was intent on the Lady Margaret Douglas. Anne smiled. That was her own kinsman, young Lord Thomas Howard, who was badly wounded with love's dart. With him was his even younger uncle, Surrey, who amused the Queen with his tomboy

87

pranks and his verse. The successive marriages of the old Duke of
Norfolk had made confusion abound in the succeeding generation;
he had three families to his credit, and his third Duchess, a
redoubtable old lady except for her weakness for her son Tom,
was at present also tending the motherless children of the Duke's
brother, who were not yet at Court. "I must make them all good
marriages," thought Anne.

She smiled to herself, pointing one foot below her robes. It
had indeed been at the plea of young Tom Howard that she had
induced the King – he would do whatever she asked – to have the
Douglas girl brought to Court from her conventual life with the
Lady Mary at Beaulieu. Nothing gay ever happened at that
establishment, and Anne had already arranged that it should
close in the autumn, when – she smiled again – there might be
alternative employment for Mary about her own royal child when
it should be born. She switched her thoughts from that event and
returned them to the Lady Margaret Douglas. Now that she had
seen the girl for herself she liked her; she was pretty, well-
mannered and gay enough when she was given reason. Any such
pleasant sight which did not threaten Anne's own supremacy with
the King was welcome at Court; and to see the girl and Lord
Tom together was like watching two turtle-doves "although the
he-dove hath the greater passion," she thought. To have such a
fair-haired beauty about oneself, with a prospect of becoming
the Queen's relation, would both set off Anne's dark attractions
and please her vanity, for the Lady Margaret was after all half
royal. A rash marriage for the King's eldest sister to have made!
No doubt the Earl of Angus, when a young man, had been ir-
resistible. Anne had met him and his brother Lord George about
Court, and had put them down as rogues, dependent on the King's
bounty. Queen Margaret – from the newest account of her
goings-on in the north, which had made His Grace frown heavily
– might well be more fool than bitch, but she had compromised
herself with that young man the King called Lord Muffin. "So
shall not I do," thought Anne, and her hand, the one with the
sixth finger gracefully concealed by the broad sleeve, sketched a
movement across her still scarcely rounded belly. A soothsayer
had told her this coming child would be the greatest ruler
England had ever known. "It does not then matter what may
become of me," thought Anne, in a moment of queer withdrawal.

How strangely these moods came upon her, in the midst of the brilliant vulgar Court she had made, with its music, jewelled chains, brocade and velvet, and all of it bones beneath! But the child she would bear should live, and rule. She would be remembered for all time as its mother, if only for that.

She thought of the King, absently though he was as usual by her side. She had never loved Henry, only now, as at all times, used him as an instrument of her growing power. He was gentle and biddable enough, like all men she had captivated. Oh, there were proud versed conceits such as he had sent her long ago, when she had still been wild with love for Percy whose betrothal to her the King had caused to be broken, and breathing vengeance at that time by any means she might find for herself. Perhaps she had found it. The list of her achievements was not small, she knew. Cardinal Wolsey, said by some in his time to be more powerful than the King himself, disgraced and dead; his houses of York and Hampton become royal palaces, and his goods forfeit – Anne herself had had her pick of the richest of them – and Campeggio, the Pope's legate, sent back in humiliation to his master after the useless trial of Queen Katharine. As for that stout, ageing, plain, stubborn, barren Spanish mule of a woman herself, and her daughter, where were they? The mother was imprisoned in the north shires, they said sickening unto death, but they had said that often. The other –

Anne's sallow face, thin with the demands of pregnancy, grew ugly. Young Mary should own herself bastard before she'd done, and her mother's erstwhile marriage to the King incestuous and invalid. My lady Mary should sign a writ denying the Pope – who was the Pope any more? – his so-called supremacy. The King was head of the Church now in England, had been since he went through that form of marriage to herself in January last. Form of marriage? "It was a true union," Anne told herself, "and I am Queen."

> The eagle's force subdues each bird that flies;
> What metal can resist the flaming fire?
> Does not the sun dazzle the clearest eyes,
> And melt the frost . . .

Those were the verses the King had written her long ago. They said his father, Henry VII, had beheaded a falcon that brought down an eagle. Anne slewed her eyes round to where His Grace now sat. He was not looking at her, but engaged in talk with that same Angus, the Scotsman, to whom, as Anne happened to know, Henry had already made a handsome yearly allowance to keep himself and his daughter. The King could be generous, but—

The wisest are with princes made but fools.

Anne shivered a little, though it was over warm in the hall. Her state induced strange thoughts and longings, she knew; she had lately had a passion for green apples. That must be why she had felt cold suddenly for no reason. When her coronation was over, then it would be time to prepare for this birth.

Her crowning. That would be the summit of her fortunes, the sign to all the world that one after the other she had conquered those who were against her at the first, who predicted that she would be only one more in a succession of pretty young women the King had fancied and taken, like Bess Blount, Richmond's mother; perhaps like her own sister, Mary Boleyn. But Anne herself had resisted Henry for so long that his appetite for her grew to the proportions of a fever, which consumed him night and day, and by the end she had only to crook her finger and he would do her desire. And soon, on the feast of Pentecost, to the sound of trumpets and chiming of bells and the sight of wonders on the broad river and the streets filled with processions of bishops and peers, she would wear the crown of St Edward and be anointed and see her device, the white falcon, honoured likewise with a crown. And then—

"Good sweetheart," said the King's voice, "will it please you to have our niece Marg'et about you daily? Her father, the Earl—" he indicated with his hand that nobleman, whose shrewd eyes surveyed Queen Anne, while his bow grew deep, "has asked it, and unless it is a displeasure to you to have so young a lady, why, it shall be done as soon as room can be found for her, perhaps after the crowning." For every room in the royal palaces was thronged to the attics for the coming spectacle, with folk ridden up from the country who seldom came to town. Anne smiled, and held out her fingers French-fashion for the Earl to kiss.

"Your Grace reads my mind," she said. "I had been watching her, and myself thought that so fair a young lady should have some diversion and pastime more often, for she becomes them well. Will you bring her to me, my lord?"

Angus bowed again and made his way back to where Madge's fresh young laughter sounded among the players. Anne continued to regard the King, the smile remaining on her face unaltered, with closed lips. He was looking at her, as he often did nowadays, less with the former lust than with a kind of protective awareness; the small eyes let their glance stray downwards to where his child lay hidden in her. He spoke softly, so that none but themselves could hear.

"Do not divert your own self too heartily, sweet, and harm our son. That is the one thing I desire now more than all the world."

He thought of the coming boy, and of the past years he had spent waiting for an heir, and the unfailing disappointments and that they were at last at an end. Nan was young and healthy. She should bear his son. His son, born in wedlock, for whose sake – rather than hers or his own – he had at last abjured the Bishop of Rome and all his works. His true-born son, as even Fitzroy, dearly as he loved the lad, could never be. His mind harked back to the time when he had hoped, by elevating Fitzroy in rank, to make him heir of England. But he had not proceeded with that beyond the dukedom; it would not be tolerated, and Henry, at most times master, knew when even his will could not prevail.

But there should no living soul gainsay him in anything when once he had his princely boy. His flesh should rule England after he was gone. "But that will be, by God's mercy, many a year yet," thought Henry complacently. He smiled his narrow hard-eyed smile, and fondled Anne's hand. "My thanks, sweetheart, for giving a place to my niece Marg'et as I asked," he said. "Her mother is far away, and not wise; and I fear my sister Suffolk, who has cared for her hitherto, is very ill." He frowned; he had an aversion to illness, and when had he last taken leisure to visit his sister Mary? Perhaps, if she should last till the spring –

"Here is the Lady Margaret Douglas now," said Anne quickly. She could tell, with the swift acuity that was hers when she cared to employ it, that Henry's mind had left her briefly, and was making its way to places which held danger for her. That he should not see, or think of, his disinherited daughter at Beaulieu was part of Anne's duty to herself, and she performed it well; and as for the King's sister Mary, she might well be an advocate for the repudiated Katharine. When the Lady Margaret Douglas was about her, the child must be made to keep silent on both those subjects. But she was young enough to be pliable; and, at worst – Anne smiled – there was always her own kinsman, young Lord Thomas Howard, to divert the young lady.

Tom and Madge had been partners together in the game. When the Earl of Angus approached, both laid down their hands. The other pair, Tom's sober brother William, and his pretty sister Mary who was to wed Richmond, continued to stare at their cards. As Madge rose up to leave, Richmond himself came over and said idly "I will take your hand, lady, if you must go to the Queen."

Mary Howard blushed and smiled, pleased at the nearness of the handsome sprig she was to marry soon. She preened herself the more in that her brother Tom looked gloomy because his beloved was being taken from him for a quarter-hour. What fools men were! Mary lifted up her fan of cards, and flirted with her eyes at Richmond, as she must remember to call him. The King's son laughed loudly. He was a boisterous, arrogant young man with a weak chest; they said he had a bullying temper and delighted in watching cruel sports. When we are wed, thought Mary, I will cure all that and his chest too.

She watched Madge Douglas's retreating back, shepherded towards the dais by her father. Mary Howard was not sorry to see her go. She was pretty enough to be a rival to oneself, with all that pale-gold hair and a complexion which never showed a spot; and she put on airs, as though she were as good as the Queen. "There is little need to puff herself up, for everyone knows that her mother, the Queen of Scots, has divorced her father, and married another man," thought Mary. "She is as much a bastard as the Lady Mary at Beaulieu, were it in anyone's interest to admit it." She returned to her cards, slightly ashamed of herself. But it was true enough that Madge Douglas should consider herself fortunate if she were permitted to marry Tom. "We are all of us kin to the Queen, and may command anyone," muttered Mary. Richmond meantime moved in his place, and cast an unlover-like glance at his betrothed.

"Will you play, or will you go on dreaming?" he said roughly. "It is your turn to cry ace."

Tom Howard brooded in silence among them all, and played badly; his mind was with Madge who had gone to the Queen. He had not persuaded the Earl of Angus yet to give permission for the match, and without that it was useless to approach the King. No doubt the old fox, the Earl, was hedging for time, waiting to see what befell before he committed himself. Tom's love ached in his throat. He had never loved anyone before except his mother; at home, with the old Duke's successive marriages and families, he had had a rough time of it when his mother was elsewhere. Now, he felt strong enough to have slain dragons for his lady whose hair was of silvery gold, like a princess in a fairy-tale; so he had seen her, that first day at Surrey's wedding, kneeling in a maze of bright colour flung upon her from the window. He had fallen in love at sight; but what was the use of that? He was powerless in this newer maze, that of royal relationships and probabilities and divorces. It might be that Queen Anne, his kinswoman – her mother had been a Howard – should be asked to speak for their marriage, or at least meantime for their betrothal, as they were so young. She alone, Tom thought, in the end, had power with the King. Surrey might have spoken for them, but he was in France. The Court was the duller for lack of his wit and splendid bearing, and the verses he would toss off as easily as any other man tossed a tennis-ball. (Surrey could do that well, too.)

"This is a poor enough hand your young Scottish lady has left me," grumbled Richmond, as he lost the game. Mary Howard laughed, fingers spread eagerly across the board to claim her winnings.

"Perhaps she is fortunate in love," she said, and Lord William winked at his brother Tom; it was as far as he could go in wit. He was a careful, diplomatic young man, who had already been sent by the King on sundry errands, and would shortly leave for Scotland. He returned his gaze to the cards again, and pushed them over for Richmond to deal. Richmond was cross at having lost, and he did not feel well tonight; his cough troubled him, and Mary was flighty and coy, and it was too hot in the hall but he would shiver if it were colder. Worst of all, his father, who had once almost declared him heir to the throne, could think now of nothing but this coming child of Mistress Nan's. Well, time would tell who was in the right of it. It would, after all, have been fatiguing to be King.

Madge faced the woman who had so cruelly destroyed her cousin Mary's happiness, but she was not, as she had expected to be, fortified by anger; instead, she was aware of conflicting emotions, so new as to bewilder her. To down them, she turned her gaze instead to the King. How he had changed! His eyes were sunk in flesh, and he looked older; the small mouth had begun to have a habit of pursing ungenerously. But at sight of Madge he smiled, and called her his niece Marg'et as he always did, and asked her how her aunt Suffolk fared. "We are informed that you visited her at Stepney."

His Grace would be informed, thought Madge, of most things that befell. That would be by means of Master Secretary Cromwell, whose minions crept out like rats into the streets and reported anything, however small, to their master. Tom had told her of it. She retained the King's glance, and answered levelly "My aunt is poorly, I fear, so please your Grace. She keeps to her day-bed, and hopes to go shortly to Westhorpe, so that the pure air may help her cough."

"Well, well, we must hope that she will soon be cured," said Henry, and turned to his consort. "Sweetheart, you know my niece? I trust that this meeting will be one of many. Marg'et, will it please you to be about the Queen daily?" He smiled, and the fleshy face relaxed into something of its former self, as Madge had once known it; but she had dropped her gaze, to hide her feelings. How pleasant, if foolish, it would have been to say "But it will leave my cousin desolate; the Princess Mary does not want me to forsake her." But one must not, nowadays, even refer to poor Mary by the name of Princess. The Earl had whispered to her of this coming appointment on their way to the high table; it would not be within the bounds of prudence, or gratitude, to refuse it. She heard, again, Lady Salisbury's voice the day the Queen had left Windsor. *The Lady Margaret hath not her own disposal; she must obey the King and her father.* And they were pensioners here, the two of them, she and the Earl.

She curtsied, and recited the words Angus himself had instructed her to say. There was nothing else to be done: and

94

she would be near Tom.

"I am your Grace's humble servant."

Henry nodded, pleased enough; no thought of her possible refusal would have occurred to him. He looked again at the girl so inopportunely borne by his sister to the Earl of Angus, who for certain reasons of his own Henry continued to treat as Margaret's spouse. It was, for one thing, useful to have a card in his hand to play, if need be, against that as yet untried red-haired boy in the north, his nephew, James V. The Scots Border forever seethed with discontent, and to have the commander of an English army who knew the country well would serve in time of war ... Angus himself had spent long enough there as a fugitive, everyone knew. But how beautiful the girl herself was growing, now that her future was secure and she had proper gowns! "She is older, now, than her mother was when they sent her north to marry James IV of Scots," thought the King, then scowled, remembering his own unwillingness, boy though he was, for that marriage. Margaret his sister had been a fine wench in those days: they had been comrades in youth. He was glad to do what he might for her daughter.

Madge stared at the new Queen, veiling the look with her lashes in order that it might not seem unmannerly. She was bereft of all power to hate Nan Bullen, as she had expected to do. She knew now what the feeling was that she felt for this swarthy, dark-eyed woman with her rich dress and her thin dark brows raised in arcs of faint surprise at scrutiny from a girl so young. Madge made her curtsy, accordingly, and went her way with the feeling she had known still strong in her mind. It was pity.

"WHAT ARE YOU thinking of?" asked Lord Thomas Howard softly.

They were walking by the river, nearby Greenwich stairs; in the hint of fog on this September day, ferries and bargemen plied up and down like flat shapes in dark pasteboard. Madge stared at the drab scene for moments, aware how used she had become to the smoky bustle and noise of London; the barges seemed no marvel to her now, even the great dragon that had belched fire from them at the Queen's coronation having gone his way. It was long, very long since she must have left the Scottish mists and gentle rains of the Border country; she no longer felt the air dull or heavy in the south.

She lifted her face to such sun as there was. She was pale, for it was some days since Queen Anne had taken her chamber, where there was no light admitted except from a single window, and her ladies must all be there to attend her in turns, for she was permitted to see no men. Madge had taken her turn and – her thoughts grew weary and sad – so had the Princess Mary, brought up deliberately for the new birth from Beaulieu, from which place her household was to be removed next month. Mary now was no more than one of Anne's waiting-women "considered as below myself," thought Madge without joy. As the daughter of the King's sister, she held prior place to the young girl now officially declared bastard by her own father's edict. But Madge and Mary still continued friends in secret. It would never be otherwise.

She recalled that Tom had spoken to her and, because she was fond of him and did not want to wound his feelings, she turned her head and smiled at him, suppressing slight irritation at the dog-like devotion in his dark eyes as he looked at her. Sometimes she wished that Tom would show more spirit, would answer her back, even slap her backside sometimes, as did Richmond his Mary. But Tom always used her as though she were a saint on a pedestal and –

She must answer soon. "I was thinking of the changes that have come since first I saw this river."

It was true; the Duchess of Suffolk had died in the summer, just after Queen Anne had been crowned. At that coronation Suffolk had ridden gaily by the new Queen on a charger all caparisoned with gold, as though his wife were not dying at Westhorpe, and . . . Frances Brandon had told her since then of a thing she disliked to hear. Suffolk was shortly to be married again . . . to little Katharine Willoughby.

"Does any love outlast death?" she said, and told him what she had been thinking. He replied, of course, that his love for her was eternal; but already she had let her thoughts run on. It was safe enough to voice them here, she knew, while she took the breath of air she was due, for Tom's jester, Folly, who was with him everywhere, and her own man, Hervey, and two of her women, walked behind, as much to protect them from the snares of Master Secretary's paid listeners as anything; they would ensure that their own young master and mistress were not surrounded and overheard. The cobbles were quiet, and yet a humming of activity came from the befogged city lying on both sides of the water; life in everyday places went on, no matter what befell at Court. The latter place had been gay enough; Madge had almost forgotten her grief for the Queen-Duchess in the round of diversions, dancing the galliard with Tom's hands firm on either side of her waist, playing cards as they often did, winning and losing wagers, racing Tom's whippet against Richmond's for more wagers, riding, playing chess, listening to Wyatt's verse as Surrey was away, watching tennis played, the more now that the days grew cooler. The King, they said, had been the finest tennis player in Europe when he was young: nobody now could aspire to his excellence. Tom did not try; Tom instead was always with Madge, squiring and escorting her;

97

G

it was accepted, now, that they were set apart for one another. Yet the King had still said nothing, though he must know of their fondness and wish to marry. No doubt he had great things on his mind.

"Here is your father," said Tom, his mouth drooping. He had only had Madge to himself for moments, as it seemed, and here came duty already, in the form of the Earl; he seemed in a hurry, being hatless and with his cheeks flushed with haste. Lord George was not with him, which in itself signified some urgent matter. Angus seldom rode or walked alone.

He reached them, and Madge swept her curtsy. "Never mind that," said the Earl curtly, "get you gone to the Queen's chamber. Her Grace is fallen in labour, and it will look ill were you not there at the birth. The tidings have but newly come, and I made haste to find you. Fortunately I knew you would be with my lord here."

"Tom, farewell now – I will send word – "

She hurried off, her women after her, and Angus and young Howard paced the waterside together, for moments, out of courtesy. The Earl did not stay overlong, for he was still in doubt as to whether to surrender the finest card in his hand, his royal and Douglas daughter, to a mere younger son of Norfolk's house. Madge might, did matters mend, make a greater alliance by far; the Howards were, to Angus's way of thinking, jumped up, since, in the early years of the century, Norfolk himself had been saddled in first wedlock with a Plantagenet wife, a daughter of Edward IV whom it suited the Tudor dynasty to marry basely. But the Howard white lion had won renown for all that, with Flodden in the balance. Angus mulled all of it over, and attempted to be jocular with Madge's sombre young man. Truly, Lord Tom was a grave fellow! They would make a worthy pair, thought the Earl, who liked his jest. But . . . he would let the matter rest, at least, till after this birth. If the Queen bore a healthy boy there would be a greater distance to bridge between Madge and the throne of England.

The throne of England . . . had that been in his thoughts? He must not, at that rate, utter them aloud; such conceits were more than dangerous. He said to young Howard instead, smiling into his beard, "Well, my lord? How waves the white lion banner? I mind seeing it in a darker mist than this, on a Border slope, another September day. A man could not see what he fought in that affray of Flodden: it was like midnight come at noon."

"My father has told me of it," said Tom quietly. "My lord, is there no word yet of permission on our matter from the King?"

But Angus only said what his daughter had thought, that the King had other matters on his mind: and soon left the younger man, who stared disconsolately at the river till his jester came to console him with wit, for Folly loved his master.

THE CHAMBER where the Queen lay in labour at Greenwich was hung with tapestry showing the parable of the ten wise and the ten foolish virgins. Madge thought that she would recall each separate virgin's pallid face to the end of her life, so long had she stood in her place and stared first at one wall, then the other. The candles in the room burned low; outside, it was still mid-afternoon, but almost all daylight was barred and the candles' heat, and the scent of melting wax, and of close-pressed bodies, made the room unbearable; yet one must bear it. *She* must bear it, there in travail on the bed, with her narrow unaccustomed body that had already strained now many hours, and surely must either soon give birth or fail. One had ceased to think of her as a Queen, hardly even as a woman; she was little more than a groaning, straining beast, having lost the cold control of herself she had kept for some time at the beginning of the pains, when pride was still with her. Now nothing but agony remained. This was what came to women; would come, one day, to oneself. Even that prospect no longer seemed real, or that there would ever be a release from this everlasting waiting, and waiting. There were so many women here, more than the room would comfortably hold; and the midwives, and the Princess Mary.

Mary stood near Madge, her eyes downcast; her cousin knew that she was praying. It would not be for the safe delivery of the woman on the bed, or for the birth of an heir. It would be – Madge thought she knew – for the ability to behave with dignity

100

in a humiliating situation, to act as though whatever befell were not one's personal concern, that this child about to be born would not oust one, completely and finally, from all due place in the King's affection and the succession to the throne. Mary would also be thinking of her mother, ill and near death, whom she was still not permitted to see, to whom this birth-scene itself was the final insult of many. And so Mary prayed; mindful, as in so much else that she had been taught from childhood, of how Lady Salisbury would have bidden her conduct herself as a royal lady, a daughter of Spain. And so she stood stiff and still, with lips barely moving, her gaze on the floor thronged as it was with brocade skirts, and no one heeded her but Madge, aware as they both were that they were here together and that when the child was born, their eyes would meet.

The child. King Henry had had proclamations of the birth of a prince ready written to send to every capital in Europe. He had asked the King of France to be its godfather. The boy's name was, it had been decided, to be either Henry or else Edward, the name of the old Plantagenet stock, the name of the Confessor. But what would the Confessor have had to say concerning the way the child's father had despoiled the Church in England? No matter. The candle-flames blurred before Madge's eyes and she wondered if, before the Queen gave birth, one of her ladies would faint . . . and if it would be herself. This was the first lying-in she had ever seen; she and Mary.

"It is coming now," said the midwife, and the sounds from the bed redoubled. Queen Anne would not remember afterwards, doubtless, that she had cried aloud. Beyond the door, the King would be waiting with his ministers for news of the boy's birth.

The boy. Some time after the head had first begun to show itself they brought out a living child from the Queen. After the long groaning and crying and sweating anguish of labour, the room held sudden silence. The midwife took the baby and wiped the mucus from its mouth and nose, and held it up by the feet to hear it cry. It did so presently, with a thin small wail like a sea-bird, waving its helpless spidery fingers which were still blue-red from birth. Instantly a lady slipped out between the tapestries to take the news to the waiting ministers and the King.

Madge's eyes met her cousin Mary's. Neither glance held any

101

expression. It was too greatly fraught with danger, at this moment, even to think lest one's thoughts be guessed at, almost overheard. But they had both seen, and both their minds were aware of two things; the baby had red hair, and was a girl.

IT WAS NOT that what happened that day in the Chamber of the Virgins at Greenwich gave immediate rise to the events which followed, fearfully striking terror upon half-doubt, certainty on sadness, and changed – how things changed, from goodwill to a kind of haunted evil so that the very words one spoke must be guarded, even when in private! How people themselves changed under it, so that where there had been thoughtless laughter, of herself and Tom and Surrey and Mary Richmond and the Queen, to the gentle notes of Smeaton's lute in the Queen's chamber, now instead there was a frequent look behind one at hanging tapestry which seemed to move, but it was only the draught from the door . . .

But that erstwhile birth of a girl had not pleased the King. 'It has made him look a fool before Europe," thought Madge privately, for she would not dare say such a thing aloud even to Tom. Yet the King wore yellow at a ball the day the news of Queen Katharine's death came, and pretended joy, and Anne cried aloud "Now I am indeed a Queen," but she was less so than she had been before. That change came subtly, intermixed with the other memories Madge had of the bitter sobbing of the Princess Mary by night in the bed they shared together at Chelsea and then Hunsdon, where both attended the red-haired baby Elizabeth, growing fast as she was and beginning to prattle so engagingly that one could not hate her, despite everything. Mary herself now was a stony-faced woman, a child no longer; she, Madge, could do little except grope her hand towards the

103

other's in the bed, and hold it fast. There was no relief for Mary's sorrow. Her mother had died of an agonising and slow illness, almost alone at the end except for her old friend Maria de Salinas, Katharine Willoughby's mother, who by a ruse had evaded the guards on the staircase at Kimbolton and had run up to hold the dying woman in her arms.

"They would not let me go to her," said Mary bitterly. And by "they" she meant the King and Anne, and no doubt the King's minister Thomas Cromwell who encouraged him in such cruelty as he had never shown before. Once a man began to be cruel it laid hold upon him and he found the next time easier, and the next.

That year the Queen miscarried, but was soon pregnant again.

Then there was a young woman about Court, one of the Queen's ladies, who kept herself quiet and prim, bearing her fine full body always in a well-bred and retiring manner; her name was Jane Seymour. When did one first hear the rumours that Queen Anne had come upon her and the King lovemaking together and had given birth prematurely to a dead boy?

Madge walked with her father the Earl in Greenwich Palace gardens, where there was a fine vista of chestnut-trees. It was late April and their young green had opened and there was a hint of coming blossom, pink and white. Madge was staring up at the trees, enjoying their stately beauty as a part of this cultured, amenable south land with its great parks and palaces. She was startled to feel a touch on her arm and the Earl drew her along another path, motioning with his head to where a woman sat alone below a tree, playing with her little dogs. Madge knew the Queen by her up-peaked hood. She repressed an indrawn breath. They went another way in silence. When they were safely alone in the depths of the park Angus said to her, "That is where she commonly sits, alone. In former days it was not so. They say she is near her fall."

"She rose high enough," said Madge stubbornly. The pity she had felt for the Queen at the height of her triumph, that day three years ago, when she herself had come to Court, persisted and had always done despite Anne's shrill high laughter, her treatment of the Princess Mary, and open contempt for Mary's mother. "This will pass: one cannot put away a wife like a dog."

104

There were even now those, she knew, who would have been glad to sit with the Queen beneath her tree; Sir Richard Norris, who had often enough brought messages to Madge herself from Tom in the early days, and maybe borne an answer back again; the musician, Mark Smeaton, who could play any gallant and tinkling air on his lute, dispersing or making melancholy as he chose: Sir Thomas Wyatt, who still loved the Queen and would divert her with verse and run errands for her. It must be her own choice to sit alone.

'Daughter, I would speak with you regarding this matter," said the Earl with caution. That he must go carefully he knew; his royal daughter had a quick answer did one venture to oppose her will, and he entertained a measure of respect for her as he had done for her mother: moreover, she had got Angus his place at Court and his pension. "The Queen's kin, the Howards," he began carefully, "may not be in favour if she goes. It would be expedient to delay your betrothals with the Lord Thomas for a little while, lest we be caught up in such matters."

She rounded on him, satin skirts rustling with a proud sound against the tended grass. Her blue eyes were dark with anger. "Sir, my Lord Thomas's brother was sent into Scotland two years since to sound my mother the Queen there on the matter, and she liked him well enough, and was pleased with the marriage-plan." How could she consider heartlessly abandoning Tom now? For the first time, mentioning her mother as she seldom did, it came to her, looking at the Earl's averted head and lowered eyes, that Angus himself had changed; the years of subservience had driven the pride inwards, and he would serve always the highest master. "He does not love me for myself," thought the girl, "but for the honour I may bring him." She was certain, however, that there were two people in the world who loved her truly for herself: Tom and the Princess Mary. She could do little enough to help the last save remain her friend, but Tom –

"I will never consent to it," she said finally, "we are troth-plight."

Angus bowed. It would not be expedient, any more than it had been with her royal mother, to try to force an issue with Madge. He had hoped that showing her the sad spectacle of the abandoned Queen might cause her to think on what he was saying; but she was headstrong, as he had once been himself.

105

He sighed, and for the first time in some years spared a thought for Janet of Traquair. It had been likewise expedient, in view of his new place at Court with the Queen of Scots' brother, to abandon Janet. Expedient was a recurring word in the Earl's cautious vocabulary. But at present it seemed to be doing him little service.

There was a jousting, to bring in the May-time revels. Each year they had had one since the King began to reign at eighteen years and ousted the parsimonious ways of his dead father. May was a joyous month and presently they would all of them ride out to Blackheath and bring home the boughs of may-blossom which were already heavy and full of scent. Once long ago, when Madge was a babe, they had met her and her mother there on their long journey south from Scotland and the King and Queen had dismounted and kissed them, and bidden them join in the May revels. "Only soon we were sent back home," Madge remembered, unable to credit fully what she could not recall: in the end, one paid for folly. And she remembered nothing at all of the time her mother had first brought her to York Place and visited Cardinal Wolsey who was then powerful, and begged his protection for herself and her child, his godchild, born in a poor Border hold in blowing rain.

He had promised protection; had sent her mother money at times after they returned north, Madge knew, for the Scots Queen would suddenly appear decked out in new gowns and bright pearl-trimmed hoods, and there would be much letter-writing and sending of her men south with letters sealed with the Queen's seal.

And, because of dead Wolsey, in the end, Madge herself sat here; secure as anyone might be, and joyous enough for May. She was nearby the Queen's place, and Anne was herself gaily clad, leaving small memory of the sad lonely figure who had sat beneath the chestnut tree, that day not so long ago. The King was by her, his head turned meantime to talk to his lords; Madge saw Suffolk among them, and averted her gaze. He was the Queen's enemy, she knew: he had never liked Anne. Her gaze wandered past his broad figure and came to rest on the place where Tom sat, Surrey by him in his customary gorgeous attire. Tom caught her eye and smiled, and pointed to his breast; he wore, she could see, the smocked shift she had lately made for him, embroidered richly with small stitches and seed-pearls, well seen beneath his doublet. He might be neither as resplendent as Surrey nor as handsome, but Madge returned his smile; it was as though a silver thread lay between them, separate from the gaudier bonds that tied each man to each woman, Mary to her Richmond, Surrey not to his wife at all but to a fair-haired Irish girl who had lately come to Court and whose father and brothers had all of them been killed by order of the King.

Why had she thought of that? It sent a chill across the blue sky of the day, the bright-coloured silk of the pavilions, the gay notes of trumpets sounding the entry for the jousts which were about to begin now everyone had assembled.

Norris was to oppose the Queen's brother, Rochford. They rode into the ring to the accompaniment of trumpet-braying and cheers; some were for Rochford, but more for Norris who was popular, a strong and wary fighter, and moreover a favourite of the King: he was said to be the only courtier Henry permitted to follow him into his bedchamber. He coursed once about the ring, then the lances were laid to rest, and the two chargers rode towards one another and passed, and turned again.

Madge found herself withdrawn from the shouts of the crowd. She did not greatly care who won this mock battle and had laid no wagers on it with her ladies. A curious state of withdrawal came to her, in which she might have been invisible, a ghost; not a flesh-and-blood young woman who clapped when the rest clapped, laughed when they laughed, watched covertly, as all did, the King and Queen in their place to see whether Henry were pleased or no, and if he followed the tourney with enjoyment. He had once been a keen sportsman and had ridden many a ring himself in youth.

The Queen leaned forward, as Norris galloped by. A white object fell into the ring, softly; a handkerchief. Norris scooped it up with the point of his spear, kissed it and returned it to Anne on the spear's point. So much everyone saw; unprepared for what came next. The King rose in his place, his great body seeming of a sudden clumsy and awkward, and thrust his way out, followed by certain noblemen. A hush fell over the crowd and then it seemed as if everyone began to talk in a low voice, discreetly. The Queen sat still for moments, and then, with ashen face, withdrew.

"What is wrong?" said the acid voice of Frances Brandon, now Frances Grey; her husband Dorset was a little mean man whom nobody liked. Madge saw the same question being asked by means of many averted, scared eyes; no one looked at the jousters, who had broken off. Presently the call sounded to retreat to the tents. A gathering of gold and scarlet waited at the barrier, with the gleam of armour catching the sun.

"What is it? Surely they do not mean to *arrest* — "

The voice fell into silence. Norris and Rochford were led away as prisoners. The crowd shifted, murmured, moved, and soon the seats about the ring were half empty save for those who, bewildered, sat on in the place where no more sport would now be seen.

"Perhaps they will have it elsewhere," said Frances.

Madge glanced at her with dislike. She herself felt as if she had received a blow from some unseen hand. She looked for Tom in his place, but he had gone; perhaps he was trying to come to her.

She never saw Queen Anne again.

They had taken Anne to the Tower. So much made itself known to those who waited, terrified of further change, not knowing how to save themselves if it came to them. Tom and Madge walked hand in hand down to the river at Lambeth, where it ran below the Howard gardens past a mass of fruit-blossom. Chestnut, apple, may; what flower would she think of as a background to what next befell? What would befall in such a way as it had done since last they walked together by the river? She clung to Tom, as if he could protect her, at the same time knowing him powerless. She saw the fear in his dark eyes, and for the first time reached up her mouth and kissed him fiercely, as though that at least were a thing that should never be taken from either of them.

"They may not harm the Queen's kin," said Tom presently. His hand reached up to the shift Madge had made and plucked at it, as though the pearls were blossom to fall unheeded on the grass.

"I Do Not hate her now," said the Lady Mary. "They say that at her trial she was brave, and at her death more so. And she sent word to me by Lady Kingston that she regretted her treatment of me, though not of my mother."

Madge nodded, keeping silence, remembering a thing Tom had told her; the King's son, Richmond, had taken it upon himself to be present at the execution. Richmond loved cruelty; he had been, also, at the hanging, drawing and quartering of the Carthusian monks last year. It was like an appetite that grew in men. Thank God Tom was not cruel.

She watched the Princess as the short-sighted eyes bent over their mending, and returned to her own. Mending now was the order of the day at Hunsdon, since both the King's daughters, Mary and Elizabeth, had been declared bastard by Act of Parliament. The work Mary was engaged on was in fact the repairing of one of her small half-sister's shifts. The child was almost without clothes now as she grew so fast, and since Queen Anne's arrest and beheading in the Tower, the throng of admiring sycophants had departed: it was nobody's business any more to see to the wants of a three-year-old girl who had embarrassed everybody by being born. Madge, engaged on her own sewing, soothed by the regular prick and draw of the needle, glanced over to where the child played, having picked up the pomander which had been given her for her diversion. Soon she dropped it again. The curious many-coloured eyes gazed at Madge beneath

109

the mop of red hair: their expression was not childlike. "One would think she was a hundred years old, and we ourselves children," thought her cousin, bending her own fair head resolutely over her needlework. She kept silence. It was better to say nothing to Mary regarding her half-sister. One moment she did her duty by the child and mended shifts, and the next she would remember – as well she might – all the harm there had been by cause of this child's begetting, of this child's mother; the latter huddled now headless in an obscure grave in the Tower chapel after the guns had fired the news of her execution over London. They said the headsman from Calais had been very expert with his sword; it had needed one stroke only, which was merciful.

One stroke. To what strange place was she herself come that she could consider mercy as such?

"You are silent today, Madge," said the Lady Mary. "Is there word of Lord Thomas?" It was like her, Madge decided, not to be able to call him Tom; Mary was always formal. Herself, she felt for Tom as his mother might have done, almost as though she were older than he; as if she must protect and shelter him from the world. Was that what young women felt when they were in love? She had no one to ask; Mary Howard, now married to Richmond, might have told her, but she was nowhere near.

She raised her head from her sewing and smiled. "A letter was brought by his man Folly yesterday." It was not now possible for Norris, who had been their go-between, to bring letters. Norris had been beheaded. So had Rochford, the late Queen's brother, accused of incest with Anne. Had the King indeed had to go to such lengths to rid himself of the woman he had once worshipped? Mark Smeaton, the low-born musician who played so sweetly in the Queen's chamber, had been hanged instead because of his low birth. "His was the only confession of guilt, and they got it under torture," the girl thought, and shivered. It was best to think of other things: perhaps of the King's new marriage. He had wedded Jane Seymour at Wolf Hall the day after the execution of Anne.

Her thoughts shied away from that. She would think of the Douglases; of her father, whose letter had come at the same time as Tom's. He had a woeful tale to tell of Scotland; James V still had not forgiven the Douglases. Poor old Kilspindie had waited many hours for him at Stirling, and when the King rode out he had passed him by on the steep slope. The old man had sunk down outside the castle gate for weariness, but no one dared give him a drink of water. Was there so much power, so much hatred, in all kings? Her half-brother now could surely be merciful, in full control of his kingdom as he was, from all one heard.

She set down her needle and stared across the room, to encounter the cool continued stare of the Lady Elizabeth. She lowered her eyes. It might after all be true what they said, that that child's mother had been a whore; what would *she* be?

As for herself, thoughts had begun to come to her in the old way in the night ... If Jane Seymour, the King's new wife, did not bring him a son, who was the next true heir to the throne now that both Mary and Elizabeth had been declared illegitimate?

Herself.

She stared down at the slender bones of her hands, stitching, stitching always. Best keep quiet, stitch on and say nothing. Everywhere lurked danger, perhaps death.

What would be her fate? Already she knew, with the queer sense of unreality which had been with her at the fatal May-day jousts, that her uncle the King meantime was like a questing minotaur, rooting about with its head near the ground to smell out kill. He had been made foolish for lack of male heirs; very well, let those who thought to step into the heir's shoes perish ... it might come to that. Devoutly she prayed that no such thought might enter her mind; if she had no ambition, perhaps the King would not think of her, quietly stitching here. With the full power of the high hot blood in her, she longed for Tom's presence; Tom, so quiet and unheeding of great events, ready only to laugh at some sally of Richmond's, to grow dreamy over the intricate lines of Surrey's verse. Tom would never have ambition to rule, any more than herself. All they two wanted was a place to live in, a bed to make love in, to make children. She stared down again at her suddenly idle hands. What fate would befall a child whose blood was Howard, Douglas and royal? What fate had befallen the Plantagenets, the two princes smothered in the Tower and buried no man knew where, and the Earl of Warwick, last of his race? There had been no pity for them because they were innocent.

The King's men were sent for her. They came the first week in June. By the eighth of that month the Lady Margaret Douglas was in the Tower, looking on one side at a dull thick wall and on the other a window and balcony below which, on the green grass, there were dark stains in the shape of a square where the block had been on which they executed Queen Anne in the previous month. At first she would not look at it and then, as if the reality of horror were better than what might grow in the mind, she sat where she could see it, staring down through the summer sunlight to that very place. There was quiet here, only broken by the wearied steps of the guards and the bell which tolled, each evening, for the prisoners who were freed to return to their cells after the day was over. Some had been here for many years. She, so newly come, was not yet permitted to leave her cell; and, in any case, not to see Tom. For Tom was in the Tower like herself, in lodgings lower and darker than her own, nearby the stinking moat which still surrounded the outer bailey, like herself seeing no one. Tom, who had loved to walk his gardens and to fly a falcon and race his whippet and listen and joust and laugh, and watch her always as if she were some goddess, not a mortal thing, was in prison.

"I am too much mortal," Madge thought, and knew great fear. She must pray for Tom and for herself, that they might be brought out of this pass and permitted – the sound had a hollow echo – permitted at last to marry. But within herself she knew that that would never happen now. They would be fortunate to escape with life.

QUEEN MARGARET TUDOR spread her white plump beringed taper-fingered hands out below her own failing gaze; her sight was not what it had been before she had the smallpox. The lustre of a thumb-ring, a bezel, she wore came to her; she had fine hands, she knew, and kept them cleanly and bejewelled, as merited a king's sister, the widow and mother of kings. She turned the ring back and forth as one of the two men spoke who was in the room with her. He was rotund, and wore the gown of a priest. Further back, by the window beyond which one could see the Carse of Perth through the drizzling August rain, stood another, taller figure, one she knew well: Lord William Howard, whom her brother of England had sent north as his ambassador almost two years ago. She had often enjoyed talk and some laughter with Lord William about the places in the south they both knew, Richmond and Greenwich palaces and the sluggish Thames where it ran amid the thrusting bustling city a Scots poet had written of, years ago at her own first betrothal. And she in cloth of gold beneath a canopy had been there, with her hair hanging, while they pronounced her the proxy-bride of the King of Scots. But by now there were other doings in London.

She swung about, the bloated face with its encysted eyelids no longer hunting, as it often did, for her young husband. Harry Stewart of Avandale, Lord Methven, was the King her son's tool, Margaret knew well; paid, with a lordship and this castle of her own, to keep her in ward, for all there was to show to the

113

H

contrary; to oversee her actions and her behaviour as if she were some common woman, not a royal princess and a Queen. They all acted against her without consulting her in any matter; even this new alliance the King her son meant to make, taking a bride out of France instead of cementing the alliance with England by marrying her brother's daughter Mary ... what did it matter that Mary had been disinherited? Such matters righted themselves in time.

Disinherited ... what was it Dr Barlow had been saying, while Lord William Howard stood silent by the window?

"My daughter the Lady Margaret Douglas in the Tower, her life in danger? And your brother also, my lord? How can this be?"

Lord William Howard came slowly forward. He had the clear brow and dark hair of his brother Tom, though his mouth over the past two years had grown pursed with diplomacy. But he dealt well enough with King Henry's difficult and treacherous sister, who liked him. It was the first time he had been personally affected by any of the matters he must bring to her attention. Anger claimed him for Tom's sake, and made his voice tremble.

"The King himself was cognisant of their wooing, and had nothing to say against it. Yet now, since the disinheriting of the two ladies Mary and Elizabeth, the putting forward of the Lady Margaret as heir to the throne has made it expedient, it would seem, to arrest her and my brother both. They are in the Tower, in separate prisons."

"My daughter ..."

The word came strangely to Margaret Tudor. A daughter meant, as a rule, one of the pretty children she had had by Harry Stewart, some of whom ran about below now in the courtyard and pestered the grooms. But that other, that she hardly thought of, truth to tell, now that the years had dulled the sharpness of deprivation since Angus had taken the girl away and would not let her come to her mother ... that girl, with flaxen hair. She had given promise of beauty, the Queen remembered, even in the long-ago time just after her birth when they had ridden together down into England and been welcomed by Harry and his kindly Spanish Queen. The child had been with her always then, a rose-and-lily creature with fair curls nodding, and her eyes blue as the harebells that grew about the moors here. She had been

114

a biddable child, causing no one any trouble, after that coarse undignified birth in a Border tower in drizzling rain like today's. But it was not seemly to blame the child for that.

"It was all of it Angus's fault," the Queen said aloud suddenly. That arrogant handsome boy she had married in the days after Flodden when life seemed like a voyage without a sail on a wide dark sea, and he had taken her in his hands and swore with an oath and a laugh to guide the ship safe to shore, but it had only foundered on rocks again, then Angus had left her . . . or was it she who had left him? "We were forever quarrelling," thought the Queen. But she quarrelled the more, now, with young Methven. She was certain he kept a younger woman somewhere. Angus also had had one, she knew, at Traquair.

"Your daughter, the Lady Margaret Douglas, madam," said the voice of Dr Barlow, Lord William Howard's secretary. His voice was censorious. How dared the priest carp at her, an anointed queen? She could understand how her brother Harry had rid himself of monks and priests, though to be sure the methods he had taken to do it were cruel. I could not act so, thought the Queen. But it would be pleasant not to have to endure censure from this fat cleric with the scholar's air; she preferred Lord William, who must be in poor case with anxiety about his brother, Lord Thomas. Not that there was anything she could do for *him* . . .

"I will write to my royal brother," she told the men. "Bring me wax, sand and quills."

Presently she sat down and wrote a letter. It was one of the few which would reach his Grace of recent years in which there was no demand for money. Margaret merely implored him to spare her child, and added, "*And 'gif it please Your Grace to be content she come into Scotland, so that in time coming she never come into Your Grace's presence . . . our request is dear and tender till us, the gentlewoman's natural mother. . . .*"

It was doubtful, thought Lord William, if King Henry would abandon so valuable a hostage to the Scots. But it might serve to save the young woman's life, and that of Tom, who had done no harm to any man.

There was another thing Lord William must do diligently; search for the truth of gossip which had it, both here and in the south, that my lord of Angus had already had a wife living when he had married the Queen. If such a lady were found, that would ease the matter for King Henry and, it might be, reduce the imminent necessity of lopping off his niece's head. For if the Lady Margaret were bastard also, how could she be heir? Yet Lord William had some trouble in ascertaining the thing. The woman had indeed been found at Traquair, where gossip had led him; but could in no way be induced to speak, until Lord William's third visit.

The young Englishman looked at her, his stolid gaze revealing a touch of temper after having ridden the damnable Border ways by night; even in summer they were bad. Janet of Traquair had refused to see anyone by daylight lest, she said, the Douglases do her harm. She was, Lord William decided, probably a witch; before she lost her teeth she might have been darkly beautiful, the iron-grey hair black as jet then, to cast a spell about a man, even were that man the Scots Queen's lover. Her clothes diverted him; they were like none he had ever seen about the Courts north or south. The bright stuffs swirled about her as she moved, without the stiffening most women wore. She would be easy to describe by her clothes alone, Lord William thought. Yet she was a lady. He kissed her hand and asked again outright if she had been married to Angus before he took the Queen to wife. Janet of Traquair gave him back look for look.

"I dare not say it, for my life. It would harm the daughter the Queen's Grace bore, that he sets much store by. *Her* he never cared for."

"If he loved you better than the Queen, surely he must have married you." It was worth while trying his diplomacy on her. He waited impassively. Janet gave her strange aloof smile and mended the candles, and turned and suddenly pointed her foot, as if she were dancing.

"He loved na her, but me, I say. The marriage was but to give him place in high councils."

"The Earl told you that?"

"He told me mony things, but ye will never gar me say them." She looked back over her shoulder with a gesture he had seen the courtiers at Greenwich and Westminster begin to use, these past years, lest someone be listening behind the arras, behind the trees in the pleasances. "It's as much as my life's worth," said Janet again. Lord William began to cajole her once more; he had met with some success on this visit.

"You have had letters from the Earl, surely?"

"Maybe."

"And you have written in reply?"

She did not answer. "Come, now," he said, "can you write? Would you send a word to the Earl of Angus in your own hand, to ask how he does? There is no harm in that."

"He'll aye dae weel enough," said Janet grudgingly. "He comes here nae mair sin' I grow auld." But she consented at last to sit down and, with much travail and passing to and fro of her tongue across her lips, wrote a short letter by candlelight, for Lord William to take with him when he went. It was worth much peace of mind to him to send it, not to Angus, but to the King in London. If there could be a breath of bastardy about the Lady Margaret Douglas, it might save his brother Tom.

A week or so later, King Henry received the Earl of Angus and his brother George in the Queen's presence-chamber at Greenwich, having withdrawn to its great round window in order that their talk might be private. The Scotsmen were summoned. Henry's small sardonic gaze noted the way they came, bowing, sidling, awaiting his pleasure, as well they might, by God! He had not withdrawn his brother-in-law Angus's pension, despite the trouble to which he had been put, and Parliament too, by Angus's ungrateful daughter. Heir to the throne indeed! Until now, he had upheld that second marriage of his sister Margaret, unwise as it had been, for the sake of decorum, taking no notice of her announcement of a divorce in 1528. But now, more than eight years later, a prior claim would settle the matter and declare his niece Marg'et bastard. He began to talk affably to the two Scotsmen, inwardly hugely amused at their inability to do aught but listen. The Earl, he knew, had been checkmated by his daughter's removal to the Tower, and was unsure of his own fate. He dared say nothing. No one dared say anything; and if Jane bore no prince by the end, he must accept it as the will of God that the crown should go after all to Richmond. Whatever happened the Scots King James V should *not* inherit, nor his half-sister either, born in England as she might have been; as if that gave her a claim!

The girl had had the impudence to entangle herself with a

Howard, his late wife's kin. That made matters worse. He scowled. Fitzroy – he often forgot his son's new title – was also married to one. Damn the whole place-seeking brood! Remembrance did not sweeten Henry. He scowled as he beckoned Angus close, without his shadowing brother. Then he looked his so-called brother-in-law up and down.

"Well, my lord, they tell me you have a wife hidden in the north parts who was yours long ere my sister."

"Sire –" Angus blenched a little; even his confidence had received a blow, and for instants he seemed confused, then adopted his habitual swagger. "They who say so lie, my liege," he told Henry, with a fine display of Douglas pride. "I am married to no woman but the Queen's Grace." By this time, he thought, it was true; his early handfasting to Janet of Traquair could not be seen as a marriage, any more than poor Madge's troth-plight to young Tom Howard. Yet Madge's troth-plight had placed her in the Tower, and they were describing her as the Lady Margaret Howard in despatches. Behind Angus's eyes modes of action shuffled briefly, like a hand at cards, while impressions came to ordinary sight despite them. How like a pig His Grace of England was growing, with his little eyes gleaming in his great ham of a face, and his paunch increasing even though the Queen's girth did not yet alter! If he gets no son this time, Angus thought, it will be dangerous to stay in England: failure makes Henry treacherous. The knowledge that he himself was standing on thin ice made him continue to look inwards, carefully; so much so that it took a nudge from George to bring his awareness back to the fact that the King was at last holding out a letter. The handwriting, blotted and blurred, brought to mind one thing, one face; Janet, seated at her table in Traquair, forming laborious characters with a hand more used to twist the spindle than to hold a quill. Angus closed his eyes for moments. When he opened them the King's gaze had not removed itself from his face. Did it hold a certain depth of sympathy for a man caught out?

"I have not read the letter," rasped Henry, "though they brought it to me. But have a care how you go, Angus; another monarch would not use you so well as I."

He stumped off to the Queen, who sat in her high withdrawn place placidly sewing a tester with her ladies, each one of whom was wearing a pearl-encrusted girdle by Jane's order. A flutter

of embellished skirts rose, curtsied, subsided and was still again.
Henry had turned his back on the Scots lords, who went out,
Angus frowning deeply. Lord George's face was bland.

"Ye seem untroubled, brother," the elder remarked to him,
when they were out of earshot. Lord George grinned a little.
"Ay," he said, "that am I."

"Events would not seem to warrant it."

"The one event ye need fear, brother, is the loss of your liberty
and maybe your head. Had Henry meant to clap us in the Tower
we'd not have seen his face this day. Tear up the letter, which he
has let ye keep; he's minded, now he has a sonsie young Queen
who may bear fruit, to be merciful; more so than James."

They paced on, not seeing the ordered summer gardens and
the sparkling river. Before their eyes was unyielding Stirling
on its high rock, where old Kilspindie – in his dotage, George
said scornfully – had of late hoped vainly to exchange speech at
last with the Scots King. "That is as we ourselves would fare, and
worse, were we in the north again," said George, who meantime
had taken to English ways and was a partisan of Tyndale's new
translation of the Bible, a copy of which he kept in his house.

But Angus felt the snell air of the north steal forever about
his heart, and wished he were home again. Would he ever see
Tantallon more, with the gulls crying above the rock and the
sea below? He would like, before he grew old, to do so ... but
Her Grace would never now forgive him, nor would her son.

MADGE WAS VERY ILL. She knew it less by events, which had become blurred, than by her thin white wrist extended on the coverlet, and by the heat. It must still be summer, then; she moved restlessly, throwing off the weight of the covers. The effort tired her; they had drawn off too much blood today: she was weak and yet still feverish. No fresh breeze could blow here, where there pressed in closely other buildings which made up the Tower, other prisons where some had been immured for the whole of their lives. Would she be so?

She had fought somewhat. The fact of being in prison had at first made her so angry, for her own sake and Tom's, that she had beaten her fists against the walls, the door. But the walls were eighteen feet thick, and the door did not yield. Beyond the window – there was a window, and the balcony – was that square place where dried blood could no doubt still be seen, darkening the grass: Nan Bullen's blood. The King had betrayed Nan. Would he betray herself?

In the end someone had come in answer to her frenzied knocking; Lady Kingston, who had seen Nan Bullen die. She had mouthed the tale Madge already knew, of how that poor soul had knelt and begged forgiveness of the Princess Mary. But Mary was far away now, and could not help her. She might never see Mary again, or anyone. She could abide here for months and years, forgotten, till she died of old age. Lady Kingston had also babbled of Acts of Parliament, but Madge could not listen for terror.

120

Once she saw an old worn woman, seated in a chair nearby, clad in a narrow dark gown and furred coat despite the warm day. Her coif was curiously broad and flat, like none Madge had ever seen. She pulled one of the long silver hairs out of her head and began to make lace with it on a pin. Madge gave a sudden cry which was flung back from the wall. The old woman, she knew, was herself. Had she run mad at last, with the heat and the attacks of fever which came, so that she sweated and shivered both?

She had never been ill before, even in the wandering days on the Border, sleeping under the open sky. Then she had still been free after a fashion. Now, lacking freedom, it seemed as if her mind and body were given up to fevered dreams and phantoms. Sometimes the need would clamour in her head to go and comfort Tom where he lay in his separate prison. She would hear herself say it, time and again, "I must go to Tom. He has need of me." He would be afraid, she knew; in greater fear than herself. It was again as though Tom were her child and not her lover. Perhaps the old woman who made lace would tell her how it had fared with Tom if she were to ask. But *she* had not shown herself again. It had been the progress of the fever.

Once there was a great bustle in the corridor, and coming and going in the outer court; the Queen's Grace, Madge was told, lodged in the Tower. The Queen's Grace ... she saw only the faces of Katharine, half-forgotten since that merry time of Yule years since, and then Nan Bullen, whose head had rolled bleeding on the grass. She hunched herself on her bed and did not try to obtain a sight of Queen Jane Seymour on her state visit. Presently the bustle died and she was told the royal party had ridden back across the ice. The ice! Why, then, it must be winter; but still she burned with fever.

They sent her the King's apothecary, Master Aske, at last, and then the King's physician, Dr Cromer. The latter told her that the Queen was certainly with child; that meant her royal uncle could be somewhat kinder to her, as she realised without speaking of it. A remembrance of the golden giant who had welcomed her to the revels that first year in England came to her, more clearly than the image of His Grace as he had now become. They told her another thing: the Lady Mary had become reconciled to her father through the good offices of Queen Jane Seymour, to whom the King could deny nothing because of her state.

"His Grace does not care for me," Madge said bitterly, and was told that indeed he cared; had he not sent his physician at his own cost?

So he cared. Her royal mother had also written letters, asking that she be sent back to Scotland. Madge heard the news as if it concerned someone else. Her father? He was well, and in the King's favour. Ay, Madge thought, Angus would walk warily enough not to lose favour with His Grace, even to admitting an earlier wife than the Queen had been, if he must; but it was not certain that he had done so, or she would be free of the Tower; they had no need to keep a bastard cooped up. She had heard of the matter through Lady Kingston.

Yet she was no bastard, she knew; pride came to her, curing a little the fit of despondency into which she had fallen. She was half royal, and a claimant to the throne. That made even Tom seem unimportant by now ... poor Tom. For herself, youth and hot blood had had their way; now they were cooled. She was become a thin tossing whispering shuddering thing, who saw old women in dreams. If they should indeed keep her here till her hair turned white, they would not cut off her head. Yet Parliament had passed an act promising the death penalty to any who should claim succession to the throne, or marry such. She understood it now. Tom and she were both forfeit. Had they beheaded Tom? No, she would have known by the sounds below, and the sight of fresh bloodstains on the grass.

The year passed and she did not mend. There were times when her life was despaired of, despite the physicians. Lady Kingston still tried to cheer her with snippets of news; her half-brother the King of Scots had voyaged to France despite the storms, and had broken his troth with Marie de Vendôme to marry the King's own daughter, Madeleine. "She no sooner set eyes on him than she would have none other," my lady said, not adding that Madeleine was so delicate no one would deny her whims while she lived. There had been, at the wedding feast, goblets of Scottish gold set out before each guest. The new Scots Queen was beautiful, they said. The pair would come home in the spring.

But the lack-lustre eyes of the sick girl on the bed took small heed of the news of royal wedded bliss out of France, when her own had been denied her. What they did not tell her, for fear of worsening her state, was that Lord Thomas Howard was also sick, and showed no signs of mending. But it had been His Grace's strict order that the two must not be allowed to meet. As for Henry of Richmond, the King's beloved bastard son Fitzroy, he was dead. It was as though what was given His Grace with one hand was taken away with the other. But perhaps soon now there would be a legitimate heir to the throne.

ABBESS AGNES JOURDAN, of the Sisters of St Bride at Syon, raised her plump capable hands in a gesture half to invoke the Deity, half to express, in discreet fashion, her perturbation at the King's letter which had been delivered to her today, and which allowed, one had to admit, of very little warning about the matter it mentioned. Choice of refusal the Abbess did not expect. It had been a condition of survival – when one thought of other monastic establishments, their treasures rifled, their precious manuscripts torn, burnt and fluttering to the four winds, their inmates turned out on the roads to swell the ever-increasing hordes of beggars who roamed from town to town – that she should always do His Grace's bidding in such small matters as that at present outlined. But to provide – and with a cold winter coming, Sister Ursula, who was ninety-six, had foretold it – fire and food not only for a half-royal young lady, but for her servants, including gentleman-ushers, was . . . inconvenient. "May God preserve His Grace," murmured Abbess Agnes dutifully, adding a prayer for the health and long life of the newly-born prince and for the soul of his mother the Queen, who had died some days after his birth. That, no doubt – the heavy-lidded, worldly gaze of the Abbess narrowed – would be why this Lady Margaret Douglas, described as the King's niece, was to be allowed safely to leave the Tower and come to what was, after all, comparative freedom to the place she had been in formerly. "She can walk in the grounds by the river if she chooses,' thought the Abbess comfortably. As regards

124

lodging for them all – well, she would consult her Bursar. When a thing must be done, God would find ways of doing it. Abbess Agnes raised her eyes to a fine ivory crucifix from France which hung on the wall by her, the tortured features of the Christ tellingly carved, the sinews prominent. Board and lodging of royalty was, after all, a species of flattery in that one was thereby shown to have weathered the late storms with diplomacy by recognising His Grace as Supreme Head of the Church in England. "And we are conveniently situated for his enforced guests to be nigh enough Court, 'thought the Abbess placidly. She would see that everything was made ready for the King's niece, including bed-linen, of which there was a plentiful store. And a brazier in the young lady's room would keep out the cold coming in from the Thames, which last year had frozen over so that Their Graces had ridden across it on horseback from the Tower to Greenwich. "May God rest the Queen's soul, she will never ride so again," thought the Abbess, who had glimpsed the procession. But Queen Jane had done her duty in bearing the heir, and had perhaps – who knew – averted a worse fate for herself by dying in timely fashion. In these days one could never be certain what would happen. The Abbess folded her careful lips, and went out to see to the comforts available for the Lady Margaret Douglas; it seemed she had been ill.

When the girl came before her at last the Abbess curtsied low; one could never tell how high a fallen favourite would rise again, come next midsummer. The wary blue eyes in the thin young face surveyed her unreadably. Lady Margaret returned the curtsy, but not too low. "How haughty she is!" thought the Abbess, in protest. "She has, one may see well enough, exalted ideas of her station in life; perhaps that is why she was kept in the Tower so long." She went about her own business, concealing further dismay at the largeness of the Lady Margaret's retinue; in addition to the menservants she had been led to expect, there was at least one more, who looked skeletal and poorly, and a half-comic creature with a starved face, who might be a jester.

"He is dying, you say?"

They looked at her helplessly, too grief-stricken to answer in words: the tears were running down Folly's face. They had come trailing after her as soon as she left the Tower precincts, and their emaciated looks had shocked Madge into letting them accompany her where she was going; surely at this protected convent there would be broken meats enough to succour their hunger? Tom himself was no longer even a remembered face: his features in her mind now were a blur, so much had fallen between.

After they had gone, taking such silver as her purse contained, she turned to her new company. Mary Howard, Fitzroy's widow, was with her here, and Surrey's Fair Geraldine. Surrey himself, she had learned, was under house arrest at Windsor for striking a member of the Court. "His temper was always hasty," Madge thought. The remembrance of Surrey was in fact stronger than that of Tom, and chiding herself for her own heartlessness she went to the prie-dieu the Abbess had allotted her, and prayed. This was the season of All Souls, and even now Tom's soul might be passing from the fever-stricken body to a place she knew no more of than he. He had been young, and he had loved her. "I have brought him nothing but dule," she thought. Would she always bring sorrow to those who loved her? Would she ever be able to love in return? She knew now, had known all through those ague-ridden months in the Tower, that Tom's love for her had been stronger by far than hers for him. She had been a goddess to him, never a woman.

On All Souls' Eve there was fog on the river. She went and walked among it past the jutting shapes of clipped mulberry trees in the convent garden. The trees were old and, said the Abbess, must be hewn down shortly to make room for new cuttings, for they no longer bore fruit. The thin cold and fog penetrated Madge's thin flesh in its fur robe, but she felt that she must walk, and walk. Her own footsteps came to her muffled by the fog. Beyond, a little way off, the same river ran where she had once strolled with Tom, a lifetime ago. The warm and eager girl she had been then had changed, she knew, in the course of her imprisonment to this cold woman who walked with her, a woman who would never more let the world see her feelings lest it do hurt. Proud and cold, they might say she was, the King's niece, the Lady Margaret, whose heart must be given to no man lest she render him ill.

Tom had been done ill by. Did he lie dead yet, or still tossing in his fever?

There were footsteps; it was Mary Fitzroy, the easy tears shining on her cheeks. "Oh, Madge, Tom has died . . . poor Tom, and our mother may bury him if she will, the King says, without pomp." After Richmond's death it seemed to her as if they were all of them dead or dying, together with the youth and happy times there had been; and here was Madge with her fair face set like a stone. Had she cared nothing for Tom, after all?

"There is other ill news," sobbed Mary. "The King's Grace – that is to say Cromwell, who lends an ear to everyone – has learnt already that you gave succour to Tom's servants, and they are to be sent away."

"They were starving," said Madge. "Could I refuse them succour?"

"Oh, you are so calm and cold, you seem to take no heed of the truth of it, which is that Tom has died of love for you, and our mother is desolate."

"Am I not desolate also?" said Madge, and turned her small hand so that the palm lay uppermost, and stared at it through the fog that still came from the river. She would write to Cromwell, the King's creature. Perhaps now Tom was dead he would secure her release.

Twelve days later they sent for her to attend the Queen's burying. The embalmed body of the only wife to bear the King a son was borne to Windsor from Hampton Court, in a coffin covered with a gilded pall and bearing a statue made of wax to resemble the late Queen, with the hair loose about the shoulders. Madge rode among the mourners and watched the nodding of the false hair with the horses' motion and the movement of the shod wax feet in their gilt shoes and hose. Beyond, all the mourners wore black, the women with white kerchiefs in honour of the dead; the Earl of Surrey, released from his arrest: Frances, big with child: Princess Mary, as chief mourner, her eyes downcast, rode nearby Madge; they had exchanged few words together. Elsewhere was the King clad in black. Madge had been taken to him before the procession started. His great face was pallid, showing traces of tears; when his wife had died he had, they said, made everyone leave him in solitude, despite the joy of the prince's birth. Madge had approached him at first without feeling. It was necessary to kneel, needful to bow one's head before this monster who had destroyed both Tom and her happiness as well as that of others. She had knelt, and had bowed her head, and once again had been taken up into those arms whose grasp was still the strongest in three kingdoms, so that lesser folk quailed under it. But the unchanged voice was that which had called out to her in pleasant greeting all those years ago at the Yuletide revels at Greenwich.

"It is my niece Marg'et. Let us comfort one another."

He too had, she reflected, as far as he might ever do, known loss. She let him fondle her, and returned his kiss.

It Was Summer Again; and again she rode in procession. The jennet ambled decorously, enduring its black trappings and the light weight of its rider, who paid it little attention. Madge's thoughts were elsewhere: unfittingly, because the corpse in this funeral was one which had in life been dear. The body of Mary Tudor, Duchess of Suffolk, was being conveyed from its temporary resting-place of Bury St Edmund's to the Church of St Mary, and a small train followed; again, Frances rode by Madge, with her younger sister Eleanor making a third beside them. Frances was growing fat, and her arrogant features contrasted sharply with those of Henry Grey, the father of her children, who looked like a mouse although his temper was peevish. But why think of the Dorset Greys today when so much else had befallen, and this ambling pace left one leisure to dwell on it, unlike the days at Court or at Hunsdon where duties filled each hour and one could never be certain, even now, of being left alone?

Even now. She, Margaret Douglas, was a bastard, the King had said lately, in the same way as his own daughters Mary and Elizabeth were still so. There had been a pre-contract of her father's and her mother was divorced. That made only little Edward fit to succeed to the throne. But Madge was weary of the talk of thrones and of the King's projected fourth marriage; it was rumoured now that he would choose a Protestant princess out of Germany, as her own Scots half-brother James's affianced second wife – his first had died – had rejected Henry's similar

129

I

offer with the remark that her neck was too small.

James ... and the horror lately in Scotland, the flames leaping up about the body of Aunt Janet Glamis, accused of witchcraft and an attempt to poison the King. Lady Glamis had died bravely. The next night her young second husband had killed himself by falling from the Castle rock where he was trying to escape from prison. James himself seemed to have a devil of vengeance in him still against the Douglases; possibly the death of his beloved young Queen Madeleine after only a few weeks in Scotland had roused it to replace his sorrow.

But James was, of course, to marry again. His second bride, the same Marie de Guise, Duchesse de Longueville, who had rejected Henry VIII's offer would perhaps by now be landing on Scottish shores. Scotland seemed far off, further even than the north parts of England where of late, this past year or so, there had been seen by many Christ Himself mounted on an ass's foal, and thousands had flocked to join Him and right the wrongs done to the monasteries, but the King's men under Norfolk had brought them to a reckoning, and there were hangings and executions now with a gallows on every highroad. They said the poor folk had rowed out in boats to where James and his first bride were travelling home by sea, to ask James to come and rule them instead of the tyrant in the south, but James had refused. "Would he have been any better for them?" thought Madge drily. Everywhere seemed to hold violence and cruelty and death. She herself could still feel nothing, and was no one. The King's bastard niece, no more.

The jennet stumbled then and Madge shot out a hand to save herself from falling. Another strong hand caught it, a hand in a gauntlet. Blue eyes, with laughter in them, met her own, and a man's deep voice said, "Steady, my lady. It is an ill road, and in summer. And your thoughts were elsewhere."

She gasped a little, blushed, and thanked the unknown courtier, who was a short stocky young man of perhaps twenty-five, clad in mourning as they all were today. The blue eyes were the only remarkable feature in his face, and held much warmth and vitality. Madge felt herself glad of him, which was indecorous for the occasion and her place; she cast her eyes down, and his mount sidled nearer.

"Never fear," he said, "the poor Duchess, God rest her, is not so great an occasion of watchfulness that we are espied here. Have pity on me, Lady Margaret Douglas, new to Court as I am and knowing nobody."

"But you know me, and I do not know you." They spoke in low voices; despite what he had said it was difficult to get away from the sensation of being watched, and Frances's ears were sharp. The young man smiled.

"I am Charles Howard," he told her. "My father is Lord Edmund Howard, the Duke's brother who fought at Flodden, but was ill rewarded. So little of this world's goods have we that he – and I with him – have been sailors, almost pirates, these past years since my mother died. My little sister Kat comes to Court next year; she is with our grandmother, the Duchess of Norfolk. You will show her kindness, I hope, my lady; she is but small, and gay for her years, and that is why I love her."

She heard little of what he said; only his name sounded in her ears. Charles Howard. She closed her eyes for instants, then said aloud "I have good reason to know your name, my lord." How long now since Tom had died?

"I am no lord, only your servant. As I said, have pity on me."

"Wherefore?" Power, suddenly, and feeling again, were rising in her veins; could this be herself, pale Madge – who cared for no one now except perhaps the Princess Mary and a little, still, for the Earl – exchanging foolishness with this man, this other Howard? Of all names better forgotten . . . what had he said about his little sister Kat, not yet at Court?

"Wherefore? Because I love you. I have loved you since the day I first set eyes on you, on Tom's arm one year in the garden at Lambeth, when there was blossom on the trees."

"You also, like your kinsman Surrey, are a poet. But write no verse to me. It will put your neck in jeopardy." She did not say the last words aloud. But they were true enough, she knew; or should have known; or would the presence of the prattling baby Prince now at Havering make her prospects differ?

"It cannot matter with whom I play at love, if the succession is sure," she found herself thinking, and then chid herself, and bit her lip silently. Who was she to think of love so soon, and with a young man she had only just met?

But Charles Howard was laughing at her. It was good to see a man laugh.

Declared Bastard Or Not, Madge was given the office of receiving the King's fourth bride, Anne of Cleves, at Blackheath, on so bitter a day in January 1540 that fires had been lit in the cloth-of-gold tents and perfumes cast upon them for pleasantness. From the perfumed air, she went out in the cold to greet the new Queen alighting from her velvet-hung chariot. Madge curtsied deeply, aware of the kindly, shy gaze of a pair of long-lashed brown eyes. "But, poor soul, she is pock-marked and big," she thought. There had already been rumours that His Grace disliked the sight of his bride so much that he had refused personally to give her his New Year present of sables and a fur muff, and had sent them by a messenger. The weather would have suited furs today, but Anne wore jewels about her neck and had hidden her hair with a pearl-sewn caul, and her gown was odd, made in the round German fashion; it was by far less graceful, Madge decided, than that they wore by custom here, with a kirtle and petticoat of different stuffs, and a laced bodice. She herself was grandly clad today; everything was grand, from the formed lines of velvet-clad merchantry and guardsmen to the Thames itself, where barges floated hung with arras and devices from the black Hainault lion to the mysteries of the London guilds, and guns boomed as the new Queen rode on her way. Madge was sad at heart, remembering that other day of Nan Bullen's crowning when there had been just such display and the sounding of cannon, and then less than three years after that a single gun had sounded for the loss of Nan's head. How pointless all such pageantry might be in the case of this poor German lady in her turn, time would tell.

Charles joined Madge when he could; they were much together in these days, and the Princess Mary, everyone knew, also had hopes of being allowed to marry Duke Philip of Bavaria, kinsman of the new Queen; they had already met and kissed in the palace gardens. "It would be well if all we new-made bastards might take advantage of our state to wed without harm, and be heard of no further," Madge thought bitterly. She mentioned something of the matter to Charles, who laughed as he always did.

"It is better not to be in high places, Madge," he said. "When you are my wife we will live simply, without state, if that pleases you. I am weary already of great occasions, and they bring you yourself little joy."

It was true; but later she was to ask herself if she would permit the denial of her royal descent enough to live as simply as Charles had always done, in hand-to-mouth fashion side by side with his hard-pressed sire, Lord Edmund. She smiled, said nothing, and continued her attendance on the Queen. The latter went to her marriage at last with sprigs of rosemary about her head, and false yellow hair streaming down over her shoulders. The sight would not please the King, Madge knew; nor did it so, for the day after the wedding he complained to Thomas Cromwell, who was to blame for it all, that the Queen was no virgin and he had been unable to consummate the marriage for disgust. "He will be rid of her, for sure," said Charles, "and Cromwell as well, grey-faced swine that he is."

"Have a care; you will be overheard," she begged him.

"You are too careful." He looked at her, seeing only her clear golden beauty in the rich gown. But she turned away; the stars would not favour this love, she knew, any more than the last.

One night soon afterwards there was dancing at Court. She and Charles followed the moving circle in a basse-dance, hand closely gripped to hand, lips smiling, bodies moving to the sound of the rebecks and flutes. Suddenly Madge was aware of chill, as though a draught had blown in through the door where the King stood, talking with some of his gentlemen who included Tom Howard's father, Charles's uncle the Duke of Norfolk. The Duke's cold, snake-dark eyes – he loved neither man nor woman nor God –

were fixed on herself, and she had the feeling that she must let go of Charles's hand and be seen nowhere near him. Their love and laughter together froze swiftly into a dead thing, a leaf blown away on the wind. She shuddered, despite the heat: and for succour looked not at Charles Howard, but at the King. His Grace's small eyes, however, were not on her; presently she discovered on whom they rested. A tiny fairylike girl, hardly more than a child, moved towards them in the figure of the dance; Charles's young sister, Kat Howard, newly brought to Court by her grandmother, the old Duchess of Norfolk who had been doting mother to Tom. Norfolk himself had shifted his gaze from Madge and Charles, as though they held no more interest for him, and was watching the little girl and, surreptitiously, the King. His expression as he did so held cold ambition and colder hope. What did he plan?

Madge felt faint. There was no mistaking the look in the King's eyes as he watched Kat Howard's small body twirl and leap. They held a clear desire she had seen in the days of Nan Bullen, of Jane Seymour; a wish to have the girl naked in his bed. Should she warn Charles? But what could Charles do without danger to himself? "If His Grace wants any matter, he will have it," the refrain of the rebecks beat in her head. Later she was able to assess the thing more calmly. The King seldom took his women lightly; his last open mistress had been Bess Blount, dead Richmond's mother, in the days when Henry himself was young. Now he was an old obese lecherous man, lame of an ulcer got with jousting on St Paul's Day in Queen Jane's time, three years back. He was no bedfellow for a fresh young girl newly come to Court. But one must accept what would happen; there was nothing else to be done. Madge was aware of a creeping of selfishness amid her horror. Would this advance her own cause to marry Charles Howard, once his kin were again in power?

It Did Not.

She had been given the envied appointment of first lady during that short-lived queendom of Anne of Cleves; now, when the good German princess sensibly agreed to the dissolving of her marriage and to live on in England as the King's dearest sister – she was in fact a hostage for the lack of reprisal by her kinsmen of the Protestant League, which accordingly dared not show its resentment at the divorce – Madge was again appointed first lady to the new Queen, Katharine Howard.

Few had been present at the King's fifth marriage. The exchequer was low after the Cleves feastings, and in other ways it was thought better not to put abroad yet His Grace's passion for the little girl he took for his wife and caressed so constantly, in public and private, that it was remarked on, sniggering, by those who were aware of His Grace's chagrin on other heads. The tall Frenchwoman to whom Henry had once desired to be married, Marie de Guise, Duchesse de Longueville, had wedded James V instead; lately news had come that a son had been born to them in Scotland. So Henry's temper would have been sullen enough had he not been diverted by his new passion, which made him feel young again. The little Queen romped about Court, displaying an innocence and warmheartedness which made His Grace indulgently call her his rose without a thorn; others, including her cold-eyed uncle Norfolk, watched and said nothing. It was the second time Norfolk had been uncle to a Queen; Anne

135

Boleyn had been his sister's child. The White Lion ascended again. The livery worn by the Duke's servants still boasted such a white lion downing the red, in memory of Flodden. Madge saw the double device often enough, in her new apartments at Hampton Court. She had been given rooms adjoining the royal suite, adjacent to the chapel.

Charles came to her there one day. She received him by the hearth, empty though it was autumn and the room grew cold. Over in the window-recess, Peter the embroiderer worked on a pair of her sleeves, to obtain the light. About them the noise of the great ornate palace which had once been Cardinal Wolsey's hummed and was never still. Charles stood frowning into the empty grate; she watched him, noticing how, since the marriage, he frowned more often and laughed less. "It is not a joyous thing to be too near a throne," she thought. Yet the young Queen was joyous enough, or appeared to be. Did she mislike an uxorious old man's caresses? But that must never be asked aloud; not here, where spies might linger. Madge smiled at Charles, to disperse his ill-temper. "What ails you?" she asked him.

"Nothing, except a cousin too many."

"Tom Culpeper?" She knew of that young man, whose handsome face wore a constant expression of discontent. He was much about the King and Queen, having lately returned to Court from the country.

"Do you know what he did while he was away?" said Charles. "He raped the wife of his gamekeeper. Had it been anyone else he'd have paid the penalty. But not Tom, whom the King loves too well."

She repressed a shiver of distaste; why had he told her of that ugly thing? "Do you mislike his coming here?" she said, carefully; knowing Charles, there would be other mislikings to uncover, that he had not mentioned except in relation to Tom Culpeper. It would relieve him to speak of them, she knew; and since the arrest of Cromwell after the Cleves fiasco one was safer, maybe, from listening ears at the door. She prayed that he would keep his voice low; the ringing sailor's tones that had called orders before the mast were dangerous here. She put a finger to her lips; he seized her hand and kissed it, then kept it in his grasp.

"Mislike it? Ay, that and other things. He's overmuch about the

136

Queen. My sister Kat is young, and – and has not always had wise folk about her. The Protestant faction would be glad enough if she put a foot wrong, with Culpeper or another."

"Another? But surely the Queen only uses them as a child might, for romps."

"Doubtless, but our grandmother took little heed to her when she *was* a child, and now it would beseem her better to be one no longer, lest worse befall."

"The King's Grace loves her childishness. It were pity to stop it for – for reasons of State." There had been so many cautionings, she thought, and fears; provided the King were well pleased other things mattered little. For no reason she thought of the pitiful Earl of Wiltshire, Anne Boleyn's father, who had offered to serve on the tribunal against his daughter and had assisted at the font at the christening of Jane Seymour's son. None dared oppose His Grace; but in his pleasure lay advancement. She must never say so to Charles; he would think of her as cautious and cold. "But I have learned to be so," she thought.

Suddenly his frown cleared and he swung about and, still clasping her hand in his own, leaned forward and kissed her on the lips. "I would have you out of here, with a sea-breeze in your hair and the colour of the sea in your eyes, as now," he said. "You were reared by it, were you not? I've sailed by Tantallon on its rock, without knowing, then, what treasure it had once held. When will you marry me?"

She smiled, pleased that he had recalled Tantallon to her; few spoke of it, but she had never forgotten the years there, before the troubled wanderings began. How much had happened since! England, the divorce, new Queens, Tom, the Tower –

"You had best not entreat my daughter as though she were any wench, Charles Howard."

The deep voice, with its Scots accents, took them by surprise; they had not seen Angus enter. He stood by the door, frowning, in the drab clothes he habitually wore, as if in constant mourning for his homeland and Tantallon. That last was forfeit; last year the Three Estates had declared it to be the property of the King of Scotland. Madge made her curtsy.

"My lord, I am glad to see you," she said; it had been long enough since Angus had visited her. With a clearsightedness which she had begun to acknowledge in herself, she knew that he would not have come today had she not been first lady-in-waiting to the Queen. As always, George Douglas was at his elbow; he waited in the shadows by the door. Not for the first time, Madge realised how she disliked her uncle: he was over assiduous.

Charles had kept hold of her hand, and faced the Earl. "May I not wed your daughter, my lord?" he said lightly, as though it were of no moment. "Is it because I have few prospects to offer except my sword-arm that you frown on me? Yet I am the Queen's kin."

"Ay, and a Howard. Madge has suffered enough from them."

Angus set his lips close, and strode towards his daughter as if she were alone in the room. "Hear me, Madge, for I had as soon the news came from me as from another," he told her. "Your royal mother is dead in the north, and on her death-bed she swore that I, and none other, am her true husband, and ye are her true daughter and heir."

"My lord –" That puffed half-remembered face, lying sick to death at Methven Castle, and surrounding the bed the Queen's children by another man, yet she had, before she died, found courage in face of them all to speak the truth. "I should have loved her better than I did," Madge found herself saying, with her eyes still dry; how could she shed a tear for a mother she had never loved and hardly known? Yet Margaret Tudor had, at the end, made restitution.

Madge raised her head and faced the Earl. Realisation had come to her what this death-bed saying of her mother's could mean. She was no longer, and dared never again be called, bastard in face of the dying word of the King's sister. She was as she had been, close heir again to the throne of England; a danger to any man she might wed, and if that man were a Howard, why, then –

Angus had turned already to face Charles. "My daughter, sir, is royal," he told him. "Royal ladies may not wed where they will."

Charles had not moved. He still stood where his sturdy height, not great, faced her own; his blue eyes were level with hers. What was it he had said a moment since about wanting to see a sea-breeze play in her hair? They would never stand by the sea together now. "I may never see him more," she thought, "he

138

is in danger from me." But Charles seemed oblivious to danger.

"Hear me, Madge," he said softly, and despite her fear she drew closer. When he spoke, it was to her alone; there might have been no other in the room. "Royal you may be or not; that is nothing to me who love you. As long as you live there will be men who love you; young or old, it will be the same: remember it. As for myself, if I cannot marry you I will never take any other woman to wife."

He turned and went out. She had not been able to utter a farewell to him. The tears she had not shed for her mother came now, in abundance; but it was too late.

There came a little cleric shortly to speak with her by the King's order; his name was Thomas Cranmer. Cranmer said nothing of Madge's newly assured legitimacy, but she knew well enough that the King had been apprised of his sister's dying message and was aware that never again could he treat her daughter as other than in the line of succession to the throne. Accordingly, her usage was to be harsh; but it was pleasanter to speak with this small abject clergyman than with Cromwell, who had taken suave delight in the misery of the victims he had trapped. Thomas Cromwell by now was a victim himself; his rough boar's head had fallen on the block. Thomas Cranmer rubbed his hands together, not looking at her as he spoke.

She was to leave Court. Her light behaviour with Charles Howard had been noted, and to curb her levity – for instants Madge felt wild laughter beset her, for the first time in long: when had she and Charles behaved with any lightness, knowing always of the fear that stalked behind curtains, in doorways, everywhere but on an open green? – to curb it, she was to be sent to that place which the Princess Mary at present occupied, being also under the King's displeasure because of the Catholic doings in the north; Syon. "You have sojourned there before," said Cranmer sadly. His mournful face almost indicated that it was as much pain to him as to anyone that she should be sent away from Court and its delights. Madge stared at him, thinking how Charles would have mocked at his subtle apology and creeping ways. But she must not think of Charles any more.

"I have indeed sojourned there," she said lightly. "The Abbess was Madam Jourdan, I recall."

"Agnes Jourdan is dead. There is a new Abbess, Clementina Tresham. She will see you furnished with all that you require."

"All I require cannot be found at Syon."

"That is levity," said Cranmer sadly.

Angus had gone out into the autumn day. He was oblivious both of George's careful talk at his elbow and the impending loss of his daughter to yet another prison. Madge would fare well enough; they did not ill-treat women "unless to take off their heads", the Earl thought wryly. But her presence seemed all at once unnecessary and unwanted, and he knew well enough why; he was a free man again. All these years, for the sake of Madge's fair name, he had acknowledged no woman but Queen Margaret as wife, nor would have done despite the insults his stepson King James of Scotland had heaped on him and his kin. He had made himself cleave, whatever was denied, to that long-ago folly of a marriage with King Henry's sister lately dead; but she *was* dead, and a hunger ate at him to ride away from these rich palaces and stale airs of the south, back to Tantallon, were it not forfeit, and to take to himself a young sonsie bride, as the King here had done, who would bear him sons of his name. Oh, it would hurt Madge, he knew; she had grown used to thinking of herself as the heiress of Angus, as well, no doubt, as the heiress of England if matters so fell out. But he himself grew no younger; it would be pleasant to be home again at his own hearth, and to take up his old ways that he had known and loved before his marriage with a Queen. But James's forgiveness would be as far off as ever: while he lived, there was no hope of return.

"I Did Not love him because he bore the name of Howard, nor he me for my name and lineage. Love heeds not such things. I can never forget him, and they will never permit us to be near one another again."

She poised her hand with its silk-threaded needle over her work an instant; what was it for, this constant stitching? "It is only that if I do not occupy myself, I shall run mad," she thought. The Princess Mary, seated stiffly away from the light, was doing nothing. How could she endure such things as must be in her mind? Mary was shortly to leave Syon. "It is not thought meet for us to be together, because we might comfort one another," thought Madge bitterly. Yet there was no comfort without Charles, and for the Princess herself Madge doubted whether she had thoughts to spare any longer for Philip of Bavaria, who had kissed her in a garden. What was love except a passing thing? Yet she knew that she had felt more deeply for Charles Howard than ever for poor Tom. Charles had been full man, with gifts of laughter and courage. Charles would not have died away of a languid fever in the Tower. Charles would live on into old age, as he had said, perhaps never marrying any other woman. "When shall I myself die?" she thought. Had she anything to live for?

The Princess Mary closed her swollen eyes. She had been crying night and day, and praying also, for the soul of my Lady Salisbury who had lately been hacked to death on Tower Green after two years in prison. "She would not bow to the headsman,"

141

Mary thought. "She would bow to no one except God and my parents." They had said they blamed my lady for the uprising in the north parts; they had said she had planned a marriage between Mary herself and her son Reginald Pole. They had said many things. But the Countess's true crime had been that she was a Plantagenet. Now there were none left. At least the cold in the Tower cellar was no longer eating into my lady's aged bones, but such a death . . . "She will be a holy martyr," Mary thought. My lady was surely as worthy of martyrdom as the saints of old who had supported one another in the pagan arenas when wild beasts came to tear at their flesh. Yet when one had known and loved someone well, it was those who were left who suffered longer . . . and there had been much suffering. Madge, her cousin seated over there, had suffered also, had lost her air of youth and was like a staid middle-aged woman for all she was only twenty-four years old; her beauty had hardened and she never laughed nowadays.

Aloud the Princess said, "Cousin, they will not give us leave to talk together beyond today. Do you remember how my lady of Salisbury said long ago that one might offer suffering up to God? She has made a worthy offering. Perhaps both you and I will suffer more than we have done. If so, there is that thought of hers for solace."

Madge saw her ride off on the morrow with the guard that was sent for her. The Princess was to be sent to her brother's place of Havering, to wait on the baby Prince. "That will comfort her somewhat," thought Madge, "for she loves him well." She herself had nothing and no one left. James V's two small sons – she had hardly given thought to them – were both dead in Scotland, and the realm without an heir. Her father the Earl, now war had broken out again, had ridden off to the north, and Madge had no news of him.

Other news came; and her own abrupt departure from Syon. She was to leave it to make room for a prisoner of higher rank; Her Grace the Queen. Katharine Howard had been arrested on a charge of adultery, with several men whose names were not yet known, but who included her secretary Dereham and also the young man Charles had spoken of on their last day together, his and Kat's cousin, Thomas Culpeper. There was much secrecy about the arrests, and of the King himself there was neither word or sign; the young girl he had married had begged to be permitted to see him, had tried to make her way to him to do so, and had been prevented by force; her screams had echoed down the length of the corridor leading to the chapel where His Grace was hearing Mass. There was no question of what would happen now; the Queen's own cousin Nan Bullen had received no mercy, and neither would the Queen. Before that there would be rackings, executions, questionings; Madge saw none of it, bundled as she was with little state to the new place His Grace and his ministers had chosen for her; Kenninghall in Norfolk.

She heard the news with unbelief, then horror. Kenninghall! "I am out of favour with the King's Grace because of supposed lightness with a Howard, and he has sent me to the place which more than any other will remind me both of Charles and Tom," she thought. Both, as boys, had jousted in the courtyards and hunted the flat Norfolk stretches, in a country which would be as familiar to any Howard as his hand. She, hitherto, had been a stranger to it; only now that she was forbidden to take the name that bore its device would she see the White Lion standard float above Kenninghall. Scorn rose in her. They said the old Duke of Norfolk had written an abject letter to the King deploring the adultery of his two nieces, Anne Boleyn and Katharine Howard. No doubt the reward of being gaoler to the King's own niece was the result.

She sat at Kenninghall, too bereaved and lonely even to sew, when news came, on a bitter day in February, of the execution of the young fifth Queen. Madge's first thought was for Charles, and how she might not send to comfort him even by a letter. *I have a little sister Kat who will shortly come to Court, and whom I love well* ...

"The thing is done, and that bitch Lady Rochford died with her. The King is grown brutal in his old age as he never was in youth," declared Mary Richmond in the safety of this remote place which had been her own home. She could remember tales of the King's youth culled from her dead husband; and she was red-eyed not only for Richmond but for the young kinswoman she too had loved well, whose short merry reign had beguiled her sad young widowhood. She glanced across at Madge Douglas,

143

so quiet and passive as always; did she even yet feel nothing?
"I wager," said Mary Richmond spitefully, "that there will be
a sixth queen soon, and that you yourself will be brideswoman,
restored to the King's favour till he tires."

"They have told me to beware of any third piece of levity,"
said Madge drily.

But the saying came true, and Madge and the Princess Mary met
again at the sixth wedding. They and the young Princess
Elizabeth, now of an age to note events, were to assist at the
marriage of His Grace the King with a pretty, kind-hearted, not
over-young widow who had been married twice before;
Katharine Parr, out of Westmorland. Madge went through her
own part in the ceremony with the feeling of a mummer who acts
in a masque. It had already been done over and over, and now
the gear was threadbare and the bones showed through. She saw
herself and Mary as old women, as the past; so, covered in a
kind of dust, seemed the King, lame of his ulcer, and his new
Queen, who had wed him out of fear. The real future was in
the young creature whose red hair gleamed in the light of the
chapel candles, and whose strange eyes surveyed the scene im-
personally, as though she imbibed all such matters for her education. But surely, now the young Prince would inherit, the
Lady Elizabeth could be of no such moment as she thought
herself.

Afterwards there came news out of the north which should
have caused Madge at least the pretence of sorrow, but she was
drained dry. James V, her half-brother who had hunted them so
relentlessly in early days, was dead: dead of a broken heart.
One could die, then, of such. The Scots force had floundered to
its defeat at a place called Solway Moss, and the King had thereafter no will to live, and left his kingdom to his girl-baby who
was only a few days old; a sorry inheritance for a woman! For
the Earl of Angus, it was at least good news; those lords who had
not been slain in the affray sent him an invitation to return to
Scotland and enter once again to the enjoyment of his estates,
and he would live at Tantallon. That name now was like a
dream; it meant little to her except in memory, and memory
held so much else that she would sooner forget . . .

She must be like the Princess Mary, and offer her sufferings to God. If she must spend all of her life alone, her faith must become a part of her as it had been for Lady Salisbury and the first Queen Katharine. She had beads now, and must tell them; unlike the young girl who had once stood by a window in a dripping Border castle and said them on her fingers. She had comfort and clothes and furs, and, again, the King's favour, for he was in high good-humour with his kindly wife, who nursed him competently. As long as that state of affairs lasted, she, Madge Douglas, was safe, provided she kept her eyes on the ground and laughed seldom. That last would be easy enough.

She was lonely, she knew. The time would be slow to pass till she was with God, if she should live to be old.

K

Interlude

The House at Hackney, 1578

"THEY SAY the salamander can live in the heart of the fire," said the Countess. "Often in my life I have felt like that creature which is our crest. Yet I myself grew cold in the midst of it; it raged round me and I took no part. My life after I parted from Charles Howard was both cold and empty. Yet no more harm befell me, and at last the wars with Scotland induced my uncle and my father to think of me as a useful pawn again."

She moved a little in her chair, so that the thin light fell on her profile. "I was twenty-nine years old when they married me," she said. "That is old in the eyes of the world. Yet now it seems as if my life had only begun then; as though all that had gone before, the suffering, the heartbreak, were nothing, only to be remembered in dreams."

Leicester watched her, aware of the charm she still had, though hitherto he had thought of her as deceitful, a plotter. So perhaps she might be; yet two men in her youth had professed a life's love for her. "You loved your lord," he reminded her, as though to comfort her for memory. She turned to him again and the red-rimmed eyes widened, to recover something of their former beauty.

"Indeed so, and he came to love me. You yourself have thought and written many hard things against him. But consider his position, my lord; as a boy, he was snatched away from Scotland and taken with his brothers to France, where he was brought up. The second brother married well, had the title of Sieur d'Aubigny

149

conferred on him – there was a drop, no more, of blood from the earlier strain of that title, and also a Stewart princess in the pedigree, which gave my husband the right to be regarded perhaps as James V's heir, failing others. All that is forgotten now. But my lord himself took no French title. He fought for France in the Italian wars, and afterwards waited for his return to the land of his birth. When it came, he – he hoped to wed the widowed Marie de Guise, who kept him waiting three years in that hope. Then he found that she had extended the same hope to at least two other Scots noblemen, in expectation of their support. That was galling for Matthew, for he was a handsome man and thought he had won her heart. But Marie could dissemble well.

"It is no coincidence that my uncle, Henry VIII, offered him money and promises at that time if Lennox would transfer his allegiance from France to England. One of the promises made was for my hand in marriage." She smiled. "I still have one of the letters he sent me at that time, filled with correct formal phrases of devotion to a bride he had never seen. It was the harder for him in that my father, Angus, had killed his – or at least had been in the field at Linlithgow, where old Lennox fell. But Matthew overcame that difficulty, and rode south in the end. I knew no more of him than he of me. Such a marriage might have been a failure. But it was not. I regard my marriage, Lord Leicester, as dividing my life into two halves; one before I met my lord, and one after."

"Tell me of it," he said. His wish to hear more was genuine. She talked on, while the light darkened outside the window.

150

III

Avant Darnlé

THE CITIZENS OF LONDON crowded in the streets to see a sight the like of which they had perhaps seen before, at times of festival and other; yet it was worth the apprentices' trouble jostling, as a rule, to be in front to catch the largesse expected to be thrown by so richly clad a nobleman as he clattered over the cobbles, with his train riding by him. Women leaned out on their elbows at the sills of the high, jutting houses to exclaim to one another across the way at his bearing, which was that of a soldier, and his handsome face: he might be thirty, they thought, or maybe less. The women came off best, having at least a clear sight of his plumed bonnet and short well-kept golden beard, his device, which was that of a bull breathing fire, and his dress, which was the white and gold of the Archers of the Guard of France. But the 'prentices were disappointed, because the narrow blue gaze roamed impassively over them and the nobleman threw no coins. After he had gone by it was rumoured that he was a Scot, which accounted for his meanness; and a bridegroom at that, come here to wed a niece of the King's few folk had heard of. There were those who scratched their heads over all of it, having heard the big handsome man address his bodyguard in terse idiomatic French as regarded their city, which he was visiting for the first time; it evidently impressed him less than Paris. Frenchman or Scot, whichever he might be, he rode on and they went back to their concerns.

The nobleman, Matthew Stuart, Earl of Lennox, had allowed

his own bitter thoughts to possess him again after the first sight of this cluttered city and thronged river lacking the translucent green of the Seine. It was beginning to be borne in upon him that he might have made a poor exchange; and word had come lately that his younger brother, John d'Aubigny, whom he had left behind in France, had been clapped in prison when they heard that Lennox himself had signed an agreement with England. Perhaps he would have been as well to hold his hand. France had reared him, it was true, and his brothers, after their father's murder by the Earl of Angus at Linlithgow years back, after which they had been smuggled abroad for safety from the murderer. Now he himself had agreed to wed that murderer's daughter, the Lady Margaret Douglas. A proud cold wench, no doubt, with her notions of royal blood, but he himself could offer as much; his Darnley-Stuart escutcheon entitled him to near heirship of the throne of Scotland, even as hers did for England, if it were true that she were not bastard as the Scots King had claimed. Lennox's gaze grew ugly as he thought of Scotland, where he had lately sojourned; ay, for too long! The treatment he had received from James V's coquettish French widow had, he thought, disillusioned him with all women for all time. Why, she had kept him long enough on a string, making pretence to be considering marriage with him, when at the same time she was offering precisely as much, no less, no more, to Bothwell's Fair Earl and others! It was all to ensure their allegiance for her precious baby daughter, but such mumming must needs have an end. Bothwell had gone so far as to put away his own wife in expectation of the exalted marriage, "but I," thought Lennox, "had none to lose, thanked be God." His life abroad had been spent in making war for the French in Italy and also in making opportunities for his own advancement, and he had always taken women when he wanted them, but had desired no nearer ties. He had known that, as with all else, he would not marry till it obtained him some preferment, and to that end he had considered it prudent to wait till his exile should be over. It was virtually so now; that was to say, if he had been right in throwing aside his French allegiance (damn that Guise widow!) in order to embrace the tempting offer King Henry had made of employment and money in England, and a half-royal bride.

"The old lecher knew well enough what he wanted me for,"

grunted Lennox to himself. "He wants war kept up on the Border till the Scots agree to the marriage of their young Queen with the King's son here, Edward Prince of Wales." But the Scots, and James V's widow, he already knew, did not agree to what was euphemistically termed the godly marriage; and in the end Lennox, baulked of satisfaction on one front, had decided to turn coat. He grinned mirthlessly in his beard; it had been rewarding enough so far. He had got his hands on the French subsidy sent across seas to aid Queen Marie de Guise in her struggles with the Protestant Lords of the Congregation. A part of it had in fact gone to equip him for this wedding of his at St James's, and to provide gifts for the bride. He would show the Guise widow that she'd have been better to have him than flout him; by God, he would!

Lennox was gratified to find that his bride was not ill-looking. In course of the formal courtship which they had pursued by letter, he had heard it stated, by her father among the rest, that the Lady Margaret Douglas was a beauty; but Lennox had put it down to the wish to seal a bargain. He had been prepared for disillusionment, remembering having heard tell of the King of England's late meeting with the reality of Anne of Cleves, whose portrait by Holbein had flattered the lady beyond all measure. But there had been neither money, time nor need for Lennox to send or exchange portraits. He and the lady must take one another on trust; and, he thought, she had perhaps not made a bad bargain. He himself was personable enough to please any woman.

He advanced, accordingly, with a certain complaisance towards the group that awaited him. He was cognizant of the ways of Courts, and bent his full attention first on the jewelled tyrant who sat, bulky and ill, in his chair of state with his pretty new Queen by him. Lennox kissed the puffed beringed hand after the French manner. Above him he heard the bluff voice roaring pleasantries, pleased to have entrapped one more Scottish nobleman in the net. "My niece, Marg'et, who is heir to me next my own flesh and blood," the voice said at last, and Lennox looked about him; he knew that he could meet his bride with complacency, as he had already, in Scotland, met her father, his own sire's murderer. He had contrived that, and had disguised his feelings; by now, he could contrive anything.

He was presented to the women present, at the same time taking in their separate appearance and hoping that the short plain creature in the too-bright carnation satin dress with embroidered sleeves was not his bride. She proved instead to be the Lady Mary, the King's daughter; small, saddle-nosed and plain. The young chit with red hair Lennox had not considered. There were two others, a young dark bright-eyed beauty and a fair, either of whom he could have taken happily enough, he thought. It appeared that the fair one of the two, whose demeanour was sober and quiet, was the Lady Margaret Douglas. Lennox was not ill-pleased; he kissed her hand, then her cheek. They exchanged the usual courtesies, he in his slightly accented English. All the time he was thinking "It is not so bad; she is not haughty, from her demeanour." He was pleased also with her clear colouring – he could barely have endured a pock-marked wench – and with her small fine hands, which he noted early. Her hair, which was mostly concealed beneath her hood, seemed plentiful. Lennox accepted his lot, only briefly remarking on the dark beauty nearby, who no doubt would have suited him equally well. She was, he learned later, the young widowed Duchess of Suffolk. Lennox smiled to himself. He had heard rumours, even in France, that the old King had an eye to her; the seventh wife?

The marriage took place. Lennox made his vows, pleased with the glitter of the St George embellished with diamonds which his bride had given him and which he wore pinned on the bosom of his white tunic. He had given her some trifle in return, of less value. He noted that she had many jewels; the Princess Mary alone, for this occasion, had given her three great brooches set in gems. It was the Princess, in fact, and not the bride, who wept when after the feasting they were escorted to their chamber and at last, after the stocking filled with salt had been flung, and jests made, were left alone in the great bed together. After the final guest had gone out Lennox turned aside to wet his lips with the goblet of wine which had been placed nearby. Now that he was alone with his bride he felt the onset of personal shyness; why should that be? To take a woman, as he knew, was nothing; but in this instance one must also, as it were, make her full acquaintance on the assumption of keeping her as a lifetime's companion. What did he know of this woman, save what he had heard? And that was unsavoury.

He turned to her half savagely. She was lying quiet on the pillows, and her hair, now that it was spread loose, he could see, was beautiful. It was impossible to tell from her expression what her thoughts were. The shining hair and the clear blue of her eyes, seen by candlelight, unmanned him. He took refuge again in his anger, saying roughly, "To have a Scot in your bed may not please ye, my lady; we are by nature less courtly than your folk here in the south. Of all those of my nation whom ye have desired to wed, in the end, as ye will see, it is myself here and none other." She had already, as he knew, refused the Earl of Huntly, to whom James V would have married her at the last. He referred to it, and to her other reputed saying that she would even be willing to wed Bothwell after his wife had gone. The widow's refusings! How could she have thought of it?

He talked on. It was as though he were determined to raise enmity in her by whatever means. Yet she answered him amiably enough.

"You are a Franco-Scot, my lord, and in France they are a courtly nation. The Earl of Huntly? He would have wed me as the Scots King's base sister, no more. That I am none, being true daughter to my parents, born in wedlock. My lord of Angus would never forsake his marriage with my mother the Queen while she lived. If you had doubts of me in such a way, my lord, why did you wed me?"

"I had no doubts of that," he grunted, not adding that he had married her because she was the best that offered. He began to boast. "Your lineage is high, but so is mine. The King of Scots would have made me his heir after his sons died, had not this girl been born. We Lennoxes are descended from a princess of Scotland, and my forebears fought with the Maid of Orléans crying *Avant Darnlé*! as death took them. Also we aided King Henry's sire at Bosworth Field. He owes his throne to us." He bragged, consciously; at the same time downing the uncertain memory of a small boy taken up terrified and crying into the saddle, to the coast by night, to France, because his father was dead; his glorious golden father, whom he had loved. The remembrance that the killer's daughter lay here by him now made

157

Lennox brutal.

"It is changed days, is it not, when such as I must take another's leavings?" he sneered. "You, my fine lady, coupled with a Howard, or was it with two of them? We need have no disguises from one another, here alone as we are." He bent over her. "Why wed me? Why choose myself, and disdain others of my nation? I bring no rich lands, and ye fare the worse for that." He thought fleetingly of the broad Norfolk acres she might have had, of Castle Howard and Kenninghall. He – they – would be dependent now on such as King Harry in his meantime humour might grant; some place in the north of England, he'd heard the name; Temple Newsam, that was it; a far ride from London. And the use of Stepney Palace while they were in town. He himself would have little leisure for either, busied as he'd be on the Borders in King Henry's war.

She had not bridled nor moved, he saw: the colour of her face did not change.

"Prove me, my lord," she said, "and that the Howards left me virgin."

"What proof have I of that till it's done?"

"If you wish so that we quarrel, why then did you wed me? I put that question to you again." She was smiling at him now, he saw; she showed neither fear nor rancour. Despite himself Lennox began to admire her: she had courage, he decided.

"Answer for yourself," he growled, "ye do not lack for wit. All of my days, since your sire put paid to mine, I have had to mend my prospects in whatever fashion. I have spent most of them as a soldier of fortune, fighting in other folk's wars. There is yet another to be fought now on the Border, where I – "

"But you will have a home to which to return, my lord." She spoke softly, and he realised that his ill-humour had already faded.

"Ever since I was a child," she said, " – and I had a harried childhood, like your own, hastened from one house to another, from one land to another, where often none bade me welcome and would see me soon gone – there is one place I remember best. It was where my good aunt Suffolk, who loved her husband well, cared for me as though I had been her own. She taught me to see to a household and order servants, and to know herbs, and brew and bake – she herself had delight in all such things, despite

158

being a king's daughter – and to make possets and unguents, to heal sickness and wounds, and the like – I could use a needle well enough already, I take pleasure in that. Always since then I have wanted a place to call my home, where I could bring comfort to my husband and to our children. I have been lonely, my lord, for long. I had hoped to be so no more."

She turned her gaze upon him, come to her after the aching years of loneliness, this fine big man who could give her sons and daughters with slim height and golden hair, and an ancient name. She knew of his bitterness over Marie de Guise, and took a moment to wonder what kind of woman James V's widow was. If Lennox continued her enemy also, could there ever be happiness for either of them in this marriage? "Can I not be your friend and ally, my lord," she said softly, "that you have vowed to cherish, even though my sire killed yours in time long gone?" Her voice trembled. "I have two examples of true wives in my mind; my aunt Suffolk that I spoke of, and Queen Katharine of Aragon, whose soul God pardon."

He tried to answer; his voice came thickly in his throat. It was true, as she said, that he had never known a home, any more than she; and the wine he had drunk, and her fair beauty, so close to him, and the things of which she had spoken, made his head swim. What did the Scots widow matter, after all? Here was his wife; he reached out to her.

"I am called Matthew," he heard himself say. He pronounced it in the French manner. Mathieu. He had last heard it on the lips of a doxy near Pavia. Everything had changed, his whole life; and he – "What am I to call ye, wife?" They could not, he thought in a sudden access of humour, continue long with naught but my lord and my lady. He was beginning to be happy; his senses sang.

"Those who love me call me Madge," she told him. "I hope that you will do so. Together we are strong under God. I will please you in all ways that I may; only, do not hate me."

"Hate my own wife? Why, lass – why, Madge, it is the best day in all of my life –"

"Then snuff the candles, Matthew, and let us make our son."

SHE WAS SO SWIFTLY PREGNANT that to her it seemed a miracle; the knowledge that her body at last bore within it a living creature of their joint making, so that she need never more be alone, brought her untold joy. The joy stayed with her after Lennox had ridden off, with five hundred men under his command and a fleet of ships, to take Dumbarton by the King's order. On his departure he had kissed Madge many times and had bidden her, in his half-foreign speech, to have a care to herself and to pray for his success. She thought nothing at that time of his errand; glad only of the awareness of being protected and loved, she had murmured against him, "I shall surround you with a girdle of prayer that you may come to no harm," and had smiled, and downed the remembrance of the prying curious eyes of Tom Bishop, the man King Henry had bidden ride north with her husband.

Now they were gone, and she was alone with her precious unborn child, and so never again alone in the old manner. She walked through the scantily furnished rooms of Stepney, seeing the dust; the King had granted her and Lennox the use of it for their time together, but now that he was gone Madge remembered older times, and voices now silent. Yet still the river ran by as it had done in the days when the Queen-Duchess presided there. Madge would sit by the window for long hours watching the water, pausing with a hand still holding the needle threaded for the exquisite embroideries she was fashioning for the baby. Letting her eyes rest on the grey Thames and the rising mists of autumn she could not help recalling how, on the first day she came with Strangeways to London, a barge had gone skimming past with His Grace in it and, by his side, a dark woman. So much trouble had arisen since by that cause, and now, thanked be God, it seemed to have come to an end except that one still heard of matters such as the destruction of shrines and convents. She turned her thoughts away from that. If only her lord might have victory in his venture, and the King also, who despite his age had sailed in the summer to make war on France, all might be well.

The King's fleet had defeated the French squadrons. Lennox was less fortunate. Madge had word of his misadventures while the Princess Mary was with her, both of them occupying themselves with gossip and with preparing for the coming child's needs. Mary had brought a gift of the rich kind she loved to give, a gemmed latticed trimming for a baby's dress. They were exclaiming over its pearls and tiny sparks of rubies, and Mary was admiring the work Madge herself had already done. The Princess had short sight, and must confine herself nowadays to making chair-seats and the like; the finer stitchery filled her with admiration and, Madge knew, a lack of envy; Mary was the least envious of women. Moreover she loved children so much that she had even shown kindness to Nan Bullen's daughter Elizabeth in her childhood, and she doted on the young brother who would succeed to the throne.

"What shall you call him if he is a boy?" Mary asked now. Madge smiled. In her dreams, as her cousin knew well, the coming child could be none other. A boy, in whose veins should flow the finest blood in England and Scotland both; of that perhaps best say nothing even to so close a friend.

"Henry," she said, "after the King's Grace."

"That will please my father. If God had granted him a second son, that would have been his name; I have heard him say it."

They smiled together, and at that moment the messenger came in with ill tidings. Lennox had failed to take Dumbarton, and had narrowly escaped with his life. When Madge had expressed her thankfulness for his safety she realised that the King would be much displeased at the news. Yet it seemed unreal; perhaps she was too greatly content with her present state to question

161

L

much, or wonder how it could have happened that Dumbarton, where her husband had been born and where his lands had formerly lain, should have resented him enough to refuse to surrender.

The vengeance came, and she was summoned to the King, who lay sick in his chair again after the unwonted expedition to the Channel. He scarcely greeted her or asked how she did; the small mouth was petulant.

"Your lord hath not well demeaned himself in the north, Marg'et. I had thought your loving fervour to have made a better Englishman of him."

The little pig's eyes roved over her body. He envies me, Madge was thinking; in the same way as he once envied youth and love, now he envies fruitfulness, the evidence he has that I am not barren like his Queen. But how could she, poor soul, when Henry was past giving pleasure, bear children? The King himself was a mass of diseased wrecked flesh. "He will not, I think, live long," she heard her own thoughts say; "but he can still do harm while he lives."

Aloud she said, meekly as she had found it advisable to do, "Sire, then permit me to join my lord in Yorkshire, the better to cheer him in his endeavours. No man can better Your Majesty in victorious war, yet my lord will do what he may."

She found the King's new title slipping aptly over her tongue. She kept her eyes downcast lest he see the dislike in them; also, lest she catch the compassionate eye of the Queen. She heard Henry's heavy breathing; the reference to France had not soothed him as she had hoped. Behind him, she knew, his wife waited terrified, now as in every waking hour; what sort of life could any woman lead with such a man? "I would to the north soon," Madge thought, "and to my own lord." She knew a great longing for Lennox. But she had not yet heard the King's answer.

"You will abide here, at Stepney, till your child is born. Thereafter go north, and use your best endeavours to persuade your lord to a fiercer war against the Scots. You will do this the more readily – " the bloated face crinkled into an old, wicked smile – "in that your child shall stay here, with us, as hostage." The King struck the arm of his chair suddenly. "I did not trust the Scots

162

in my youth, and I do not now," he roared. "Lennox will betray me if he can."

She caught her breath on a sob; was the child in her very womb to be a pawn in the game, taken from her as soon as she had given birth? "My lord would never betray Your Majesty," she said. "He is too greatly sensible of the honours you have done him, the domain of Temple Newsam itself, and my own hand – "

"The hand of my bastard niece, whose sire was wedded already when he begot her on my sister." The King's breath still came thickly. Madge drew herself up to her height; a flush stained her cheeks, despite all caution.

"At my marriage feast, sire, you said openly that heirs of my body should gladly be heirs of your own. Have you forgotten it? Do you seek now to destroy your sister's honour, and mine?" Speak gently, pleasantly, Madge, she was thinking; one shrill word, one false move, and he will have your liberty, if no more. But the King had already turned his great head aside to where his wife, as always, bent over him gently, considerately. She dare do naught else, thought Madge with compassion.

"I have mine own sweet heir Edward, and need no other," he grunted. "Get about your duty, niece; bear your child, then as soon as may be ride into the north parts to spur your sluggard lord. Am I to have every beggar Scot batten on me without recompense? Lennox should have taken Dumbarton with ease; as it was, Tom Bishop says he had to force a Moorish pike on him for the escape they both made, neither of 'em clad in armour."

So Tom Bishop the spy had done this, she thought: and all the promises made to Lennox when he took her as his bride were come to nothing. How would her husband take the news that he had wedded only a bastard of the royal line? The bleak thought of losing Lennox's love occurred to her. She took her leave without further speech with the King, and returned to Stepney in low spirits.

When she was alone she wept, again wishing her lord were by her. What purpose was there in her life if everything were to end in uncertainty and fear? Was she even to wish this child dead that she carried? "He may be heir to nothing now," she told herself. The King had disowned him except as a hostage, and – this added to her bitterness – her own father Angus had married again, this time a marriage that could not be doubted, to a young girl, a daughter of Lord Maxwell, who, he had lately written was pregnant. Neither the Douglas nor the royal inheritance was to be her son's, "and yet I myself and the child's father cannot be let alone to enjoy the freedom private persons have," she thought. As long as the King lived her rights depended on his caprice; she had ample evidence of it.

"Yet I need hardly pray for his death. That will come soon enough, and he will go to his account." It was a far cry from the memory of her first visit to Court in girlhood, where a merry hospitable giant with a red-gold beard had tossed her in the air as if she were a feather.

"My niece Marg'et has grown tall" . . .

"And now I will soon grow thick," she thought, looking down at her body. Well, she must bear this child and love it while she had leave; after that, it was at God's disposal.

The child was born at Stepney at last after a short easy labour. It was a son. The Princess Mary, who had come to be with Madge at the birth, bent over his cradle afterwards, her plain little face full of happiness. What a transforming change joy makes in her, Madge thought, turning her tired gaze to watch her cousin. They had sent word of the birth to Lennox and to the King. She herself felt nothing of the expected gladness; as soon as she was fit to travel, she knew, she must leave her baby. He had all necessary attendance; the wet-nurse waited. "We will christen him as early as may be," she heard herself saying, "in your jewel-trimmed robe you gave."

Mary was playing with the baby's fingers. "See how he grips me! It is pity you must leave him so soon, Madge, to go to your lord. But I will have as much care to him as though I were myself his mother. That you know well."

That she knew; but might it not wring her heart that the baby would not know her, his own mother, when they should meet again? She closed her eyes and willed sleep to come; strangely, after labour, it had not. It was as though she had suffered too little through it all, and without reward. It might almost have been another woman who had borne her child.

Some weeks later, after Henry, Lord Darnley, was christened at

164

Stepney Palace, his mother made her way north, alone except for servants, to the Yorkshire place the King had given her and Lennox for use while his mood might last. It was, as she had already learned, part of the spoils of the Pilgrimage of Grace. Its former owner, a Catholic lord, had been executed.

At First The Sight of Temple Newsam depressed her. It was a great red square block of a house built round a courtyard where grass now grew, giving the place a desolate and abandoned air. In the paddocks more grass blew, brown with winter and neglect. Riding up from the south through the bitter sleet it had not seemed as if she could ever be warm again: now, courage came to her aid and she determined to kindle fires in the damp grates and brush the mildew from remaining furnishings. Most of these had been pillaged. Outside, not a beast grazed, and she began to wonder what they would do for food when the stocks they had brought ran low. It did not sustain her spirits that there were other properties in the King's grant to them which would be, no doubt, like this; the ruins of Jervaulx Abbey, the other houses of Temple Hurst, Silkstone and Beckay.

By night she sank exhausted into a damp bed, remembering to say a prayer for the murdered Lord D'Arcy, who had owned this place. In his day it must have been richly furnished, cared for, and beloved; could she make it so again? Even the chapel had been rifled, and she had already placed there such things as John Dicconson, the priest, might need. Mass should be said daily when the chapel was reconsecrated. She frowned in the dark. She had heard Dicconson say that Lennox himself had been made to swear an oath to acknowledge the King as head of the Church in England. God was English, no doubt. She herself had never been asked to swear; would she have done it, with prison as the alternative? She did not know. "I cannot blame my lord," she thought. But here in the north parts they would have freedom in their faith.

On the following day she had the servants unpack her gear. There was among it a bundle of furnishings for the bedchamber she would share with Matthew. She shook out the contents and spread them to air, then hung them with pride. Much of the embroidery was her own work; the bed's tester was of cloth of gold and purple velvet, showing the arms of England. There was a quilt which delighted her because it changed colour with the changing light; and a great hunting tapestry to hang on the wall. Elsewhere, on the panelling now washed and polished with beeswax, she hung two portraits; one of Matthew's brother the Sieur d'Aubigny, the other of her own mother, the Scots Queen. "She acknowledged me," thought her daughter, staring at the portrait. "It is fitting that she should hang here in my hall." Already the house was beginning to feel and look like her home. She had had none since Tantallon.

She pinned her golden images about the bed-curtains, which were of crimson velvet. Downstairs the feather mattresses were drying out before great fires; the servants had scoured the country for wood to build them. Tonight they would all be warm. The apple-cheeked Yorkshire maids whom she had employed on her way were, she discovered, not afraid of work. They made a pleasant change after the sometimes slatternly service she had had to endure in London. She and they cleaned, dusted, swept, polished, everywhere; the chamber and the closets, hall and cellar, buttery, pantry, kitchen, larders, wardrobes, brewhouse; there was work for a month in any of them. It was too early in the year to fold away dried herbs with the linen; Madge found the place where she would clear the nettles and make a herb-garden; meantime she aired the linen frequently lest it lose its sweetness before her lord came riding home. She set the serving-men to scythe the fields, and wished for stock to fill them; but wishing had to do for the time, as there was not much money.

Aid came to her in an unexpected way. One day she was turning out the room which would be Darnley's nursery when he came north. She was brushing tapestries, one of the Holy Family and others of figures representing the virtues, which she would hang there; as soon as he could understand on what his

167

eyes rested, he would be told of it. While she was at this task one of the servants came to say there was a visitor below.

Madge bit her lip. She did not look her best, she knew, in a linen cap and apron and straggling hair, and dust on her face as like as not. The room had been full of cobwebs. However, she went down. Standing in the courtyard, with his mount still held by the reins, was a tall man with grey eyes, surrounded by his servitors. He swept a bow, smiling gravely.

"My lady of Lennox, I believe. I am the Earl of Westmorland." She nodded; she had known him from his device. "I rode by Leeds today," he went on, "and it occurred to me that there might be certain matters I could send you, from my house; nothing here was in readiness after poor D'Arcy was taken. Do you lack for meat, wine, or aught else?"

She flushed with pleasure, not only at his offer, but at the effect she knew she had on him, linen cap or no; he looked at her in a way that took no heed of cobwebs and aprons. Madge would love none but her lord, but it was pleasant to rouse admiration in a personable man; what woman felt otherwise? And it was evident that this nobleman, who had ridden over out of neighbourly duty, found her person much to his taste. The grey eyes lingered on the gold of her untidy hair; she put up a hand to tuck the loose lock under her cap. "You are kind, my lord," she said, "but why should you do this for us?" The presence of Lennox was implicit in her words; she would never exclude him.

"It is no favour, but what I owe. When poor D'Arcy went, I drove off his beasts and took certain of his wine-casks, to keep till an owner came. Otherwise, they would have vanished, as has so much else in this part of the country."

She accepted with gratitude, and before long a drove of cattle, well enough fed over the winter, came to graze in her fields, and a cartload of salted carcasses to hang in her cellars. Lord Westmorland rode over thereafter at her invitation, and together they broached the wine. It was good, and well matured; Madge grieved at the fate of the late owner.

"Was he a young man?" she asked of the late Lord D'Arcy.

"Young, and ardent. He had great faith, for which he died. In these parts there were many such, as is well known."

Her fingers turned the flagon. It was unsafe to talk overmuch of such things, even though the spy Tom Bishop was away with her husband. She thought again of Lennox, and raised her cup, and smiled.

"Let us drink to my own lord in the wine," she said, "and may he ride safe home; and when he does so, may we all three have a merry meeting, for you have shown much kindness to me, and will always be welcome in our house."

Westmorland gazed at her, and smiled. That she was a beautiful woman he had seen at their first meeting; now, he was filled with admiration for her courage in dwelling here alone, and making the place a fit habitation for her absent lord. He raised his own flagon, and replied to the health. "To call you friend, my lady, is a matter near my heart," he said, "and may I never forfeit my welcome here."

"You will not. Good friends are like good wine, and improve with keeping."

He wished her many of both, and soon rode away, that there might be no gossip from their too frequent meeting in the absence of her lord, whom he could see she loved.

Lennox rode home and she greeted him with a loving embrace, a good fire and food. He was pleased and bewildered, looking about him.

"Ye have worked miracles here," he said. "When I rode by on my way to the north it was desolate enough; now it is a comfortable house, and warm."

"Did I not say I would make a home for you?" she reminded him, and he laughed, and kissed her. "Ye have not failed of any promise, Madge," he said, and held her away from him that he might gauge her health after the child's birth. "How do ye fare, wife?" he said. "I grieved that ye should ride north without my company, through the bitter weather; I would have come south sooner, but affairs on the Border are rough and unsettled. The Scots like not the marriage of their Queen to Prince Edward, and have hid her away, no man knows where except her mother's folk."

He sat down and pulled her to him, and asked about their own child. "Oh, he is well," she said, "and my cousin Mary writes to say that he tries to talk, and has a tooth," but at the back of her mind, as she talked, was the fear that Lennox might have heard of the King's withdrawal of his promise of heirship; how did my lord feel his wife's degradation and his own? "Yet we are not degraded in truth," she thought. "My father would not lie to me."

She dissembled, and asked about Angus; had my lord met with him? Lennox growled that her father was too greatly content with his sonsie new wife and their bairn to see anyone, but he had had kindly messages from the Earl, and sent others in return. "He is for the English alliance, or so he says; but will do naught to foster it, and the King sent him a sharp lesson lately, and has laid waste all his gear."

"He has regained Tantallon, and will be busied with repairing the lost years there, whatever the King may do," she said, and for the first time in long thought of Tantallon, but only as a place she had once known; here was her home, and her own lord sat by his hearth, and if only their child could have been here with them, she would have been content.

Looking back, she found her love for Yorkshire assail her in certain ways, strange at first as pertaining to a strange place. She loved the sharp air, appealing to some part of her that remembered her Scottish childhood. She would walk, with Lennox by her, about the fields and moors, glorying, as the year passed, in the bright colours of the heather and harebells and the blowing northern grasses, and the frequent sight and sound of the hunt in full cry. There was, too, the knowledge that in this region the old faith had flourished long after it had died in the south, and by degrees she found others who would help her sustain her creed. Lennox himself preferred her company to riding off again to war; they would sit together by their fire, secure in one another's love, and the knowledge in time that Madge was again with child. Yet amid the long northern vowels and the solid kindly friendships, and the freedom of knowing that many miles lay between her and the Court, there were two things not welcome. One was Tom Bishop's presence: Madge knew he continued to spy on them, sending word south of any supposed indolence of her lord's, or on occasion his hasty speech or her own. But Lennox would not entertain suspicions of the man, who, he said, had saved his life at Dumbarton.

There was a matter which brought Madge deeper grief. Word came of it from London. Her child was dead. The small hostage to King Henry had not fulfilled his promise "nor," she thought, "will they keep him captive now." There was that for comfort. Lord Darnley lay in his grave in St Dunstan's, Stepney, and the Princess Mary's jewelled robe wrapped the tiny body in its coffin.

How could she weep for him? They had not known one another. God grant that she never again bear a child who might be taken from her.

SHE GAVE BIRTH to her boy, when the time came, in the great
bedchamber where there had been, in old days, rites of the
Templars who had been expelled for taking part in unholy
mysteries alien to their faith. Remnants of such ceremonies still
covered the floor and ceiling; the Pentacle, and the great double
circle with its half-erased names which must never be uttered
without dread. The very number of thirteen was there, which
Edward III, himself said to be a leader of covens, had incorpor-
ated in multiple in the leopards of England. Madge cared for
none of these; her beloved saints' images, who had brought her
through so many troubles, made a guard about her and the
child she laboured to deliver. The saints gleamed gold against
the crimson bed-curtains in the candlelight, on this dull Decem-
ber day. Between pains she thought of the Christ-child, whose
birth was later this month; and rejoiced that she herself had
made all ready for a cheerful Christmas, with the chapel con-
secrated and the larders filled, this first year here with her lord
and her son. That he must be a son Madge was again resolved.
Yet he was longer than the last in coming, and caused her
much pain.

She held him in her arms after it was all over, a long-limbed
lusty baby with a fuzz of light-brown hair which, when it dried,
would be gold. She was so filled with joy and triumph that she
could scarcely find words to speak to Lennox, when he came
into the room to kiss her and the child. "We will keep this one

by us," she heard him mumble, and she echoed his thought in silence with all her heart. This child should be no hostage, sent south to placate the dying old man in London; he should bide here with his parents, and know their love, and learn much, and grow to be a fine man. A man to reckon with, he should become, she was resolved, her royal son; royal on both sides of his pedigree, for was not his sire the heir-presumptive of James V but for that girl-baby at present hidden away in Scotland by her mother?

Yet even thoughts of Marie de Guise did not disturb Madge now. The Frenchwoman had borne sons, it was true, but they had not lived to rule. *Her* son, Lord Darnley, should live, she was resolved; his healthy crying cheered her. Soon he would suck.

She bent over him where he lay by her, her loose fair hair mingling with his. "He will soon have ringlets," she thought. He was beautiful as well as high-born, her son. He also, they had decided, should be named Henry after the old tyrant, who might be pleased that they had remembered him. But the child should have all of his great-uncle's gifts, none of his vices. Soon she would find preceptors, confessors, body-servants for her boy. The time would pass swiftly till he should be a man. Then –

Lennox, with them in the room again, smiled at her earnest plans. "Leave the bairn be till he can eat pap; till then he is like other babes," he told her. She did not contradict him in words, keeping it meantime to herself that this child was to be like none other. A man would not understand such premonitions, would say she was fevered after the birth.

Like no other; her Darnley, her son. She cradled him close against her so that the dazzle of the candles might not hurt his eyes, so newly opened; or lest the devil's signs of star and circle invade his mind before he should be christened. She herself would keep such things at bay with prayer, she knew. There should be no evil thing come nigh her son.

173

SHE WAS TO BE deprived, this time also, of the right to watch her son grow out of babyhood. In later years she would look back in unquenchable bitterness as she recalled how soon she had to leave the second Darnley after his birth. Word came again from London; her uncle the King was dissatisfied with the progress of the war against the Scots. His niece Marg'et, he implied, was not using all of her persuasive powers upon her husband. Desperate lest she herself, Lennox, all of them, be hauled south again to prison with the loss of their lands, she rode north at last by her lord's side, among his men. More she could not do to show a zeal she hardly felt; the godly marriage, as it was called, had been much discussed in London, but the Scots themselves were stubborn in their refusal to part with their little Queen. It began and ended as all wars begin and end; she saw the black smoke and curling flames they had kindled about the castles and abbeys and farms she had known in her youth, some of which had sheltered her. She knew also that her father the Earl, turned patriot with the rest now he had won home again, rode against his son-in-law and herself; cheering on his Scots with a bravery the more remarkable in that his age was now great; he had never been so formidable a warrior when young. What ailed all of Scotland that it would not yield?

She did not see Angus nor he her. It was possible that she might not know him now; his hair must be white. At the end of

174

the campaign she and Lennox and the men rode wearily home again; there had been little worthwhile plunder in a land so poor. She was left with a memory, which she never lost, of blackened fields of stubble and a dour unrelenting hate for the English who had set tinder to roof and byre. That she was herself one of that loathed race had never seemed strange to her, till now. She conjured with herself over the matter; need Christian blood have been shed at all if this marriage had been agreed upon? But it had not; the Scots would never agree.

She tried to leave the remembrance behind as the Yorkshire moors broadened before her; it was good to be home. At Temple Newsam she found her son taking his first steps, devotedly watched over by the man Taylor who had been appointed his body-servant, and would be with Lord Darnley always. Madge held out her arms to gather the child to her; he screamed, and she knew that her travel-worn looks were strange to him. Later he would accustom himself to her, his mother. It could not but be so.

It was so, and the child began to run to her and chatter against her skirts, but against this joy was to be set in the balance the news from London. The black campaign on the Border might never have taken place; she could have stayed at home with her son instead of riding across fords and disputed ways, camping like a soldier and watching the horror soldiers could make of a land once fair. She could have done as she would in all ways except one, and the end would have been the same. The spy Bishop loathed her, the more that she knew him for what he was; and he had the ear of the King. He had poured out tales to the dying tyrant of the Lady Margaret's Papistry, that it was safer to practise in the north; her anger with him, Bishop, because she said he was a heretic and had threatened to cast him out of the house. "I would cast him out because he betrayed me and my lord, and would have continued in it; but so he has done in any case," she thought when the word came.

It was slow in coming. The King had died at Christmas. His will had been read; by the time she and Lennox heard of its contents they were common knowledge. She, the daughter of Henry VIII's elder sister, was cut out of the succession. It was the state of affairs that had pertained at the time of her long-ago betrothal to Thomas Howard; but this time there could be no redress. After the issue of the King's own body, the children of his younger sister, Mary the Queen-Duchess, were to inherit. "Frances and her children, Jane Grey and the rest, stout Protestants all; yet that would not have pleased His Grace in other years, when he professed himself Catholic as any except for allegiance to the Pope."

Madge found herself in a state of black Douglas rage, turning up and down her great hall; she struck her hands together as though to hurt the palms, and gritted, "He is gone to his account. When his coffin rested, they tell me, overnight at Syon it burst open. A dog came and licked his blood from the stones of the floor, and none might drive it away. Did not one of his reformed preachers liken him in his lifetime to Ahab, whose blood was shed at Ramoth-Gilead?"

Lennox watched, helpless to aid or calm her; he had never seen her in such a mood of anger. Perhaps, he was thinking, they had best show themselves in London. It might be as well to make known their allegiance to the Protector Somerset, who had charge of his young nephew Edward VI, lest the new King himself be influenced to become their enemy.

They went to London, traversing the difficult muddy ways of winter. Afterwards Lennox realised that it had been a mistake. Neither with the young King, a pale cold-eyed boy, nor with his uncle, who was entirely given over to the tenets of the Reformers, did they make headway. Everywhere they were treated with coldness, and in the end returned the poorer to Yorkshire. At the least, there they were at home among neighbours who did not greatly care that they had been cut out of the old King's will. Those who were left to enjoy the inheritance – but joy was absent from their faces, Lennox muttered – were the young Protestant Edward VI and after him the Queen-Duchess's daughter Frances Brandon, now Duchess of Suffolk in her own right; and Frances' tiny, scholarly daughter, who suffered naught but pinching and slapping from her mother, yet endured it; Lady Jane Grey.

THE GREAT OAK on the lawn at Temple Newsam shaded the sunlight that fell on the bright hair of a little boy seated beneath. It was a remarkably fine day, so much so that Lord Darnley was learning his Latin out of doors. His tutor, John Elder, was still at Temple Hurst, from which they had lately come because of the press of Douglas relatives which suddenly filled it, some of whom had also followed them here. But Darnley's body-servant, Taylor, who never left him, was nearby. "Taylor knows no Latin," thought the boy gleefully. In the distance he could see his small sisters playing with their nurse. Further over, his mother, still in her riding-clothes, walked about with Lord Westmorland, while his father, silent as always, made a strolling third with Archibald Douglas, who had been ill. Cousin Archibald was always ailing, and Darnley remembered his mother throwing up her hands when she heard they were riding in as fugitives, and saying, "But he has nine motherless bairns! Where shall we put them all?" The bairns, whom Darnley found rough and ignorant, were thankfully still at Temple Hurst. As for James Douglas, Lord George's son, he had been taken south to the Tower. Darnley did not understand all of it, but he recalled his mother's face when James was taken away, and afterwards she had come and kissed him with unusual fervour, and he had seen tears in her eyes. Asked if she wept for Cousin James, she said, "Yes, and for the place where they are taking him. All of his boyhood he spent in disguise,

177

M

pretending to be a farmhand, and now the English have taken him instead of the Scots."

It was all very regrettable, but no doubt James would be set free before long; he always escaped from trouble. Darnley's fair brows drew together. He could not understand the housing of so many Douglases when his own father, the Earl, had lately driven his grandsire, another Douglas, out of his house in Scotland and burnt it behind him "and Drumlanrig Castle also," thought the boy, proud of his knowledge of so long a word as Drumlanrig. However it had happened, the Douglases had crossed the Border and invaded Temple Hurst, and Darnley was glad of the peace and quiet here at Temple Newsam; all of last year the strange Scots voices had made babel of that other home. Lord Archibald's children had been the worst, having no mother "yet she was governess to *my* mother," thought the boy, in fresh astonishment at anyone's ever having attempted to govern so august a personage as the Countess of Lennox. That his mother was beautiful as well as gracious he knew; he knew Lord Westmorland thought so too, and a great many other persons who came here to hear Mass when they might. All of that was his mother's doing, not his father's; the Earl was so silent and withdrawn nowadays as hardly to speak to anyone, even his son.

"My young lord is not paying attention to his lesson," he heard the voice of Taylor say gently. "The young King in London will be far and away the better scholar of the pair of ye."

Darnley pouted. They were always reminding him of his scholarly cousin, King Edward, and the King's scholarly sister, the Lady Elizabeth, and of course the Lady Mary who had been the best Latin scholar of all in her youth long ago. Then there were the Grey cousins, who were worst of all, being only girls but knowing Greek and Hebrew as well as Latin. It was hard to be expected to keep up with all of that when he was so much younger. "I have finished my construing," he said slyly. "May I ride my pony now?"

"If your lady mother permits it. Run, my lord, and tell her you are finished your lessons, and take her this," said the serving-man, smoothing the paper on which a translation of Caesar's Commentaries were transcribed in an even and beautiful hand, correctly as far as he might tell. No pains had been spared to turn my young lord into a paragon of learning, and as a rule young Henry Darnley repaid the effort; but the sun was so hot today that a small boy might surely be permitted a gallop on his pony, as the thought of playing with his sisters on the lawn would be far beneath his dignity.

Tom Taylor watched his young master's strong legs take him across to the place where his mother was. Her fair head bent towards the boy's own and they conversed earnestly over the Latin, while Lord Westmorland watched. Presently Lord Darnley ran back again, his face wreathed in smiles.

"My lady mother says that I may go. She knows less Latin than I. Who is it that was wroth with her?"

The devoted Taylor frowned a little. "My lord, I know not." It would be someone of great importance who would dare to be wroth with my Lady Lennox. No doubt the little boy had overheard what he should not, either from his mother and her constant friend or, more likely, from that other sombre group who walked the lawn. Taylor's frown deepened. That purveyor of mischief, Tom Bishop, had been dismissed the house by my lady, or he might well have been the one responsible for creating such a state of affairs, or the rumour of it. As it was, perhaps it would be best if my lady herself were told of what had been said; Taylor was a true servant, and devoted to the welfare of his mistress and her son. He had viewed with trepidation the influx of Douglases after the war in the north; rumour had it that my lady's grace had had much trouble to obtain permission for them to cross the Border after their homes had been burnt by my lord. "A sorry coil,' thought Taylor, "and all because the Scots would not wed their little Queen to the young King of England." But that "rough wooing" had been purposeless, for all the harm it had done and the folk it had slain; Mary, Queen of Scots was now safe in France.

The child slid his hand into Taylor's on their way to the stables to see the pony saddled. He chattered unheedingly in answer to the man's discreet questioning. "Wroth with my lady mother? It was the old King of England, the one who is dead. He cut my mother out of his will because he said she did not cause my father to make fiercer war on the Scots. But the Earl made

179

savage war, did he not?" The blue eyes searched Taylor's face, anxious for reassurance. The man nodded gravely. "Ay, your sire burnt towns and kirks up and down the Border, and your grandsire the Earl of Angus defended them." He could not refrain from praising the brave old man, who had saved the Scots guns at Coldingham and had led the van at Pinkie Cleugh where the Scots army had been defeated the year of the old King's death. "His pikemen drove back the English horse, but their archers drove *him* back; and later, when he had rallied his men, he beat my lord Wharton and forced him back to Carlisle," he said proudly. Like many folk, he thought, the Earl of Angus had returned his loyalty to the land of his fathers, the land where his wife had borne him sons, but those children were now dead. "My lady will be the inheritor there, still, though she has lost the English throne for herself and her posterity," the man thought. But he did not say the last aloud to the sharp ears of Lord Darnley. He saw the little boy into the saddle of his grey pony, and rode with him about the Temple Newsam fields in the sunshine.

Back on the lawn, the boy's elders continued to talk. If Taylor had known, the Countess and Westmorland were engaged in nothing more onerous than a discussion on the gifts of Surrey the poet, who had lost his handsome head on the block as the old King lay dying. "If my uncle had lived a day longer, Surrey's sire would have gone as well; but Norfolk escaped. Would that it had been his son who had done so! He was a marvellous rhymer, and a wild fellow." Madge smiled with sad eyes, remembering the gilded days when she and Tom and Surrey and Mary Richmond had been young together, and now what had become of them all? Even poor Mary had been examined by the King's Commissioners as to her religious beliefs, for being a Howard she adhered to the old faith; and the rest, save for herself, were dust.

"Here is your lord," said Westmorland in a low voice. He disliked the Earl of Lennox, but acquaintance with his lady would not be possible, he knew, were he to make that fact manifest. Tales of Lennox's brutality in the north had reached here; had he not hanged children who were hostages? "Perhaps that is why his mind is afflicted," the Earl thought. The dark-clad, bearded figure came solidly across the grass now, in search of his wife; he would never forswear her company for long.

"My lord is sick of war," said Madge in a low voice before he joined them. "He has seen so much death and carnage that it troubles his sleep, and waking he cares not to be left alone. I divert him as I can, but sometimes tasks – " She was unable to finish, because Lennox came up to them and smiling, as if she had not been speaking of grievous matters, his wife reached out a hand and laid it on his arm.

"Have you left our guests alone so soon, my lord?" she said, and Lennox jerked his head as if to be rid of a fly.

"I am weary of them," he told her. "They can speak of naught but James Douglas taken to the Tower, and Archibald Douglas of the pain in his vitals. I cannot listen to more of it; I trust they will soon be gone."

"Soon now," she said soothingly. "I did but house them because my father asked it of me, as you know well; and he is an old man, and at that time himself had no home."

Lennox grunted, recalling the time when he and none other had deprived Angus of a home, burning it over the old man's head as he rode out towards Calder. Madge and her father had, however, been better friends since the death of the two young heirs at Tantallon, some years back. That the heirship of Angus was dear to his wife Lennox knew. He recalled the insinuating words of James Douglas, who before they took him away had been trying to purchase it. "They know well enough that we are pressed for money," Lennox thought. Since the affair of the late King's will had become known, credit was the less easy to obtain for folk who would never wear the crown of England. Lennox looked at his wife, not caring. How fair she was, and how greatly frequent childbearing, which made some women plain and bedraggled, enhanced her beauty and made her like a goddess, fruitful and golden! Their home here, that Madge had fashioned with her own hands out of a few neglected acres and a ruin of red stones, was dear to Lennox also. He had not relished leaving Temple Newsam to go south as they had had to do at the late King's death. He would as soon be done with Kings and Protectors. They had got little good of the visit to London.

That night, with the children sweetly sleeping, Madge walked

181

about their beds with a lit candle in her hand, shading it carefully with the other. The little girls slept all together, limbs and fair hair entwined, even breaths scarcely lifting the quilted coverlet she had herself fashioned with such care. They had the bright complexion of her race, its rose-leaf texture of skin flushed now with sleep. "When they are grown they will be comely women," she thought, and drew their curtain. She passed on, treading softly, to where Darnley slept, in the glory of sole boyhood alone in his bed. How he had grown! The gallop on the pony today had tired him out, and he lay still. Madge raised the candle higher behind her hand, using the light to survey her son as he slept, careful not to wake him with the direct glow of the flame. As she stood there she was aware of a third presence by her in the darkness; Lennox, come in silence to be with her as he often did. In the same silence they gazed down on their sleeping son.

Afterwards she became aware that Lennox's eyes had turned to her after they left the boy. They held the mixture of supplication and loneliness she had half come to dread since the war on the Border; how it had changed him! "They said in London that I did not incite him to it hard enough, and that lost me King Henry's goodwill before he died," she reminded herself for the hundredth time. But how could any woman's word have made that black assault the more fierce, or left deeper scars on the man who had launched it? Lennox now was like a child in the dark. "When I married him, he feared neither man nor devil," she thought. Yet had the early memory of his father's killing perhaps made Matthew less certain than he had seemed in those years? She tried to look back, and could not; she saw only the man now before her, the victor defeated, with grey in his beard and hair which had once been bright.

She set the candle down. "He grows tall, our son," she said lightly. Always now she made the effort to appear unconcerned and light, the better to cheer Matthew. But he answered absently and made no comment on their son's long limbs, promising as they did a giant height, like the old King's, in the end. Lennox plucked at her sleeve. "This is fair stuff," he said, like a mercer appraising wares.

"You have seen me seated working at it often enough. It is blackwork, of the kind Queen Katharine brought with her out of Spain." By day, she knew, the uneven colours of the vegetable-dyed threads made for hues more varied than plain black on white, having green and brown, violet and blue and even yellow tones among them. She had taken much pleasure in fashioning the pair of sleeves; it pleased her that he should notice them. She reached up and kissed him, stroking his cheek.

"Made you no cheer with my kinsmen today?" she asked tenderly. "I know they spoke of James Douglas the rough of tongue." James Douglas, now a man, had been the boy who, all through the time of King James's outlawry, had stayed in Scotland disguised as a farm-labourer. Some of the earthy quality of that occupation had stuck to his tongue, which was foul. Lennox did not reply; instead, he put his hands one on either side of his wife's face, and drew her to him.

"I would sooner have your company than that of any other," he told her, "and I grudge it to Westmorland."

"We must show courtesy to a neighbour, Matthew; he has been kind, as you know well."

"Ay. But I grudge the time it takes to show it. Only when you are with me am I myself again. Do not leave me, Madge; stay about me. Without you I amount to but little now."

She tried to think of ways to reinstate him in his own esteem. "I have disappointed you of a royal dower, which you were promised with me," she said. "You do not reproach me with that, Matthew; few men would fail to do so." She was grateful, and had been from the time of the black news about the King's will, to Lennox for his continued love and care of her. Most husbands would have considered themselves deceived, and would have acted accordingly. She had much for which to be thankful.

"If we had been beggars we had maybe had more joy," said Lennox. "Yet with you by me I'm content." He spoke with the shyness common to men not apt of tongue, and she laughed softly over the pleasure it gave her that he should love her for herself. "Why," she told him, "had we been beggars, so fine a boy as we now have would have been nothing and no one. Now, despite my uncle's testament which disinherits us, I do not despair of making Darnley a great future."

"That may well be, Madge." He watched her in their chamber, as she divested herself of her coif and kirtle and began at last

183

to comb out her hair; she had dismissed her women for the night and as a rule, especially if Lennox were with her, liked to do such tasks for herself. "Yet there's still a King of England," he said, "and he is young."

"And delicate. They keep him too close at his books. But I was not thinking of England."

"Then – "

"Mind, though the Lady Mary is ageing and has no husband, there is Elizabeth, bastard or not as they may decide in time." She dissembled, fingering her hair. "Our Harry will be as fine a scholar as Edward at his age," she said irrelevantly. She turned to Lennox suddenly, on an indrawn breath. "Now that the godly marriage, as they called it, has come to naught, and the Scots Queen is safe in France and betrothed to the Dauphin, what befalls if the Dauphin dies? He's sickly too. There is much sickness in the royal houses of Europe."

"Your mind runs on where mine would walk," he said admiringly. "If Dauphin François dies – "

"If he dies, where may the Scots Queen marry? There will come a time when she must come home. If so, what then? Might not our Darnley, when he has come to man's estate, be as fair and high-born a consort as ever graced a throne? Might he not – with the rights he has through your blood and mine?"

"Ye speak truth and wisdom, maybe," he murmured, "but it is all of it perchance, and who can foretell what may befall? The other boy died."

"Darnley will not die till he has fulfilled his destiny. Of that I was certain at his birth."

"We are all but mortal," he said, and his eyes darkened; from contemplating the future he had turned again to the past, and the hanged faces of the children at Carlisle dangled before him. One had had rose-leaf cheeks and golden hair like – like –

"I had to do't," he told himself defensively. "I had sworn to their sires that if their body of horse should fail me, the boys must hang." The sires and their horse had failed indeed, had deserted to the other side at a critical moment in the Scots war, and was he, Lennox, to have spared their sons thereafter? Yet often in the night he would wake sweating, groping with his hand for his wife who lay by his side. Since the Carlisle hangings he dared not be alone.

184

He saw his wife by candlelight now, fine hair a long, crackling silver-gilt veil beneath the comb; a fragrance like the summer day came from it. Lennox dropped on his knees by her.

"You are all the world and more to me," he said, and did not add the thought that came unbidden even as he strove to outdo its coming; had he known his own boy Darnley dead among the rest, how great would have been his grief!

But Madge was smiling at him, and Lennox forgot his mind's demons in loving her.

"It Is Not *comme il faut,* they tell me, to travel as we do now in a litter in England, and not in a barge upon the water. But I have endured enough of that, and am thankful that God has brought me to dry land again, though to be sure I do not regret my journey."

Marie de Guise, Queen Dowager of Scotland, raised her long lidded eyes beneath her modish coif, and surveyed first her near neighbour, the Countess of Lennox, whom she had particularly requested should sit by her in the litter, with Frances Suffolk and her meek little daughter, Lady Jane Grey, opposite and then turned her head once more to marvel at the citizens of London who had come out to see her. *Comme il faut* or not her progress by road had been marked with great enthusiasm it was known already that she had made fast friends with the little King. But what a motley red-faced crowd! thought the Dowager; they must live on pudding. Most wore flat caps, and gowns something longer than had been worn of late years in Paris. Her agile mind harked back there for instants, and sighed she had had to say goodbye once more to her little daughter her Reinette, who, it seemed, had only just begun to know her own mother again after an absence of almost three years at the Court of France. Marie de Guise had lately visited her there, and had stayed on and on so long, for love of her child that by the end it had had to be made evident that her welcome in France was wearing thin. "So I voyaged back," thought the

186

Dowager, "and I may not see my Reinette again till she is a grown woman and Queen of France, when surely she will welcome me." Meantime there was Reinette's northern kingdom of savage intractable nobles to subdue, no task for a woman; but for her daughter's sake James V's widow would not shrink from attempting it.

She returned her gaze to the pleasant fair-haired noblewoman beside her, who was, as she knew, both well-born and a Catholic. For both reasons Marie had made sure Lady Lennox should occupy her litter with her and not, as would otherwise have been the case, the thrusting wife of the Protector Somerset. It was bad enough to have the unpleasant Suffolk woman and her poor little daughter, but the cheering of the crowds ensured that one might speak in private to whom one wished.

"You, as a mother, will know well, my lady, what it means to part with a beloved child." Almost, as she spoke, the Dowager forgot that Lady Lennox's lord was the traitor who had absconded with the French money that time at Dumbarton, and had since then served England so well as to make that terrible series of raids on the Border, some years back. She frowned a little, and surveyed her long well-kept fingers. Having regained her composure she continued to talk, as she loved to do, about Reinette; about the child's red-gold hair, so like her father's; her beauty and cleverness; her love of birds and animals, and the prowess she was making at her studies as well as with dancing and music.

"You also, Lady Jane, are proficient in languages, so I hear," smiled the Dowager, addressing the child on the opposite cushions; it was ill-bred totally to ignore the other couple in the litter. But Lady Jane's forceful mother replied for her, as she usually did. "My child both speaks and writes Latin, Greek, French, Italian and Hebrew," she announced triumphantly. Marie de Guise professed surprise and admiration, at the same time feeling sympathy for the bullied child. "They are all of them so learned, these young royal people!" she said. "It would not do for the Queen of Scots to grow up ignorant of dead languages when the King here and his sister the Lady Elizabeth, and Lady Jane now by us, are so proficient. Do you know what King Edward said to me? We had some pleasant converse, and then he told me with reproach, 'Madame, you would not have me to your son-in-law.' That is true; it is better for Reinette," and her voice dropped again, "to be married in France where the faith is strong, and they deal hardly with reformers such as speak freely here in England."

"My son Darnley is also a Latin scholar," put in Darnley's mother with diplomacy. She regretted not bringing the boy with her to greet the Queen of Scots' mother, but neither he nor Lennox had come south. Marie de Guise turned her bright bird-like gaze upon her for instants before she spoke again, still quietly. "Your son is reared in the Catholic faith, my lady. That I know. It is perhaps easier in the north of England. Here they will talk of nothing but sermons and the Bible." She made a little *moue*. Madge agreed fervently, adding that their chaplain at Temple Newsam said Mass daily with none to hinder him "and many from that part of the country come to take part." "This Reformation is like all new things, and will pass or modify itself," said the Dowager, as the spire of Paul's gave slow place to the Palace of Westminster and Frances Suffolk stared ahead of her and thought how frivolous the widow was, with those scarlet sleeves. "Many have died, however," Marie de Guise murmured. "When will it cease? I have tried to make a friend of the English King. That may help. But he is not of an age to have power for himself."

There need have been no blood shed had you married your child into England, Madge was thinking; but said nothing of that, for it was too late to mend and in any case, Frances or even little Jane, whose ears were sharp, might overhear. Within her mind she was turning matters over swiftly, not hearing the noise of the crowd. The Kings here, both old and young, had treated her scurvily; would not it be advisable to cement the Dowager's evident liking for her by healing the breach with Scotland and with her father? "Much good may come out of France for my son," she thought, reflecting that later, when Darnley should be grown, they might move nearer a seaport. Temple Newsam was too far inland for direct journeying overseas. There were other places. Now she must talk, pleasantly, about unimportant things to her half-brother's widow. She thought the Dowager looked older than her true age. No doubt affairs in Scotland made youth difficult to retain.

The long eyes and long throat and long fingers were balanced by a full yet cautious mouth; the Dowager wore a black gown which opened to show the bright sleeves. Madge thought of a thing to say which would not offend the company. Queen Marie's portrait, in this same gown, had been painted lately on this English visit, with her parrot on her arm. "I can recall my half-brother's parrot he had at Stirling," she said. The Dowager laughed a little.

"He loved all such things, as does our daughter. He liked nothing better than to go out, dressed as a plain man, a poor man, and meet the common folk. They loved him, and he them. He would write verse about it."

"A dangerous ploy for a King; did you have no fear for him, madame?"

"I liked him to do what made him happy. He had much sadness in his life. I like to think that when he was free, when he was among his people, his heart was gay." She made a little movement with one hand as if to dismiss the intimate recollection. "Do you return to the north soon, Lady Lennox?"

"As soon as I may, for my children miss my company."

"And your lord? I pray you commend me to him."

The bright oblique gaze met hers. Can she indeed forgive Lennox what he has done to her daughter's land? Madge wondered. If so, there might be much to be accomplished now that she and the Dowager had met and had become friends after their fashion.

THE EARL OF ANGUS lay gravely ill at Tantallon. He had expressed a wish to see his daughter. Madge fretted to be gone at once, but letters had posted back and forth between Yorkshire and London without bringing the desired safe-conduct to cross the Border. "What harm are they afraid that I do if I see my father?" Madge asked Lennox, with tears in her eyes. He looked at her sombrely.

"They are afraid that you will never return; your dower lands from me are there, and if Angus dies you will inherit his also." It was true about the dower lands, but she had forgotten it; certain domains with names whose pronunciation she found difficult, and which were hardly by now Lennox's to give, had been appended to her marriage-settlement. She blinked away her tears incredulously; she could not understand how it would occur to anyone that she should ever now desire to leave England.

"Write and say that I and the children will be left here, as surety for your return," he told her, and she wrote, accordingly, to the Protector in London. This was no longer Somerset, who had been executed, but a cold and much disliked nobleman called Dudley, who had lately induced the young King (they whispered that the boy was ailing, but nothing was certainly known) to create him Duke of Northumberland. A reply came at last, after further letters. To her relief the safe-conduct was enclosed at last, when she had almost ceased to hope for it.

190

"They will have their own reasons for wanting you out of their way in Scotland meantime; trust me to contrive here," Lennox grunted, when he read the letter. Madge shrugged her shoulders. "How can that concern us?" she said. "I let it be known at last that I am with child again, and desired to make this visit before the birth; that may have hastened the matter."

She laid her hand on Lennox's shoulder as they both scanned the letter again, with the terse signature it bore of the new Duke's secretary, Cecil. Why should such a name stay in the mind?

"Return as soon as you may," said Lennox, embracing her as she rode off. He had sent as many serving-men with her as they could spare and the children — Darnley now was grown very tall for his age — with the little girls, made a bright-haired cluster about the doorway to wave her farewell. How dear they were to her! She would spur her mount on the way to make haste the faster, and return the sooner, as Matthew had bidden. She had little concern for her own state. Her pregnancies were always healthy, and gave no trouble to herself or the child.

After they crossed the Border she thought less of her family and more of her father, if only out of duty now that he might be dying. It seemed strange how little he had come to mean to her. How many years it must be since they had parted, he to take his own way, she hers! "Yet there was a time when he was all the world to me," she thought, remembering a tear-stained child gazing out of a window at Berwick, looking at the broad water of Tweed. Now, Tweed was left behind; they were coming to the land she had known in childhood, before the exile. It was as green as ever, and the signs of Lennox's fires had been grown over long since with bracken and bramble. She would not think of the harm that had been done; he had been under orders, and had dared not fail in his duty to England. To England! That country itself seemed remote here; the very air was different, fresher and colder, with the sea wind in it now she neared the east. Would she have come sooner had her father not made that second marriage, both sons of which were now dead? She had been angry, she recalled, at the marriage, thinking it might take away her rights as heir.

But the lands of Angus should still be hers, and the Crowned Heart her banner alongside the bull of Lennox and the Tudor rose and the crest of the salamander. No doubt Angus wanted to see her regarding the disposal and management of his lands after he was dead. That he desired to look on her face again for any other reason, after so long, was unlikely.

Riding across to Tantallon it seemed smaller in some way, as though her child's memory had made of it a giant's abode full of red caves. Beyond, the sea glittered coldly. She was led past the fortifications green with grass, and through the gateway and across the inner court and then through corridors and up winding stairways where men-at-arms stood about with the Crowned Heart worn on breast or sleeve. Their frank stares reminded her that here, where every man's name was Douglas, none was called master except the head of the clan who lay in his great curtained bed. The young Countess of Angus had already greeted Madge downstairs, making a deep nervous obeisance like the provincial she was; a comely, red-cheeked young woman who had failed in her duty. She said gently to the old man in the bed, "My lord, your daughter, the Lady Lennox's grace, is here," and he made a gesture with one hand to show that he understood, and wished her to leave them alone.

"I would have speech with my daughter in private," he said clearly. "See to it that we are not disturbed, except maybe to send some refreshment; my lady has travelled far."

Madge refused food and drink; the room was close and warm after her ride, and she had brought provision for the journey. After the young Countess had gone out she seated herself nearby the great bed and looked at her father. His features seemed sunken and his hair and beard grey, and he had a rash which covered his face, arms and neck: but otherwise he was less changed than she had thought; and, as she could remember well, there was still mockery lurking in his eyes and mouth for himself, the world, and her. A great love came over her for him; why had they not seen more of one another?

"How fare ye?" he said, as though they had parted yesterday. His sunken gaze roved over her, seeing her cheeks bright and fresh with the wind of riding, her hair somewhat dishevelled beneath her hood. Her body, which by now was thick, she had concealed in her long surcoat. "Well enough," she said, and told him of the coming child. "How is it with you, my lord? I grieve to learn that you are sick."

"Ye do not grieve in truth. When I die the lands will be yours. Land is worth more than folk. I strove to beget sons of my name, but it was not God's will that they should live. God must have a special eye to ye, daughter. Perhaps it will be remembered that your issue have royal blood of both north and south."

He moved restlessly. "It will suit the Douglases ill that a woman should have the land," he said. "Does Lennox treat ye well?"

"He is a loving lord to me, and I am glad to be his wife."

"In any event he will have a care to your inheritance. George my brother, who was aye about me – George, and James, his second son, for the first's as naught – and my own bastard of the name, may try to make it their own by some deceit."

"Fear not for that," she said, "my lord and I can guard our own."

He lay on the pillows and laughed. 'Your lord and you! Do ye rule Lennox, then?"

She was about to say "My lord needs me by him, by reason of his sickness of the mind," but she did not say it. Instead she told him, leaning forward so that she could look into his face, "Talk not of the inheritance, my father. I would see you well yet for many a year, and in enjoyment of your lands. You were long enough away from them, in the south."

"I was wrong to trust King Harry," he said, speaking with difficulty as if his breathing hurt him. "Much befell in England that should not have done, for you and for me. I could not take your part as I'd have wished to do, when young Tom Howard died and ye were placed in the Tower. Yon was wickedness; but had I said a word out of my place, the tyrant – ay, he was that – would have stopped the pension he gave me – "

"I got that for you, my father."

" – and I'd have been powerless between him and the wrath of the King of Scots. I havena been as good a father to my lass as I would." He spoke as though he faced himself in his own mind at last; the gnarled discoloured hands lay still on the coverlet. Presently he began to talk again, as if none heard him except his own soul.

193

N

"Is it not a daft-like thing that I had to lead out armies against my own son-in-law? Lennox made such havoc in this land that he will never be forgiven." One of the children hanged at Carlisle had been kin to Angus's wife.

"He also had to do as he was bid," said Madge, "or we would both of us have suffered, and our children too." She added, after thought for a moment, "And you, my lord, and your new lady, might not have made us welcome had we come as friends then."

"Do not speak so," he said testily. "I said, is it not a daft-like thing? The two countries so near, and with but the one Border between them – there's aye been trouble there, folk not knowing to which land they belong – and yet the substance of both is spent on war, where there could have been peace. What could Lennox and Angus not have achieved had they been together, instead of enemies? From the beginning I was for the marriage of our young Queen with Edward, as all know. Yet being a Douglas I was suspect as being in the pay of England." He struggled up in the bed. "Yet I would not thole Lennox any more than another, in his burnings and slayings here. We are not a land to be forced into what we've no mind for; in Bruce's day another Edward found that. Nevertheless I think myself that that marriage would have been right, godly as they called it, could it have been brought about by fair means. The more harm may well come to Scotland by reason of this marriage of the Queen with Dauphin François. France is a far cry from Scotland, for all they talk about the Auld Alliance. How can she be Queen of France and Scotland both? Her own land will suffer, never doubt it. And the old faith, that her mother still fights for, is sick to death here like myself, while the new grows strong. They say there is a man Knox that preached before King Edward; he will be a power in the land when I'm gone." He laboured for breath, and she sought to ease him.

"They say Dauphin François is delicate," she said. She grieved for the dying man, and yet within herself she knew her own hope that his mind might be brought to echo hers, before he went. It was true the Dauphin might die; but were he to do so, who then should marry the Queen? King Edward? He might die also.

"All of the Valois are rotted with the pox from birth," grunted the Earl. "King Henry's son will be little better; why, they say he's like Richmond, and his chest is weak, and he may never make a man. Oh, they've tried to conceal it from ordinary folk, seated in their closets in secret council as they are, but *I* know for news is brought to me. When Edward dies, the devil will have his way with the succession in England."

The sunken eyes, suddenly bright, regarded her. "Ye have a fine boy, Madge, so I hear. Ye have reared him like the prince he is. Even George Douglas, who's spare of praise, had enough to say of Lord Darnley when he came riding back across the Border. Ye didna grudge the homeless Douglases bite and sup, and they should not forget it when the time comes to succour you and your boy."

She was thinking that the Douglases were unlikely to succour any except themselves. Aloud she said, "If this were known in England, my lord, it would mean trouble and maybe imprisonment for me and my lord and our children."

"Trust me; it has not been spoken of to any. Yet I'd be glad of a trusty messenger to come and go between us two, while I live."

She thought of John Dicconson, her priest whom she had brought with her, supposedly to succour the Earl. He was trustworthy, and would carry word if and when it was needed; but would this old man live so long? She said gently, "The only messenger I could send hitherto, my lord, at your request, was a falconer, and even in your own stronghold here, there was nowhere but the middle of the castle green to talk without being overheard. Someone may be listening even now, behind these curtains."

"Ye are canny and wise," he mumbled, "not like your mother. Why, she'd courage, if naught else besides folly. I mind when she and I and the young King James – he'd be but a bairn then – and his brother who died, who was but a babe in arms, faced the crowd outside Edinburgh Castle who would have had our blood, and she – my wife the Queen – spoke to them as was most fit, and they grew quiet. There are not many women will turn back a crowd. Then she said –" his smile grew wide, like a death's head "– and I can hear it yet, in a voice like her brother King Harry's, 'Ring down the portcullis!' and it rang down, between the crowd and ourselves; and every man

195

went home to his own place soberer than when he'd come. Ay, she was a fine woman in her way, for all we quarrelled from the first; it was my grandsire arranged the marriage. I never wed another, Madge, while she lived; nor before, though when I was little more than a boy I had a young wife died in childbed the time of Flodden. Janet of Traquair was my love, but never my wife. They brought King Henry her writing to force me to say otherwise, but I did not do it. Whatever they say now or in the future, remember this; ye are no bastard, your mother herself swore it as she lay dying, and I swear it now. If any are heir to the English throne after King Harry's issue, it is yourself and your son. The will he made can be set aside; it was wickedness, like so much else of his."

There was silence in the room except for the distant sound of the sea. Nearer, Madge could hear the movements and shouting of the Douglas men and her own, below on the green. Her folk would have eaten and drunk well; Douglas hospitality was famous. She looked at the old man, symbol of so much power and changing history, who lay drifting towards death. Would the Crowned Heart banner maintain its glory after his passing? "He has not disgraced his name in the end, for all his intrigues and that he was a pensioner of England," she thought, and realised that her thoughts were strange to her. Why should she think as a Scot? "But he would never have left Tantallon," she thought, "except for me."

"The Queen's Grace, as she was then, Marie de Guise, used to ride often over to Methven to see your mother," the voice on the bed whispered; he was weakening, she thought. "They say that before Queen Margaret died Queen Marie restored her to her faith. Poor soul, it was as well; she was neglected by all at the last, except her son's French wife."

"I met the Queen's Grace in London, but she said naught to me of my mother." Her own voice sounded cold; within herself she was aware of shame. Her mother had written to defend her while she lay prisoner in the Tower, and she had never sent her line or word. Now Queen Margaret was dead, and it was too late; but here was her father soon to die also.

"Shall I send John Dicconson the priest to you, my lord, if you have done with all you had to say to me? I will kiss my son for you." She sought his hand, and in defiance of etiquette

196

put her lips to it. There was, she knew, so much more that should have been said by both of them; but it would never be said now.

"Ay. When your son's son wears the crown of Scotland and England both, let him remember me."

She thought that his mind wandered, and rose and left him; presently she saw the priest make his way into the room among the close-drawn curtains.

Shortly after she returned home Lennox came to her, his face grim. "There is ill news from the south," he said. "Northumberland and his man Cecil knew well enough what they were doing, hurrying ye into Scotland before a lying-in when ye could take no part in state affairs. The King is dead – they say it was not made known for some days after – and Northumberland has married his son to Lady Jane Grey, and has proclaimed her Queen."

She stared at him. "My cousin Mary will have a word to say to that," she said, then groped for Lennox with her hands. "Matthew, were you glad to see me return? Let me hear you say it."

"I had never a day's nor a night's rest till you were safe home again. Let us leave great matters to settle themselves; what have we to do with who wears the crown?"

She remembered Angus's words to her, but said nothing. Matthew had been solitary in her absence, and she made haste to cheer him as best she could. It would not be long before their next child's birth; she hoped for a boy.

THE CHILD was a girl. The Earl of Angus rallied, and would not die for two years. Other things befell to which Madge, in her lying-in chamber, could give neither heed nor help, though she prayed as always for the Lady Mary, the rightful heir to England. If her prayers were heard in no other way, if she had no living son but the one to succeed her, perhaps she could succour the friend at whose side she had shared danger and sorrow long ago. She would stare down at the new child's golden head, then up at the golden saints pinned about the bed-curtains. Shut in here as she was, there was nothing she could do but pray, while the world went on.

It was Lennox, again, who brought her news as soon as might be. His face was less troubled than she had seen it for many a day. He took her hand and sat by her, smiling, like a child who has a secret. "What is it?" she asked, in a low voice. It was necessary for them day and night to speak thus; there were spies, she knew, in her house, for Bishop had been sent back to them. But Lennox let his words ring out joyfully.

"We have naught to fear now, Madge. The Lady Mary has led a royal force to London, and the people have acclaimed her rightful Queen. Does not this bring ye cheer?"

"I thank God for it. I have prayed these many years that she should see her rights. How does she? How do they all? Will they send for us?" She had struggled up in the bed, her cheeks flushed; he laughed, and stroked the new child's head

198

with a finger.

"Be at peace, till ye are mended." He told her of some things which had befallen. Lady Jane Grey and her husband were in the Tower of London, though it was said the Queen would do them no harm. Northumberland himself had been beheaded. "Merciful as she is, she could do no less, for he would have had her throne from her."

He got up and began to pace about the room. "The country they say is in a ferment of loyalty," he told her. "For years she has been kept hidden, and they know little of her, except that her father treated her harshly for the sake of her mother, whom they loved. They still speak of Queen Katharine as a saint, despite the fact that it is nigh on twenty years since her death."

"May I mend soon," she said. "I would ride to London by you, to find out there what things may be for us, and for our son."

"The Queen's Grace will not forget us," he told her. Presently he left her to sleep, but she could not. Thoughts and memories filled her mind in procession, like a tapestry. Above all was the knowledge which was almost certainty, that she, so long outcast, might now be the Queen of England's closest friend as well as nigh relative, for Queen Mary would never deny her her rightful birth. Queen Mary! The name had a strange ring; it was still difficult to think of plain-faced, gruff-spoken, honest, learned, downtrodden Mary as Queen. "I would I were by her now," thought Madge restlessly. "I doubt me we will not reach London till after the crowning. What joy her mother, and our good Lady Salisbury, would have made this day! What a Queen she will make, after all! For nothing deters her from what she believes to be right, whether it be to her comfort or her confusion."

If Lennox had still been with her he might have told her that that was a parlous state of affairs for the ruler of England. But Madge meantime resolved to have done with one form of expediency. Before she was out of her bed, she sent again for Tom Bishop, and told him to leave by daybreak. "I will have no more heretical spies about me and my house," she said, and saw the hatred in his eyes. He had always hated her.

GIFTS WERE SHOWERED on the Lennoxes from the moment they found lodging in London. On the day of their arrival a resplendent figure, who was Clarencieux Herald, waited upon my lady with a great diamond "for good luck" as the Queen had bidden him. Madge was touched, as it was known that Mary's exchequer was almost empty. Already before riding south she had surveyed her own wardrobe ruefully and had brought the best of what she had, as had Lennox and Darnley. But for herself, the few caps and much-worn gowns which had stood her in good enough stead in Yorkshire would make a poor figure in this new, bustling world. With the crowning of the Queen so lately over, everyone still wore magnificence; cloaks were shorter, gowns richer, coifs had changed their shape to resemble flattened hoops of velvet and brocade in the fashion that had come over with the Dowager from France. For men it was no easier; there was already creeping in the small high ruff which later would become broad, worn as it still was with a narrow-necked tunic below, and less padding than had been seen in King Henry's day; men now were tall, slim, and swaggering. Shabbily, as they themselves knew, the Lennox family waited on the Queen, Matthew lending a fine presence despite his old-fashioned long dark gown, and Darnley with his slender height and golden head causing not a few others to turn and ask who he was. But there was no need to tell the Queen. A small gaudy figure, in the bright gear she loved, almost ran down from the

200

steps of her dais to greet them, and kissed Madge affectionately
on both cheeks.

"Cousin, it is long since Syon!"

She had changed a little; she was older and paler, and sorely
troubled with her headaches; at the recent state entry into the
City she had worn so heavy a jewelled caul that it had made
her ill, and the coronation itself – "they had no precedent, none,
for a Queen Regnant, so they had to do as best they might,
but I am glad it is over" – had tired her. But she did not
forget old times. Straightway two gowns of gold and silver
tissue, embroidered kirtles and other gear, were sent to Madge
at her lodging. Lord Darnley, who was given several suits of
clothes belonging to the dead King Edward, was less pleased,
although his height already permitted the gear of a sixteen-
year-old to fit him. "I care not for dead men's shoes," he
grumbled, but smiled again when Edward VI's Venetian lutes
were put at his disposal. He could already play well for his age,
and sat with his long legs negligently disposed in Edward's
silk hose in their lodging, tinkling French airs while his elders
talked together. Madge was glad of the diversion for her son; he
was surrounded too much by servants and his sisters. She wondered also when the dead boy King could have been given
leisure to enjoy himself on a lute; he seemed to have been kept
at his studies or else made to sit by the hour listening to
preachers. There was no sign of Master John Knox in London
now, although the Queen had issued an edict that each man
might worship as he pleased within reason. Nor was there
anything heard of Lady Jane Grey, kept close prisoner in the
Tower still, although allowed to walk freely in Her Grace's garden
there.

Lennox chafed in London, feeling himself idle though he had
been given the best jennet out of the late King's stables. However it pleased him to see Madge by Her Grace's side on great
occasions, clad in her gold and silver, and on terms of such close
friendship with the Queen that she preceded the Princess
Elizabeth. "Yon chit likes it ill that my wife goes in before her
to dinner and to church," he thought. Concerning church itself,
he pursued Her Grace's creed, which was his wife's also, less
from conviction than habit. The Lady Elizabeth was, he suspected, like himself, and attendance at the Mass of the Holy Ghost

201

in Westminster meant little to her: or again it might mean much. Nobody knew what she was thinking. She had grown into a nunlike, scholarly, secretive girl; her dress was plainer than anyone's now that the fashions had brightened; and she spoke hardly at all except when spoken to. No doubt she was watching her steps since the rumoured affair she was said to have had with the late Admiral, Somerset's younger brother. They had executed *him*. Lennox thought he would not trust the minx herself an inch, and that she would have been better removed also, or at least hidden away; but the Queen was merciful, and had Elizabeth much about her.

Madge knew her husband was unhappy and chafing, and accordingly she forsook her grandeur and her great occasions; in truth she was somewhat weary of them. They rode back to Yorkshire at last with a promise made to come south again to spend Christmas with Her Grace; but before that much had befallen.

THE SUNLIGHT GLINTED on Madge's hawking-glove, which was set with rubies, garnets and pearls great and small. She was provided for now by wool-revenues and other gifts of Her Grace, and had no longer need, for the first time since her girlhood days at Court, to stint herself or her family. She rode by Lennox's side over the moors about Wressil, while the wind whipped their mounts' manes and tails into a frenzy and bent the strong stems of the heather. The hawks flew high in the bright day. Madge, close-hooded, raised her head and hand to recall her tiercel, which was newly-trained. When the bird had perched again on her wrist she turned to Lennox, reining in her horse and shading her eyes from the sun. A fine day was rare at this season of the year; how like their own fortunes! Chance had favoured them as much as the Queen's generosity; it had kept them in the north all through Wyatt's late rebellion, and they had had to take no part and see no sights of terror, such as the citizens hanged each man outside his own door, and the Queen's great bravery within range of fire while all her ladies wailed and screamed. Madge shivered; she had not yet accustomed herself to think of one other necessity, the child Jane Grey dead, beheaded at last on Tower Green.

"Do not take cold," said Lennox, his eyes on her. She was, as he knew, with child again, but would take no heed of his advice not to ride out, only laughing at his fuss and saying, "Did ever I lose a child yet?" before her eyes clouded over and he

203

knew she remembered the dead boy buried at Stepney. They both wished, again, for this coming child to be a son. "If he is so," Lennox said aloud, "we should maybe call him Philip after the Prince of Spain."

She nodded; they were never far apart in their thoughts. "I hope the Queen will be happy if it comes to a marriage," she said, stroking her tiercel's back with a finger. "Eleven years is a fair difference in age between husband and wife, if the man is the younger." She and Lennox were admirably suited in this way; he was a year older than she.

"Princes marry for policy only," he said, adding "Philip of Spain is a widower already, and has a son."

"The Queen's Grace may not bend her mind as readily to policy as a man would hope," said Madge. "I remember when she was a child she told me – oh, long before her open torments started, for she knew well enough then – that she had already known sorrow; it was when the Emperor Charles V failed in his engagement to her, and now she is to marry his son. May *he* not bring her more grief than she has had! If he does so, I think I shall want to kill him."

"Do not do that; we are bidden to be present at the wedding, if it takes place," he said drily. They both knew that there was much opposition to the marriage in the country. Lennox's eyes narrowed as they gazed over the brown moor. "I wonder," he said, "that that young puss, the Lady Elizabeth, kept her head in London when the Lady Jane lost hers. It was for her, they say, that Wyatt gave his life; and when thrones are the prize there's small argument."

"That one will keep her head on her shoulders whatever befalls, I doubt not," said his wife. "She is like and yet not like her mother; wiser for herself, no doubt. I cannot care for her, but it is maybe by reason of the hurt her coming brought the Queen's Grace. The Princess Elizabeth has done me no harm."

The hawks swooped in the clear air above them, and brought down their prey.

THE WIND AND RAIN blew mercilessly against the Queen's
Spanish bridegroom as he was rowed inshore by a crew in the
Tudor white-and-green livery. Philip was feeling slightly sea-
sick. The gale continued to blow, and he was obliged to don a
cloak of scarlet felt and a broad hat under which to convey his
dripping person towards Winchester. The few passers-by were
not impressed with him, though his following was grand enough;
they saw him as he was, a short-legged, fair-haired young man
with a protuberant lower jaw and the eyes of a prawn. In his
train rode his mistress, disguised as a page. Philip had not felt
himself capable of enduring both the vile climate of England –
a storm had raged there in his grandfather's time that was still
remembered in Spanish history – and the future embraces of a
thirty-eight-year-old spinster without this occasional solace.
Everything would be conducted with discretion: his father the
Emperor had been so greatly anxious for this marriage, and the
consequent conversion of a heretic country, that he had had
Reginald de la Pole, who was indeed no heretic, imprisoned in
a German monastery until the wedding ceremony itself should
be concluded. It was whispered that de la Pole and the Queen
had had a *tendresse* in their youth, fostered by the Cardinal's
Plantagenet mother, Lady Salisbury, the Queen's early governess, and the Cardinal had certainly been making his way homeward now that Mary Tudor was safely on the throne. Philip
reflected vaguely on the situation as he watched the raindrops

drip from his hat's brim and also observed a messenger riding towards him armed with a long white wand, and carrying a message from the Queen's Grace at Winchester, where the wedding was to be solemnised. Philip received the contents with absent courtesy. He was not seriously concerned with the subject of de la Pole. Queen Mary had, he was reliably assured, taken an oath on her missal at Westminster to the effect that she would marry no one except himself. He had come, accordingly, to perform his duty: but he would be glad when it stopped raining.

Another suspect was under restraint: following Wyatt's insurrection the Princess Elizabeth had been brought from Ashridge and placed in the Tower. At first she had been under close guard, but this by now had eased. She turned her smooth scholar's head to look at Lady Lennox, who had just come into her chamber on some pretext; the Princess was careful not to show her dislike of this cousin who had the ear of the Queen, and who had lately been put in charge of her in prison. Things might have been worse than that, Elizabeth knew; she was well aware that only her own circumspection, and plain luck, had allowed her to escape death when Jane Grey had died. Her own worst moment had been endured when she sank down on the stones by Traitor's Gate, when they brought her in by water: nothing could be more wretched and without hope than that, remembering how she had heard of her own mother entering there "and she never came out," thought Anne Boleyn's daughter. But there were minor annoyances unconnected with losing one's head. Aloud she said "My lady, need there be so great a noise made overhead with the throwing about of logs and pots and pans? If the tocsin rang to tell London I had escaped, I swear no one could hear it. I believe you do it to disturb my days." Lady Lennox's kitchen was abovestairs, for she had been granted a suite of rooms in the Tower. Elizabeth looked eloquently at the bare walls of her own room, from which my lady had lately removed all hangings. "There is a draught here, cousin," she said plaintively.

Ay, and no space for your admirers, Robert Dudley and others, to hide themselves, thought Madge, who from observation and report had convinced herself that the Queen's young sister – she could hardly bear to call Elizabeth Princess – should be strictly looked to, though Her Grace seemed now to require less supervision. There was not only the danger of Elizabeth's escape – children in the garden had brought her flowers, and might bring messages – but, after the long-ago affair of the Admiral, the girl might be more wanton than her mother, and Northumberland's sons were imprisoned in the Tower and Elizabeth had somehow made their acquaintance. Madge downed recollection of her own imprisonment here – how glad she would have been at that time to make friends! – and dealt summarily with the matter of the kitchens. "The work of my household must be done, and no one can expect rough serving-maids to use care whenever they must throw a log," she said roundly. The strange jewelled eyes regarded her in their familiar way, as if Elizabeth were a hundred years old. "Then there is no help for it?" the girl asked pertly, as Madge thought, and she returned a sharp answer; after all, she was older than this puss, and in rank her equal and more so.

"There is no help for it, and you are well enough lodged." Her annoyance flared into anger. "The Queen's Grace has been a merciful sister to you, and it becomes you ill to complain of the way you are treated here, where you have every comfort."

"Except my liberty."

Madge closed her lips firmly; she would not enter into argument with this chit, she had said too much already, it was the child moving in her and making her heavy and fretful, and there was much to do and little enough time before she must ride to Winchester, where she must stand by the Queen's side at her wedding. As if she had read her thoughts Elizabeth said, idly as if it were of little account, "So my sister weds the Spaniard after all? I pray God they have fair weather."

She looked up; the wind howled in the chimney, and below whipped up the waters of the Thames into waves. "Blessed be the bride the sun shines on," said Elizabeth. "At this rate my sister will have small blessing." She looked and spoke as though innocently, but her cousin frowned.

"You should pray for all blessing on the Queen's Grace and on her marriage, that it may result in sons who live to wear the crown of England." Her voice sounded strident in her own ears. Elizabeth was smiling.

"But that would suit you ill, would it not, my lady?"

"I?" Madge spoke indignantly. "Nothing would bring me greater happiness than that Her Grace should be blessed with children. No one who knows her can wish her else. I must leave you now, Princess, for I have my journey to make to Winchester."

She left the chamber, flustered, while Elizabeth continued to smile her enigmatic smile and to warm her spidery fingers at the brazier, whose flames the wind fanned wildly, red and blue. She herself knew that she had said nothing that could damage her if it were repeated to the Queen. "But I do not think," she told herself, "that my sister can bear children. So it behoves me to wait, and to say little."

The wind howled on.

The royal wedding was splendid in spite of the rain. Both bride and groom had sent patterns of the stuffs they would wear to one another's tailors, and each complemented the other when they returned from the scarlet-clad way to the Cathedral altar, Philip's trunk-hose echoing Her Grace's white satin gown worked in silver, and his brocade tunic studded with pearls her kirtle, whose own great sleeves were caught with clusters of gold, and the stuff itself gold-embossed. Being Mary, she had added customary touches of her own fondness for bright colour in her shoes, which were red, aided by a scarf of black velvet. They had been married, the bride and groom, in the selfsame place where Ethelred the Redeless had married Emma of Normandy, five centuries before. The ancient church was full of Spanish and English splendour. At the end of the exchanging of vows, when the ring was placed on the Queen's finger ("a plain gold ring I will have, like any other maiden," she had said to Madge earlier) the bridegroom's gift, which signified his bestowing of worldly goods, was placed on the missal. Philip had placed three handfuls of gold mixed with some silver. Everyone saw the Queen smile as her matron of honour, Lady Lennox, who was well known never to have had enough of this world's goods any more than Her Grace, darted forward and scooped up the offering into the Queen's purse. That memory of shared laughter was to be their last. Madge never forgot it.

Afterwards she went back to Temple Newsam and in time gave birth to a boy. He was called Philip, in honour of the Queen's husband, as they had agreed that day out hawking seven months since. But she had almost forgotten Philip of Spain for the time: it filled her and Lennox with joy that they should again have a living son. Darnley, a trifle wary of the newcomer, came into his mother's chamber when bidden and stared wordlessly down at the new baby's head. "Have no fear that he will ever take your place," said his mother.

But she cradled the baby against her gratefully, as she had done his two brothers. What were the great matters she had left compared with this happiness? It was true the Queen said she was also with child. Madge spared time to hope that it was indeed the truth.

But the baby Philip died, and soon Madge's daughters began to ail. As they laid the tiny coffin in its grave it had already begun to seem as if the brief ascent of happiness in all their stars was broken. There was ill news, she knew, from London; the worst news of the Queen. Cruelly, as Mary had believed herself with child, she grew big and went ailing thus to term and beyond, towards the last seeing none except a very few. Jane Dormer, her lady-in-waiting, who had been Madge's friend since their girlhood days together in the Duchess of Suffolk's house, sent word north when she could. The Queen's swollen body gave forth, in the end, with great pain, only diseased matter: there was no child. Philip had never loved her; she was only an ageing woman who had given him her heart; and in the end he abandoned her to prosecute his wars in the Low Countries. He left Mary alone with the name for cruelty and bigoted blood-lust with which his acts had branded her when the burning of Protestants gained in fury while he and others governed England in her name. Mary Tudor was to be remembered for little else; any mercies she had shown were soon forgotten. By the end she had neither fame, child, husband nor happiness.

Worst of all, from Madge's viewpoint, she and Lennox had lost the Queen's trust. It had happened because she herself urged her son Darnley constantly towards France. She took the full blame for what befell then and afterwards.

209

o

The House at Hackney, 1578

THE DOOR HAD OPENED; it was the grey-haired servant to announce that the meal was ready. Leicester brought himself back to an awareness of where he was, here, in Hackney, in the reign of Elizabeth. He saw Lady Lennox rise, taking her little granddaughter by the hand, and made ready to follow her. "You may leave your cloak here, my lord," said the Countess. He left the gold-embroidered conceit on the chair where he had sat, and followed her downstairs to the hall.

Here an array of food had been set out, Lenten and frugal as he had feared; bread, eggs, small-ale, and fish. There were few at the lower board besides his own servitors, whose faces expressed disgust at the poor quality of the fare. Leicester was placed by the Countess's right hand at the upper table. He saw that she sat at a raised dais, and maintained the state of a princess of England. "Well, and is she not so?" he asked a voice in his own mind, that would have queried it.

He cast his eyes over the few among her own household who sat at the lower board. Among them – he should not have felt shock at this, for he remembered hearing that Cecil had placed them in her house – were the man Nelson and his wife, eating with downcast eyes. For instants indignation rose in Leicester; how could she endure the daily sight of that man? He had been the only one present to escape death at the appalling business of Kirk o' Field, where her son Darnley had been murdered, eleven years since.

213

"She has endured the fire," he thought, remembering the crest of the green salamander. He turned his gaze, mouthing some courtesy, to the jewel at her breast. He could see it more clearly now that candles were lit. It was a sapphire heart, for mourning, with an emerald and ruby crown. She saw his look, smiled, and turned the jewel about so that the obverse could be seen; it was a pelican shedding blood from its breast. She kept silence except to talk of other things.

He answered, contributing to the small-talk; but his mind was on the jewel. He must ask her about it, he thought, later. He must ask her about many things. A kind of excitement had risen in him that he had not known since youth; he, Robert Dudley, about to be displaced from the intimacy he had held about the Queen from the beginning, might – might perchance – possess the secrets of matters fifty years old, ere this night was done. He, of all men, might hold the key to past and future regarding the Crown. He might –

"Have you eaten enough, my lord?" came the voice of the old woman by his side. A feast such as this must have stretched her lean purse almost beyond endurance; why had she made such a sacrifice for him? True, she had unburdened herself of much that no one now living could know, or remember . . .

He answered in the affirmative, the dry stale taste of the fish still in his throat. "Then we will go upstairs again," said the Countess, and rose and preceded him. She had both begun and ended the meal with a blessing according to the old faith. Amusement rose in Leicester faintly that he had both witnessed and acceded to it.

They reached the room into which he had first been shown, the child Arbell following them with her usual silence. His cloak lay undisturbed in its folds on the chair and Leicester took hold of it and laid it aside, anxious lest his wearing of it seem discourteous. He had the impression both that everything he did and thought was clear to his hostess, and yet mattered nothing. She seated herself also, and the enigmatic jewel swung against her; she put up her hand to still it, and went on with her tale as if the meal they had eaten had been a mere interruption, which had not mattered.

"One good thing came out of that Spanish marriage," she said.

214

"Jane Dormer, who was the poor Queen's lady and with her when she died, married the Count de Feria, who was Philip's ambassador, for love. She went with him to Spain."

"You will have heard, then, from Spain, now and again."

"Why, yes; and also from King Philip. He was never my enemy. You and Cecil know that well, my lord; why do you ask?"

The room had grown darker while she talked, and Robert Dudley listened; seeing himself again as he had been so many years ago that he had half forgotten; that young man in the Tower after his father's execution, who had somehow made assignations with the other State prisoner, the beguiling, secret, maddening creature who had been the young Elizabeth. Still herself in danger, and knowing it, he and she had danced on thin ice together, then and later, God knew; although at that time his own peril had been small. He had been released shortly after, never in any case having had suspicion thrown on him other than that he was Northumberland's son and the brother of Guilford Dudley, who had married Jane Grey.

The Countess was holding out her almost transparent hands to the low fire. "Let them bring in more logs," she said. Leicester rose and went to the door and called, and presently one of her dark-clad elderly servants came in, carrying a load of wood. "You may cast it all on, John Phillips," said Margaret Lennox. "The room grows cold."

"All, my lady? But there is little enough left in store." The man spoke more as a friend than a servant, as though he watched over her. She paid no heed.

"Do as I say," she said imperiously, and the old man bent and mended the fire till the flames leaped and sent reflections through the room. "That is warmer now," said the Countess. "While I live I may as well be warm. I have dwelt with enough cold in my time." She laughed, and drew her threadbare robe about her.

The child Arbell had been in the room with them all this while, playing quietly with her rag mammet. She crept closer to the hearth now to taste the warmth. "I had forgotten her," said her grandmother, and called John Phillips back. "Take my lady Arbell away; it is her bedtime." The little girl came obediently and kissed her hand and then her cheek, dropping a curtsy. Then she was led away, carrying her mammet carefully.

"God knows what will become of her," said my lady sadly. "I have little to leave her, and there is no one left, when I go, to care. Maybe my lady of Shrewsbury will leave off her building in Derbyshire stone for a while, and take some heed to Arbell; she is her grandchild too."

A spice of malice suddenly lightened the drawn face. "That was the third time I was put in prison," she told him. A smile lingered on her lips with the pleasure it gave her to be able, at last, to jest openly without fear. He had a glimpse of what she must have been when she was young, fair and gay. "I always said," she went on, "that I was in the Tower three times for love: once for poor Thomas Howard's to me, once for my son Darnley's marriage to the Queen of Scots, and last of all for the love – and it was a true love, though short, poor children – that my son bore towards Elizabeth Cavendish, Lady Shrewsbury's daughter. They made Arbell between them. You will remember my son Charles, my lord? I bore him last of all my family."

Leicester inclined his head; he could just remember having seen the young Earl of Lennox, who had died even before his young wife; a sickly youth a full head shorter than his brother Darnley had been. It was easier to recall, for he had witnessed it at close hand, Her Grace's rage at the final insolence of my Lady Lennox, who had gone north on some pretext and secretly arranged the Cavendish match for her son with old Bess of Hardwick, who had bartered her daughter for the name. The Queen had arrested Lady Lennox and brought her south with the newlyweds, and for a while again to the Tower. "They loved much," he heard the Countess say softly. "Arbell is the very child of love; is she not lovely, my lord? Yet who will love her in turn? Whoever it may be, they will incur the wrath of kings. Such is our fate."

Leicester moved restlessly; he was not concerned with probabilities or with the future of penniless children of royal blood. He said aloud, out of courtesy, "That last imprisonment would be the worst, at your age?" And as suddenly as the change from sun to rain, he saw the tears come into her eyes and run down her cheeks. She did not wipe them dry.

"No – ah, no! The second time was the worst by far! They came and told me then that Darnley was dead, and in such a manner! You know of it well . . ."

216

IV

The Lion's Mark

SIR NICHOLAS THROCKMORTON, the new Queen Elizabeth's ambassador to the Court of France, wrote to his mistress in 1559 of how well "a young gentleman, an English or a Scottishman, who had no beard" was received by the equally new King and Queen, François II and Mary of Scotland. The young gentleman himself was Lord Darnley, aged fourteen: he was so tall that he seemed older to the diplomat. Darnley himself was still possessed by the hazards of the sea-voyage he had made from Burlington Bay, which was not far from his new home in Settrington, Yorkshire. His wit was quick enough to perceive that this convenience, which allowed her to send messengers readily to and from France, was the reason for his mother's having uprooted her family from Temple Newsam and Wressil, both of which Darnley regretted, as he had many acquaintainces there from coursing and hunting all about the countryside. But, his mother told him, he was to be more than a country squire; and to this end, he knew, she had once or twice despatched his tutor, John Elder, on sundry errands to the Court of France. Darnley could in fact remember, with disgust, how a specimen of his own handwriting had been taken over, when he was eight years old, to the Queen of Scots to let her see how fine it was. The Queen was not much older than he; why should she judge his handwriting? It was almost worse than the time he had been made to translate More's *Utopia* for a gift to the late Queen Mary of England; at least she had sent him a jewelled chain in reward. But this other Queen had sent nothing; and now it was considered time for Darnley to go himself and pay his respects to her. This he was nothing loth to do, for the journey offered some excitement, away from the constant company of his sisters at home and young Charles, who was beginning to run about after him on spindly legs. It was a manly feeling to take part in the cloak-and-dagger arrangements whereby he must ride to Burlington and set sail by night, with his mantle wrapped high in folds about his face and his cap pulled well down over his head to hide his golden hair, while his mother let it be known (he knew) that he had gone on a visit to Lord Westmorland. The voyage had not been smooth, tossed about as he'd been in the boat; then the landing, the knowledge that he was at last on foreign yet friendly soil, and the horses waiting to convey him to Chambord, where François and Mary were holding their Christmas festival. It all partook of the adventurous and braggart stuff of which Darnley felt himself to be made; was he not Douglas and Tudor both? He was enjoying the secret journey. It was somehow all of a piece with the ploys there had been a year or two back, just before the late Queen died, when his father's brother, the Sieur d'Aubigny, a fat man whose fate it seemed always to be taken prisoner, had had this happen to him again while he was fighting on the English border in the service of the Queen Regent of Scotland, Marie de Guise, then sick unto death; she had in fact died soon afterwards. Darnley's uncle, ignominiously prisoner in the north of England, had sent for aid to his brother Matthew, to the latter's embarrassment, but money and aid had been forthcoming. "I do not think, however," Lord Darnley ruminated, "that Queen Mary of England ever forgave my father and mother for that, as it was trafficking with the Scots." No doubt what he himself was doing now was something similar; a Frenchman was the same as a Scot to any Englishman, especially since the loss of Calais. But Darnley was finding the visit to his taste, especially when the Château de Chambord came in sight and he was unable to repress an indrawn breath at its magnificence. He had not hitherto seen, or imagined, the great Renaissance châteaux inspired by a former King of France's warlike incursions into Italy. The wars had been expensive, but had garnered this magnificent heritage built by imported Italian craftsmen.

Darnley was sufficiently recovered not to gape at the Archers of the Guard of France as he was ushered into the presence of the young King and Queen.

They sat side by side on high chairs, with a background of fleurs-de-lys on blue cloth so that they looked, at first, like stiff heraldic figures. Then they moved and smiled; and presently, as Darnley bowed over hands, he began to compare this boy and girl with others he knew. The Queen was pretty and graceful, he thought, though not more so than his own sisters if they could have been as grandly dressed, with bell-shaped skirts all glittering with gems, and sleeves puffed at the shoulder. King François himself was nothing to remark upon, except that his height threatened to equal Darnley's. He had a pale, puffy face with lines, unlike a boy's, that stretched from nose to mouth, making him look tired always. He seemed amiable enough, and they talked, while Darnley aired the French he had learned from his father and from John Elder. One thing he noted; at almost every word the boy King uttered, he would turn to his young wife to see if she agreed, which was not singular to Darnley. His father at home seldom spoke at all, and followed his mother about almost like a child, and could not bear to be long absent from her. Perhaps, Darnley thought, it was common enough for men to be subject to their wives.

The next time he saw Mary Stuart much had changed.

He had won home again safely and, after much questioning about his journey and his reception, the answers to which seemed to please his mother, life settled into its usual pursuits. Darnley was growing used to Settrington, with the enhanced state of its household and the figure of his mother, like a matriarch of mediaeval days, at its centre. Two of his sisters had died; this made the Countess cling to him and to young Charles, more than to the two remaining girls, as if the latter were currency whose value might drop, while he and Charles were pure gold. The vacant places at table were soon filled. Two young lady wards, named Mabel Fortescue and Mary Shelley, who were kinswomen of someone in London, and others too, came to encompass his mother about like a flock of imitative goslings (not that one would ever compare his pious, busy, dignified yet tender mother to a goose) to learn stitchery and

the manners of great ladies, and how to run a household, which
meant, Darnley knew, mysteries connected with the brewing of
wine from elderflower and fruit, and making of herbal unguents
which healed hurts – his own when a boy had been rapidly
healed by some matter his mother put on them, but of course
now he was almost a man he was no longer addicted to grazing
his hands and knees, like Charles – and supervising the baking
of bread, and basting of joints over the great fire in the kitchens,
for my lady did not believe in leaving all such things to servants
without overseeing them for herself. All these and other
matters went on despite his morose father, who was as often
as not by his mother's side while she was about these tasks, or
alone with her lord in her solar. There – this at Darnley's age
seemed no more than a slight addition of spice to the whole
excitement of living – one had to learn to keep one's voice
lowered, as at certain other times and in certain other places
in the house, when a man named Forbes passed by, who had
used to be trusted by my lady but was so no longer. That such
as Forbes should remain in the house against the will of even
Darnley's powerful mother seemed natural enough, when one
grew used to it. He had been sent on the instructions of the
Queen's Grace from London, or rather through her secretary,
Cecil, who knew all the Queen's affairs and most other folk's
as well.

"Is Forbes a spy of Cecil?" Darnley had asked his mother once.
And over her face had instantly fallen a kind of smooth mask,
and she had guided him out before her into the knot-garden.
Stooping to pluck a herb as though it were of no moment, she
said to him, "Do not ever speak aloud of such matters; remember
that in your position, and mine, we are always followed and
always spied on, even by those we may trust at the first. There
are ways of evading spies; the first is to learn to hold one's
tongue."

So it was, often, in her solar; Forbes might well be behind
the arras, listening. "Can we not kill him?" Darnley murmured,
and was reproved; if such a thing happened, they would all be
sent for to London, and imprisoned, and later another spy
would be sent in Forbes's place. So the spy continued to listen,
and eavesdrop, and follow one, and send letters; concerning
what? One day again, about a year after the visit to France,

Darnley's mother had bidden him come to her in the open, away even from trees behind which Forbes might hide. Her face was full of suppressed excitement and her eyes sparkled like sapphires.

She said to him, "The young King of France is dead."

Darnley thought of the sick boy with lines on his face. It seemed a pity that François II had had to die; he had been pleasant. Darnley was about to say some such thing when his mother started to talk again, as if the news had not yet come of which she would speak; as if the death itself had been only a beginning. "The young Queen of Scots is a widow," she reminded him, and waited for instants lest he should interrupt, but Darnley said nothing; what was there to say? If a woman's husband died, then she was a widow. It stood to reason. Why did his mother look at him so intently, as if trying to read what might be in his mind? For the first time, Darnley felt uncomfortable with her. It was as though she were trying to turn him into some person whom he was not.

She waited for instants and then suddenly stood up on tiptoe and kissed him, as though he were a child again. She said, "My great tall son must take a wife some day; why should it not be Mary of Scotland? But do not let our friend Forbes hear you say it."

Darnley considered the matter. It did not concern him greatly that Mary Stuart was a Queen. He himself had a grandmother who had been Queen of Scotland, and on his father's side there had been another Scots King's daughter, generations back. Royal folk were the same to each other as the rest of the world; he already realised this. If his mother wanted him to marry Mary Stuart, no doubt it would happen. "Do I say so to her?" he asked, thinking of letters. His mother laughed.

"No; you had best say nothing. It is for her to speak of this first, but it will do no harm to let her see you now, when she is bereaved and lonely. You must go to France again, Harry."

He nodded; he knew she was pleased with him when she called him Harry, as if they were any mother and son. "You must take letters from me," his mother said, "as secretly as you did the last time, and deliver them to Her Grace who is a *reine blanche,* in mourning, keeping her chamber."

"If she is keeping her chamber how will they let me see her?"

He had fleeting recollections of the times of his brothers' and sisters' births, when his mother had kept hers. Perhaps a mourning-chamber would be less inaccessible. His mother said, quickly as though she feared being overheard, "She is not as isolated as most Queens in white dule; being Queen-Regnant of Scotland, she must see those who come to her on her country's business. They will admit you, Harry."

So he had taken ship again, in one of the small anonymous trading vessels which came and went within sight of Ravenspur Head. He rode this time not to Chambord, but Orléans, where the Queen kept her mourning. The Court was there also; the new child King, Charles IX, a boy of ten, they said visited his brother's widow every day. Darnley hoped that the little boy would not be present when he himself was admitted to see her. It would almost be like having his own brother Charles listening to everything that was said.

He was fortunate. Except for her ladies, who kept a discreet distance, Darnley saw Mary alone. The chamber was all hung, not this time with fleurs-de-lys, but with black velvet, in folds so thick that no daylight could penetrate, and the place was lit with candles. It was like a tomb, Darnley thought. Mary herself was in the high-barbed coif and enveloping white robe of a French royal widow. Her face looked out with eyes bright as a fox's, and the hand Darnley kissed was, he noticed for the first time, exquisite and fine, with long tapering fingers; not so small as his mother's. He was aware of queer feelings rising in him that he had never known before. But when and where else could he have encountered a *reine blanche* in her black ghostly candlelit room, giving it, and her, an air both of being unreal and matchless anywhere in the world? But she was real enough; the young body beneath the smothering folds of *deuil blanche* was no phantom, but fashioned of flesh. Also, he was glad to find that she made no play of weeping and wailing for the deceased young King. Darnley was young enough to be embarrassed by emotion. She might have been fond enough of François, he decided; but made no fuss about it.

She spoke to him as if she were glad to see him. "It is always pleasant to meet a Scotsman, my lord; and you are an Englishman as well, which makes it better still. That is – unusual." Her voice had the slightest trace of foreignness, emphasising her difference from other young women he had known; from all other creatures. Darnley had risen from kissing her hands, and began to brag a little; his voice sounded young and clear in the velvet-hushed chamber.

"My home is in Yorkshire, madame. But my parents both have land in Scotland which they never see."

"And it would please them to return there?"

The question was put gently, but he was aware of the sudden bright appraisal of her eyes. He felt a creeping of discomfort. What if he had said the wrong thing? His mother should have told him what to say. But the late Regent, Marie de Guise, he knew, before her death had promised to restore his father's lands, and as for his mother's –

He thought of the right answer. "It would please them to be near Your Grace, if you yourself should return home."

She smiled. "A gallant! How old are you, my Lord Darnley? Perhaps I should not ask; although it is only women who dislike stating their ages." She began, as if in atonement, to ask many questions about his parents, his home; how was her good aunt? How much better was my lord of Lennox's malady? "I heard that he had been ill," she murmured. She seemed to know everything.

Darnley had mumbled that he was fifteen. He was still feeling foolish – he knew that everyone expected him to be older, to match his height – when suddenly Mary began to talk, rapidly, intimately. "My own mother died, you see, just before my husband," she told him. "They brought her coffin back here, to France. I was allowed to see so little of her when she was alive; then they brought back her dead body. She wore herself out keeping my kingdom for me. Then François – then the King died, although he was so young. It has made me feel that life is very transient, perhaps unimportant. Shut in here I was thinking only of sad things, then you come in here – aged fifteen." She gave a little sound between tears and laughter. "When I do come home, Lord Darnley – as perhaps I shall soon do, for there is no place for me now in France – why, then I hope we shall meet again."

Darnley had handed her his mother's letter. She started to read it now with a murmured excuse, leaving him no time to answer; turning herself half away so that the candlelight shone

225

on the opened seals, and on her exquisite profile, which, Darnley saw, was like the carved angels in churches which had not been wrecked by the wars. Only, she was made of flesh, as he had already noted; not of wood or stone or mourning-stuff. She –

Mary Stuart faced him again, and smiled. "I will write to your mother," she told him, "and you shall have the letter before you leave. Divert yourself a little, if you can, while you are at Orléans. The Court is in mourning, but you need not be."

She was smiling at him still, with a smile which seemed to convey a special meaning; what had been in his mother's letter? Darnley felt the corners of his own mouth lift in a returning smile. With rare insight into the mind of another, he thought of Mary, left alone here after he'd gone. It couldn't be much fun for her, cooped up in a candle-lit darkness.

He did not see Mary again on that visit, but the letter she had written to his mother was handed to him, sealed with her royal seal, before he left. Darnley put it in the bosom of his shirt with a sense of importance, of conspiracy. It was almost as though he were an ambassador ... for whom? For his father and mother? For himself?

It was his mother who greeted him on return, running towards him more swiftly than was her stately wont, kissing him, plying him with questions, seizing the letter from him at last with small eager hands. Forbes must be elsewhere. "So she wrote? She put pen to paper regarding what I asked?"

And when she had read the letter through she seemed more than ever pleased, and called him Harry. From that day – or so Darnley afterwards thought – everyone, even his father, seemed to treat him with even more deference, as though he were a King.

NEMESIS FOLLOWED. Afterwards, in the long perspective of memory and regret, Madge used to wonder how she could have thought it would be otherwise. They had been too long carefree. She herself however had used the utmost care, maintained constant caution, in her correspondence between France and Settrington, Scotland and Settrington, even on two occasions Philip of Spain and Settrington. It was all to help her son. She had made a point of using messengers she trusted, not Forbes after the first; men like Arthur Lallard the schoolmaster, men like Ralph Lacey who were known to her, who would never betray her, or her lord or her son. But Forbes . . . Forbes, proved to be the tool of Cecil after he had been discovered in some minor matter of reporting what she'd said! It was long now since she had ceased to trust Forbes, but he was in the house; watching her, reporting every movement and saying of hers, even that inadvertent one when she heard that the young Queen Mary had won home safe to Scotland despite the English ships lying in wait. Madge had held up her hands and given thanks and exclaimed, "How God preserves that Princess at all times!" It would all be, by now, in Cecil's despatches; also the journey Lord Darnley had made to Orléans (though not, please God, its result) and his earlier one that time to Chambord. Cecil would have everything duly noted and filed away in his cabinet.

But nothing happened openly amiss until the following Christmas.

They were all making merry after the meal, and Darnley had chased staid Mabel Fortescue into a corner and was tormenting her, and little Lord Charles ran about after his brother tugging at his doublet, and their sisters, who had been ill again, seemed to have revived bright hectic colour for the occasion with some gaiety, and even Lennox, who had been surly and strange since his illness with everyone except herself, talked together and laughed in good humour after the Christmas fare she had made ready over the past weeks. There had been roasted fowls and baked meats and pies and oranges and raisins and cock-ale and marchpane, following on the fast they had made until, that morning, they had attended the simple Mass said daily in Settrington chapel, and as she had seen the light from the window shine on Darnley's head as he partook of the Sacrament, Madge had again vowed fiercely that he should not become as she had been in her own youth, relegated to obscurity, forbidden to marry a royal bride because of his royal blood. The letter Mary Stuart had sent from Orléans had itself shown that that young Queen had recognised, in worldly enough fashion, the existence of a partner suitable by birth for herself, when she should marry again. That was as much as could be hoped for until she, his mother, could get Darnley by some means into Scotland. How was she to spirit him across the Border without being prevented by the ever-watchful Queen in the south? It would have, she had already decided, to be in some manner connected with the Angus and Lennox inheritances. Perhaps Matthew should go also, if he were well enough, to avert suspicion. What she herself must do, whether to go with them to guide them, or stay here to guard the English interests, was not yet clear. God would send all things as they came.

She stared down at her plate, forgetting the gaiety all about her, no longer even hearing the comical mewling of Tom the fool, who was adding to the laughter brought on by cock-ale. Madge had let her mind stray back. How foolish – more so than the hired fool – she herself had been to listen to the old woman to whom she had given shelter and houseroom, two years since, when she came to the door in rags, without flesh on her bones, and so poor! Ever since the time long ago at Syon when she'd succoured Tom Howard's folk to her own hurt, Madge had had a merciful heart for beggars and the destitute. That woman had

228

stayed on with them at Settrington till she died. It had not been long; she had been found seated one morning by the night's cold ashes, cold as they, with no more life in her. Before that, she'd looked at Madge and said . . . and said . . . *Ye shall be in great trouble, and yet do well enough, for ye hope for a day which I trust ye will never see, your doings being espied betimes.* That might have warned her, at the time, about Forbes; perhaps it had; but in other ways what did it all mean? "It was to occur about now, the trouble," thought Madge, "for she told me of it at that time she came, and said so; yet here we are, and even my lord is merry."

She cast a glance of affection at Matthew; how much better he looked now that he had risen from his sickbed! The physicians had been able to do little for him; it was she, his wife, who by daily and nightly care had brought him out of the deep pit where his mind seemed to wander, and made him walk among men again, see the light of day again, talk and sometimes laugh. It was a pitiful thing that such a big handsome man could not endure his own company . . .

The fool screamed and danced. They would pay him well, and this was Christmas. "God save us all from ungodly passion," he cried, and began to make play to imitate Her Grace and Robert Dudley, whom everyone said was her lover; portraying in such a degree, by twisting his body and countenance, a coy long-nosed spinster and a forthcoming nobleman with no time to waste, that the company dissolved in laughter. "And, mind you, he had his wife Amy Robsart pushed downstairs as well, to break her neck that none might say he was married. God forbid that all fine gentlemen should behave so, or we are in fear of our necks, ladies, all of us!"

Madge frowned a little. Was it wise to allow such talk in her house, even in jest? Her eyes sought out Forbes to see how he was taking the sally, but he was nowhere to be seen. Perhaps this gave her her first taste of unease; perhaps it was the voice of Mabel Fortescue, still teased by Harry about the window.

"Lord Darnley, keep your hands to yourself, I beg . . . why, what a body of horsemen are alighting in the courtyard! Why, they are in the Queen's livery . . ."

THEY HAD ARRESTED everyone in the house. Lennox and Darnley were mounted and put to ride between the guards. Madge herself would have ridden also, but pleaded that one of the girls was sick and Charles, her youngest, little more than a baby. She had, therefore, been put into her litter, with the three children; this delayed their journey and also gave her time to think; less to remember what had happened than what might still do so. Of what use now to worry about the new-milled flour not yet in crocks, the newly churned butter, so scarce in winter, and the few cattle kept alive for spring? And the main part of all her gear at Settrington, the serving-dishes and knives and ladles and cauldrons, and the plate, had had to be left behind; they were permitted to take only what could be carried readily. That was the least of it; they were bidden to await Her Grace's pleasure in London. To Madge the words had a grim echo. She had already awaited the pleasure of a monarch in the Tower, for many weary months with never a sight of him. Would the Queen lodge all of them there? "If only we may be together," she thought, "it will not be so bad." The remembrance came of that balconied room looking out over Tower Green, with the phantoms that came to haunt her and the sense of being, always and for ever, alone . . .

The journey was harsh, the winter ways hard and rutted with frost. On the way the sick younger girl started to shiver and cough; the colour that had come into her cheeks for the Christ-

230

mas feast was still there, hectic, making carnation patches one
on either thin cheek. She was too thin for a child, and so was
her sister. Madge hugged Charles to her against the litter-
cushions as if to protect him from whatever disease was ravaging
his sisters. Within her own mind she knew, and would not
admit the memory of the Queen-Duchess, coughing her soul out
at Stepney long ago. Two of the girls were dead already; these
two might also die; but her sons should live.

"They will not secure Charles in prison at his age," she
thought; but there was Darnley, and the promise he carried.
She parted the curtains of the litter and looked out, through
the blast of cold, to where his still arrogant figure could be seen,
riding between two of the Queen's men. His father drooped in
the saddle nearby; such a journey would be tiring for Matthew.
Madge closed the curtains again and began to think and plan.
They might, she knew well, spend years awaiting the pleasure
of Her Grace. Darnley must not be taken prisoner. Darnley
must escape. But how? When? Not now, when their every
movement would be espied by the guards and Darnley's figure,
mounted on his grey horse, would be seen for miles among the
frost-rimed hills even by the light of the moon. No, it must
happen later; in the moment's confusion before they were put
wherever Her Grace pleased. It must happen in London, that
place of rabbit-warren dwellings and swift easy travel by water.
Once among the jumble of houses and streets Darnley, if he
moved swiftly, would be safe. But how to tell him, prepare him,
give him money?

She thought of a means, as the girl nearby coughed always.
It was heartless, but the only way. Presently what she had
known would happen again did so, and the child coughed up
blood. Madge nipped Charles hard in the buttock. He screamed,
then began to wail.

"Cry out for Harry," she whispered, "cry for your brother."
She could always administer another nip, she thought, if he
stopped too soon. She thrust her head out of the litter again,
calling the near guard. The procession slowed; the guard's face,
red with cold and anger – the damned litter had added days
to the length of their journey – bent above her.

"You can see what has happened," she said, "and my son is
afraid of the blood. Let his brother come, pray, to comfort him.

It will not take more than moments."

He demurred; they had had orders to keep the prisoners strictly separate; but Charles continued to howl and in the end his brother came, dismounting and putting his head and shoulders into the litter. Madge moved quickly; she thrust her purse in his hand; it contained all her money. "Not Scotland," she said, "not yet. Make for France."

His fingers pressed hers and the purse had gone; had he taken her meaning, and would he contrive for himself, young as he was? "But he would grow older in the Tower," she thought; the risk had been worth taking. Charles had ceased to cry under her comforting caresses; presently, when the litter-curtains were still again, Madge set her mouth against his hair. "Hush, my darling," she murmured, "hush. You have seen Harry. You shall see him again, I swear, when . . . when we are all of us together again."

Lord Charles Stuart's sobs lessened. But he was confused and incredulous. His mother had nipped him, and it had hurt. Such a thing had never happened before. And she had said he was afraid of blood, which he wasn't. He stared, letting his breathing settle evenly, while the slow miles passed and his sister lay and coughed and brought up more blood. The other girl lay quiet.

They reached London at last, all except the younger girl. She had died on the journey.

No time for grief. No time, almost, for seeing to the care of the sole surviving girl out of four, who was almost as sick by now as her sister had been. Lennox had come to comfort Madge when he could. They had been set down, the party, in divers places according to Cecil's instructions; some at the Gatehouse in Westminster, others to the Palace there; at least it was not, or not yet, to be the Tower. When they were left alone, and Charles put to bed between sheets that might be damp for she had not had time to air them, Madge found herself in her husband's arms; the rough feel of his cloak, which he had not yet cast off, comforted her. "At least we have one another," she thought. "At least we have that."

"Where is Darnley?" said Lennox at last, looking round. The guard had gone and they were, as far as might be known, unobserved. The sick child's coughing came from the curtained bed; beyond her, Charles already slept. Madge put a finger to her lord's lips. She was smiling, despite their situation. Nobody else was there. Darnley had gone, alone into London, at the first instant he might. She would pray that night that he reach the coast. "John d'Aubigny will have a care to him, once he is in France," she whispered to Lennox, who still held her close. "He owes you that for the aid you sent him when the English held him prisoner."

"As now they hold us. I am glad the boy is free."

"As yet . . . as yet! We must pray."

Prayer was answered, and no sign of Lord Darnley was found by the many searchers sent out through the city by Cecil and Her Grace. With failure, their anger mounted; the chief prey – they knew well enough, had known from the beginning what was afoot between my Lady Lennox and the Queen of Scots – had eluded them but there were still the parents in their hands; and they said the Earl of Lennox was ruled by his wife. Perhaps when the couple were separated for a while, some truth might emerge.

They came to take Lennox away, alone. They would take him to the Tower. When they came – the Master of the Rolls was sent, with all due courtesy, to collect this prisoner who boasted that some of his own Scots blood was separately royal – when they came, they were met by a distraught woman with her whitening hair half-loosed below her coif, her mouth slack with terror.

"My lord cannot be left alone. He *cannot*. He will go out of his mind. He has a sickness – "

"Her Grace's orders, my lady." That was all they said; and she could hardly see for the blur of tears as they led Matthew's big figure away to his solitary prison.

There came to her, some weeks later, a crumb of comfort in what had begun to seem like the blackest time of all. Darnley was with the Sieur d'Aubigny, safe in France.

AFTERWARDS she came to realize that those years were an apprenticeship for loneliness. She had once thought that about the time long ago in the Tower. But now it was brought home to her what it meant to lack a presence which had been beside her daily, nightly; a man who had become part of herself, who looked to her, as a child did, for supply of his needs, his food and cheer and clean linen. So it had been between them for many years, and now she was not even certain that Matthew was kept in cleanliness, or comfort; word had reached her that he was allowed no exercise in the Tower, that it was cold. and damp, that he had been questioned, had failed to answer, had been questioned again. "What is our fault?" she asked, in letter after letter to that omniscience, Cecil. He sent her evasive replies, or none. He would not permit her to see the Queen. "If I could but see her," thought Madge, "I could soften her heart, even hers." But it was not permitted, and once Lady Sackville – she and Sir Richard were, as if of intent, Howard kin and related to Anne Boleyn, and were to be Madge's gaolers when she and the children were taken at last to Sheen – once my lady hinted to her that the Queen had always disliked her since she, in her turn, had acted as Elizabeth's wardress in the Tower "and you took down all the hangings". Yes, and threw logs and pots and pans about over her head; of such things are treason compounded.

The winter passed, and summer came to the tumbledown

palace: the green grass sprang in the park and flowers came out of their bud. Madge's last remaining daughter lingered on all year. She watched the child's gradual weakening with a kind of stony passivity; if there was a curse laid on all her kind, it should spare Darnley and Charles. Of the former she never heard, for letters were not permitted to reach her. But Charles was her joy. He was an agile thin child now, not so great in height as Darnley had been at his age, nor so forward in his learning, "for God knows," she thought, "I can barely pay for our food and keep, let alone a tutor for him." She needed, if only for the boy's sake, his father by him; time and again she wrote to Cecil to beg him to permit Lennox at the least to share their imprisonment out of his "close keeping and lack of comfort". For herself she hardly dared think what state Lennox might be in by now, sick, alone, cold, and weakened in mind and body. How had they questioned him? What questions had they asked?

At other times she would tell herself, "The fault is mine, all mine. Matthew had no part in it." For it was becoming plain, although no open accusation had been made, that the matter of the Queen of Scots was at the root of it. She was glad she had counselled Darnley meantime to go into France; but perhaps she should never have counselled anyone to do anything. They had begun to level shafts at her for having governed her husband. That, she already knew, was what many folk thought. She replied with a flash of spirit, "Since his coming here he has needed no such schoolmistress."

But it was a schoolmaster who saved them. Lallard, the man who had taken sundry messages for her in the north, was brought before Cecil. "As for Scotland, I never was there before or since," he said roundly at the end of several hours' questioning. It was, as though he had known it, the right thing to say.

The Queen fell ill. (If the bitch dies, Madge thought, they will be perplexed again about the succession.) It was the moment to write and protest her devotion to Her Grace and her hopes for her recovery, and she did so. Her Grace mended, and Madge wrote again. It was autumn now and the leaves were swirling down to death about Sheen. Would Matthew endure another winter alone in "that house both unwholesome and cold"?

Her pen never rested. She begged, cajoled, pleaded loyalty, pled for Lennox always. She let it seem as if her true interest lay with the Queen, but asked again that Lennox might be imprisoned with her and their children "and I shall be content".

Perhaps Master Secretary Cecil had had enough letters; also, he and Her Grace had had little satisfaction out of the solitary confinement of Lennox himself, who had behaved with great dignity and no little spirit, and said that he would answer for his crime when he knew what it was. They had not broken him, any more than they had broken his lady.

So, on the twenty-sixth of November, at last, at Sheen, there was brought to her a big pallid man with bowed shoulders and a grey beard and hair. He held out his arms; then she knew him, and ran into them. At the same time she was thinking, my God, he is grey; and my own hair is white: we are old, both of us. But he was with her again; the nagging poverty and cold, the lack of freedom, the hints of the Sackvilles to whom she now of necessity owed money, mattered less, an infinity less than they had done. Matthew was with her, and she was no longer alone. He was with her and – this was the strange thought she had – stronger now than she was herself. His solitude had brought out a vein of iron in him, and had borne him up.

MADGE'S APPARENT CONCERN for the Queen's health bore slowly ripening fruit. After some months she and Lennox were permitted to leave Sheen and reside where they would in London; so deeply in debt were they that a place was hard to find. In addition, lawsuits had started in their absence over the ownership of their lands in Yorkshire; Madge fretted to be gone, to repair the havoc there.

At last permission came, and she rode north. She found herself again confronting fields of blowing grass, with not a grazing beast in sight, or a man left to cut hay. Inside the house things were worse. Damp and mildew had taken their toll of anything that was left, and not much had been; every single object of any value had been pilfered, chests opened and left yawning to the tainted air, cupboards ransacked, trails of thieves' feet showing through the dust where they had dragged the spoil away in sacks, then dust had settled down again.

"I do not know where to begin," she thought, and a great dreariness of spirit possessed her. She went to what had once been her oratory – the statues and crucifix were missing – and knelt down to pray. She was reminded, through her weary grief, of the impermanence of worldly goods. Moth and rust doth corrupt . . . thieves break in and steal . . . So it was with her; and all her children were dead now except the two boys. I must count my blessings, she thought. They were four; Darnley, Charles, Lennox, and the hopes she had in Scotland. Kneeling

237

still, she found plans circling in her mind, while her fingers moved by habit over her beads. Darnley and Scotland, Darnley and the Queen of Scots. Would it be safe yet for Darnley to return to England from France? "Not till I have seen Her Grace," she thought. Perhaps the Queen could be sounded by asking permission for Lennox himself to go north to see to his Scottish inheritance, restored before her death by Marie de Guise and never yet visited. They had written to him then, "If ye may come to your estates now, it shall be with honour, but later it may not be so." He should go indeed with honour, if it might be done; and then –

She was intriguing again. She must be a born plotter, here in supposed communion with God, and thinking of inheritances and her son's marriage.

She would be glad to see Darnley home. It was over a year since he had gone to France; would he have changed, acquired the polish and independence of a young well-travelled noble-man? The Sieur d'Aubigny and his wife would have been good to him and would have seen that he was introduced to the ways of the Court, the ways of life.

Madge sighed. She did not want Harry to know all of the latter quite yet. But there had been no means of preventing it; and she must stop thinking of her eldest son as though he were a baby, when he was turned seventeen.

Lennox acquired permission to go to his Scottish estates. The smoothness and speed with which it was granted astonished her. No doubt she had grown inured to delays and refusals; as it was, there was hardly time to think what it would be like, again, with Matthew no longer by her. "But at least this time you are a free man, and may ride where you will," she assured him, as she folded his scanty linen and mended clothes; so threadbare a great lord to arrive to claim his heritage! "I would we had the money to buy you a new coat," she said sadly. He laughed, with the new confidence he had gained during that time in prison, and kissed her.

"They will know their liege lord, and where there's land there's money. I'll maybe come back to ye in French finery bought of one of the Queen's folk that followed her from France."

"And the castles themselves, will they not be damp without firing for so long?" It was many a year since Lennox had been hurried out of his native country, a little boy in fear of his life from his father's murderers. She remembered again that one of them had been her own father, and said a quick prayer that Angus's soul might rest in peace. Then she turned back to her husband, the anxious look still on her face. He had been ill again at Sheen, though not the appalling former sickness of the mind, more of a tertian ague such as she herself took at times. But men never had a care to themselves without a woman by them. "You will keep warm?" she said. "You will not sit about in wet hose and shoes, and sleep between covers that have not been aired, or –"

"I will have small comfort, no doubt, but only because you are not by me. But have no fear; it will not be long till our next meeting, and then I hope to come not as a beggar, but as a man with gold in his purse of his own getting. We have lived from hand to mouth all these years; even the Queen's Cecil saw that it would be less of a charge on him were I to come into my own."

For instants he was almost an unfamiliar, featureless stranger. He was going into a land which she herself could recall only from her childhood, and that had been unsettled enough. She blinked back her tears and said in a low voice, "And Harry's interest? You will not forget?"

"No more than my right hand can forget my sword-hilt. But it is yourself who must be the means of it, and not I. I will be there, though, if – when the lad comes north."

He had altered the phrasing quickly. Madge must not be left with doubts and fears beyond those she already possessed. He looked at her with pride and affection. What a woman she was! He had more faith in her than in anyone else on earth. If she wanted this marriage of their son with the Queen of Scots, it would happen. Lennox himself was hardly more than her servant in the affair.

Darnley came home that year. After Lennox had ridden off a tall figure in a cloak appeared at Madge's doorway in Sackville Place. The servant asked his name.

"Tell my mother it is the devil," said Harry's voice, grown

deeper in absence. Darnley pulled off his plumed French cap and gave it to the man, combed his crushed fair curls out with his fingers, and came to her with great strides across the hall.

"My mother!"

A smile of great joy transfigured her face. "Why, son, you are grown so tall that I cannot well kiss you," she whispered, anxious not to weep lest he think her a fanciful old fool, yet filled with such triumph that tears seemed the only relief. "Then I will aid you," said Darnley, and put his two hands about her waist and lifted her as though she had been a child. She could feel the roughness of his cheek, a man's, and the prick of his ruff and his hands' hard grip. "Ah, Harry . . . Harry!"

Then she began to fuss over him. Had he eaten? Were his shoes wet? What kind of a crossing had he had? How had he left my lord of Aubigny? What had he been doing with himself? Above all, how was he? "You are thinner," she said anxiously. "Did they not feed you well in France?"

"With the best of fare. I lacked for nothing, mother, but you – we heard – I am sorry – "

But the past hardships did not matter, now she had him home again. She drew him to the fire, and bade them put on more logs. Now her son was with her once more there must be nothing lacking, nothing stinted, everything fine and dainty and warm as he had been used, no doubt, to it in France. "And when Her Grace sees you!" she said, running her hands over the silken stuff of his doublet, and looking up again into the face which was no longer a boy's, yet not quite yet full man; not quite yet; she still had a little of his boyhood left to her, until . . . until he went north.

Favour Continued to shine. Perhaps she herself had appeared willing to court it. She had stood together, with Her Grace, as godmother to Cecil's newborn child; she had discouraged any favour shown to her by the common people, for there were those who resented the harsh treatment of the King's remaining heirs, despite his will. But Madge had remained discreet, taking none of the bait offered; and as a result, she was bidden to Court, and told to bring her son Darnley with her.

Once there, she herself knew that she had grown old. It was much as it had used to be, with everyone competing for the notice of the arbiter, the monarch. Only now it was no longer a big man with a red-gold beard, but his daughter. Meeting the Queen, kissing her long beringed white fingers, one could no more mistake her for an ordinary mortal than a snowdrop could be compared with a pasque-flower. Her Grace now relied on her appearance to a far greater degree than even her father had done; she was bedizened and bejewelled, clad in great ruffs and farthingales which stretched her skirts to make the breadth seem equal to the length; she wore a wig since her recent illness. Only the eyes, in the high-boned painted face, were the same; strangely coloured, of no one colour in especial, like opals. Her Grace might have been any age. "From this time on," Madge thought, seeing her, "she will look as she does now, whether she be thirty or seventy." Elizabeth was no longer a woman; she was a Queen.

Or was she still a woman after all? Lord Robert Dudley had

241

her ear; he was never far from her. It was whispered that he had lain with her one New Year: and if once then why not many times? At any rate, he was spoken of here and abroad as her paramour; and when word came that he had been suggested by Her Grace as a husband for the Queen of Scots, Madge could barely control her anger.

"It is an insult," she said to Darnley, who was much with her when not occupied at Court, though, being to all intents the next heir, he often had to bear the sword on state occasions. "It is so gross of itself that the Scots Queen will refuse it; that is certain."

"Her Grace is creating *him* Earl of Leicester," said Darnley, concealing a yawn behind his hand. He had found Court life diverting at first, as all new things; it had been the same in France; by now it wearied him, and he wished the ceremony of creating my Lord Robert a peer was over. If he had cared to examine the reasons for his weariness, which he did not, he would have admitted that it had come upon him because Lord Robert and the Queen, and not himself, would be the centres of attention and glory.

Sir James Melville, the Scots Ambassador, was in full view of the procession which would make an earl of Robert Dudley. He recognised many faces, among them Lennox's wife, looking her age; he had already made the acquaintance of Lennox in Scotland and had been entertained by him at his pleasant castle of Crookston, on its green hill nearby Glasgow. Lord Lennox had sent earnest remembrances to his own wife, of whom, Melville had noted, he seemed very fond. He would pass on the remembrances, but meantime, in the capacity of watcher, assessed for what it was worth the pageant of the upcome nobleman. It went without saying that his own Queen would refuse the offer; what intrigued Melville was the reason why it had been made at all. Her Grace of England could not seriously entertain the notion that the proposal of her lover as a husband would be acceptable to his mistress. "For Dudley himself, it might have been a different matter, thirled as he is to the spectacle of royalty here," thought Sir James, recalling the loveliness and grace of his own young Queen. No need for wigs and white-leading there! She was so beautiful and gracious that it should not be a hard matter to find her a suitable husband; and yet, owing to her position in Europe, it was damnably difficult. She could not marry her deceased husband's brother, though Charles IX would have liked nothing more; and she had already refused Philip of Spain and his strange little-known heir Don Carlos. But here, in the assembly today, was one whom Queen Mary might marry; Lennox in his oblique way had spoken of it. Sir James cast a particular eye over the young bearer of the State sword, Lord Darnley.

Handsome enough, he thought; tall enough for the tall Queen; and young; a trifle too young; who could say yet what he would become when he was older? But there was one heartening thing; Lord Darnley proclaimed his royal blood both by his colouring and the height which came down from Edward IV and had belonged to Henry VIII himself. A big burly man in the royal mould, this slender boy might make. With proper advice – and would he not have had that from his mother? My Lady Lennox was known to be discreet and wise in the ways of the world, from which she had suffered more than enough – with that, Lord Darnley might not make the worst possible husband for the Scots Queen. He would report all of it to Edinburgh.

The procession came back with the new-made Earl. Afterwards the Queen called Melville to audience. She was disposed to be jovial, and laughed much, showing her blackening teeth.

"How like you my new Earl?" she said; it was as though she could attend to no other subject than Robert Dudley for long. Melville sought for a veiled diplomatic reply, and found one. "As he is a worthy subject," he said, "so is he happy in serving a Princess who can discern and reward good service."

The hooded gaze surveyed him. "Yet you like better of yonder long lad," said Elizabeth. She was smiling now, with closed lips. How much did she know of what folk only thought as yet? he wondered. Her Grace must be well served with spies.

He answered, traducing Lord Darnley as far as he was able. No woman, he swore, would make choice of such a man. "Beardless and lady-faced!" swore the diplomat, remembering at the back of his mind how he had been instructed to obtain leave for young Darnley to have a safe-conduct into Scotland, to see his father. It would be the more easily come by if Melville abused him now.

243

MADGE LEFT DARNLEY behind to fix his interest with Cecil and Her Grace, and took Charles with her back to desolate Settrington. His prattle on the way diverted her thoughts; but once there she was obsessed with the ruin of the place and the necessity, which was becoming urgent, of selling some of the land for money. "By ill fortune, it is Crown land," she thought wryly. Neither this nor Temple Newsam had ever been hers and Matthew's outright. Their hold on it had depended, as both knew well, on how they conducted themselves. Now, Master Secretary made difficulties over any sale, "And yet," she thought, "he does not recompense me for what I have lost through him." She had hardly any goods left, and no money. Her jewels – a flash of pride went through her at the recollection – she had sent with Lennox to Scotland, some in gift for the Queen. No one should say Harry rode north as a beggarly bridegroom. But it had left her, his mother, all the less to sell. Alone in her bed, she would lie awake and worry till the dawn showed coldly through the shabby curtains. She no longer had the heart to take her needle and embroider more; so much of that kind had been stolen.

She and Charles were at their supper on a bitter February night when the wind outside howled as though witches rode it. There were few servants, but Madge had not dispensed with her state; however poor they were, Charles must know, and she herself remember, that she was an English princess, here in

244

England. Charles's manners gave her cause for anxiety; he was growing fast, and wild without a tutor or his father.

"I hear a horseman," the child said, setting his knife down with a clatter on his place. He licked his fingers, and Madge frowned. "Do not do so," she said, "but wait for the ewer to be brought. There is no horseman, child; it is the storm."

Charles wriggled rebelliously. What was the good of waiting for a ewer when there were only the two of them to serve, himself and his mother? "I wish," he said aloud, "that Harry had come. Why did he not come to Yorkshire with us?" Harry, so newly seen again and so godlike, was a nonchalant example for a small boy to copy. Harry never cared for anyone; not even their mother, for he knew he could always get his way, most of all with her.

He heard his mother answering that Harry had business in the south; and then the door was kicked open and Harry himself was with them, followed closely by the man Taylor who was his body-servant and had been from the time when he was a child. While Darnley was in France Charles had gleaned many tales of his brother from Taylor; a being so favoured and glorious could hardly exist. But now here he was, and mother, forgetting her state, had risen up in her place to greet him and bid him sit down and sup. Afterwards Charles remembered that although she had been pleased to see Darnley, she did not seem surprised.

"Must You Leave tomorrow? It is as though we have hardly had a sight of you."

Darnley stretched out his long legs to the fire. Charles had been sent, against his will, to bed; the two of them were alone after supper. "Before daylight, if it is possible," he said. "That will give us a start of Secretary Cecil's fellows, if any followed. I doubt if they did; but in case it was so, I rode first to Temple Newsam, and bade farewell to the old place, before coming here." He kicked at a log which had rolled, glowing, out of the fire, and lifted one eyebrow. "Farewell," he repeated, "and so far as I and my five men know, we were not followed from there. If we were, they will expect me to bide a day or two with my lady mother –"

"Which I wish you would do."

"– and may be in a tavern, thinking they have some days' grace. I tell you, I had some experience of evading English spies when I lay hid in London, and later got across to France." His tone bragged a little. He was, very slightly, drunk on Madge's best cask of wine, which she had brought with her from Sackville Place and would only have broached for a special occasion. This was such a one.

"Have you clothes for the journey – and after?" They both knew she referred to his meeting with the Scots Queen. Darnley shrugged his shoulders.

"What I lack, no doubt my father will furnish when I win

246

across the Border and west to Crookston. Otherwise I am not badly off for gear, for my uncle saw to it that I had a shift to my back in France. And, God knows, the Scots are not the best-dressed of folk; no doubt they will think I come in the latest fashion." He surveyed his high soft boots of Spanish leather, not without satisfaction; they had been a parting present from his affectionate and well-dowered aunt, the wife of the Sieur d'Aubigny. Otherwise he must make do with what he had until . . .

Madge rose and went upstairs to her chamber for some moments; on the way back she looked in on Charles who, despite his temper on being sent off to bed, was sleeping peacefully. She returned to the hall to find Darnley helping himself to more of the wine.

"Sweetheart, do you not think you should keep a clear head for tomorrow, in especial as you are leaving early?" she said. He laughed, and tossed the wine back down his throat. "My head will be clear enough, never fear," he told her; but she noticed that his speech was a trifle slurred. She watched him drink the wine and then firmly removed the cup. His laughter grew louder.

"My beloved lady mother, I am no longer a boy; I can hold my wine."

"No doubt; but I have a present here for you, and then we must both go to our beds, for I will rise to see you off in the morning."

"No need; the mornings are cold." He shifted restlessly in his seat; what had she brought him? He had hoped it was money; and at first the glister of what she held led him to hope that, despite all that had happened, she had secreted some gold coins at Settrington. He was going to have to ruffle it a trifle at the Scots Court, for that finicky young half-French creature would doubt-less not take heed of a shabby suitor. But his credit would be good in Scotland, at least for a while. He pretended to curiosity before he saw what his mother held in her hands; the feeling turned to shame when she cupped her palms and kissed what they held. "Mother – you will not part with your saints! Why, they – " As far back as he could remember, those gold figures had been pinned round the curtains of his mother's bed. She always said they had kept her from evil; they were her talisman, almost the last she had left, for she had sent away her jewels with his father, and now –

"When you are in your bridal bed, I ask that these be set about you and the Queen."

She thrust them into his hands, and he sat a moment awkwardly, staring down at the tiny figures, thinking of all they must have meant to her. "They have guarded me through more danger than I hope you need ever know," she told him. "They give strength and meaning to prayer. Promise me that you will never forget your prayers, Harry."

"I promise. And I will value these above any other thing I may obtain."

"Except your bride," she smiled. "I wish you and the Queen every contentment, fine children and a long and happy reign."

"It isn't settled yet," said Darnley uncomfortably. Sometimes he felt that his mother expected too much of him, while at others she watched him as if he were a child, like that business just now about the wine. Well, he would soon be his own master in Scotland, and might drink and do as he would. She would be lonely here, in Settrington, his mother. He put the little saints' figures in his doublet and went over and kissed her.

"That is for all you have done," he said. "Never man had such a mother."

Her tears, he knew, were not far off. "When you were a little child I planned a great destiny for you," she told him. "Now it is to come true, but how I wish I were there with you all!" She came to Darnley and kissed him three times. "One is for your father," she said, "and one for your bride."

"And the third?" He knew very well.

"For yourself, and to show that I never forget you day or night. God send we may all meet again." She began to cry, and dried the tears angrily with the back of her fist.

"Why should we not?" said Darnley cheerfully. "You shall ride north soon as the mother of the King of Scots, and lady of Crookston Castle as well as all the Angus lands."

"Harry – do not speak openly of it yet, the Crown Matrimonial. It is for the Queen to decide, and she – "

"For a woman? No woman ever ruled the Scots. When I marry *I* shall be King." His lower lip thrust out stubbornly. Madge gave up trying to warn him and tried gentle persuasion instead.

248

"Do not be too rough a suitor to Her Grace; treat her gently. It is not gentle to insist, from the first, that you be King. Let her say at the beginning what shall be done and then, as happens, you will obtain the mastery in your marriage. You have seen how happy your father and I have been together. I want such happiness for you, my son."

"I hope to obtain it. I could not have a better model than you and my father." It was true; he knew Lennox had never had eyes for any other woman since his wedding-day. "I wonder how he fares alone at Crookston? It would be better were you there with him; would they not permit it?"

"They would not, for caution's sake, allow three folk who are heirs of the blood royal to leave England together. I must stay here, to guard our English interest." It was true; whereas her son and Lennox had their sights set on Scotland, she still, with the English blood in her, held to her position here as next of kin to the Queen of England. It meant more – ay, more even than the Angus inheritance, disputes about which were still raging. "And there are lawsuits here as well, and the matter of the land-sale not yet settled," she thought. She would have a dreary time of it after Darnley had gone to join his father.

She rose to see that he breakfasted and to bid him farewell very early on the following day. The five men-at-arms, including the faithful Taylor, were already mounted when Darnley went out. His horse waited. He and his mother embraced, then she saw him leap to the saddle. It was true enough, she thought with pride; his head was again clear. Youth could discount wine. And he was young; so young to be riding off to a fair fortune and a throne, without counsel ... but there would be his father. And, as he had said, they should all three have a merry meeting ...

She watched until the grey February dawn hid him from sight, and long after.

THEY CAME to arrest her soon, with a command for her instant presence at Court. She had been in the stillroom, giving the maids instruction about making young nettle-beer; outside, the shoots were tender and green, and set in great jars would soon ferment. She had been so greatly occupied with the task that she had not heard the horsemen come. Charles was away, on this fine April day, across the moors on his pony, with a single servant. He had recovered from his disappointment at the going away of Harry, and as small boys will had grown happy with the spring weather and the longing to be out of doors now the frosts were past.

The young lady charges were in the solar. Madge was warned of some matter amiss by Mabel Fortescue's scream. She would not have heeded it – Mabel had shed her stolidity after Darnley had left, and was become an irrational, giggling young woman who needed a good slap – but at the same time there was a stir in the house; one of the girls she was instructing ran to the window and came back, goggle-eyed.

"My lady, my lady, there's armed men in the yard. What can it be except war?"

But they had not come to make war; only to take herself. It was much like the last time.

She was hustled away; they would not give her time to change her gown, or to put a few necessaries together, or even wait for Charles. The child was her worst anxiety; who would see to him?

She asked if the young ladies might remain at Settrington till their relatives came for them.

"All are to go back where they belong; the place is to be emptied," she was told callously.

Emptied! Her house, their home, on which, over the years, she had bestowed more loving care even than Temple Newsam, for she had had the more leisure after all her children were born! "Who will come to do it?" she asked the captain of the guard. She rode by him, hemmed in on all sides by guards in the royal white and green. The captain did not turn his head; he had his orders.

"Her Grace's officers of the Star Chamber. It is no concern of mine." He spoke gruffly, for he had had a glimpse from the corner of his eye of the stricken woman they had put on a palfrey in her rough hodden gown. They were using her like a condemned prisoner, he thought, and her the Queen's kin; not that that said anything, with the better part having their heads struck from their shoulders long ago. This old woman, though, he'd heard, had taken much to do with arranging a marriage between her son and the Scots Queen. Those were high matters, too high for a plain man like himself; but everyone knew the Queen of Scots was next heir to the Queen of England, notwithstanding she was a Papist like this lady who rode by him. Stiff in her Poperies, folk said Lady Lennox was; even now, as they rode, he saw her lips move in some prayer, and her beads hung at her girdle with her household keys. He'd have to take *those*. Keys and beads jangled with the speed at which they rode, and he was beginning to feel, himself, that they'd ridden far enough and he wanted a meal. But he had had orders to bring Lady Lennox safe to her lodgings at Westminster, and not to delay on the way.

They kept her confined at Westminster from April till June.

She was beyond despair; there was no news from anywhere, no letters from anyone; Matthew had surely written? Had the marriage taken place? What had become of Charles? "He is only nine," she thought repeatedly, and a wild memory of the disappearance of Darnley at the time of their earlier imprisonment in London came to mock her. Charles was in no such case; he was too young to fend for himself, and would a servant, without pay, do what was needed for the child? "I am power-less," she thought, and again, "I am powerless to alter or avert," and she would wonder whether Her Grace's officers had come yet to Settrington, to make it finally desolate.

In Scotland, Lennox himself fumed, angry and helpless. The Queen of Scots – his thoughts switched for instants from his wife to his son, and he agreed that the betrothal was going very smoothly, after a courtship among the winds and waves below Wemyss between two young folk who, after all, had already met in France – the young Queen had written to her cousin, begging her to release the kinswoman who would soon become her mother-in-law. But from what he heard, that in itself might make matters worse for Madge. Anger mounted in him; what had the times come to when a helpless woman could be carried off to prison for no offence but her blood?

He saw the Queen's Master of Requests ride off into England, with letters from Queen Mary touching her future mother-in-law. Lennox frowned; he himself was not sure of the good faith of John Hay. In this distracted country where everything was like shifting sand, he and his son had enemies, he knew; one was the Earl of Moray, the Queen's bastard half-brother, who wished to be King. Lennox had his own suspicions of a plot which had been formed between various of the Protestant lords to kidnap him and Harry and send them back to England, to their deserts, as no doubt it would be put: but it had not happened. He was too wily, and Harry too well protected by his betrothed and her favourites, for it to have come to pass. Lennox stared into his fire, and wished he had his comfortable wife by his side. Had his letters ever reached her? He had had no reply.

John Hay's arrival was the signal for Madge to be transferred to the Tower, despite – or maybe because of – all pleading in her favour by the Queen of Scots. For months she had had no sight beyond the tapestry-hung walls of her own palace cham-ber; now, suddenly, there was the Thames again with its grey water, and a barge which waited, and herself hustled into it with her hood drawn close. She knew well enough where it was they were taking her. The cream-coloured turrets of squared monstrous stone reared soon enough above the wharf. They helped her up the slippery steps to the gate through which Anne Boleyn, and Elizabeth herself, had gone before her. "And I too," she remembered thinking, seeing a girl of long ago. Her servants followed. At least this time she had two good women about her, and three menservants who could, she knew, do much for her sake. But this was a prison from which few ever escaped alive. Would her death follow, or would she be here till she died?

MASTER SECRETARY CECIL transferred his narrow, omniscient gaze from a scroll which gave orders for the removal of young Lord Charles Stuart to the care of one Lady Knevet and her husband, in Yorkshire. The room was full of such scrolls, each one neatly piled and annotated, with the royal seal and fantastic, arabesqued signature *Elizabeth R.* Cecil's life lay here, among these papers; also the lives of many others living and dead, including that little-known but widely guessed at secret life of Her Grace herself with Robert Dudley, Earl of Leicester. But it was not that which interested Cecil now. He reached out to draw the candle nearer, so that its light fell on a letter addressed to his wife by Matthew, Earl of Lennox. Like many others sent to Lady Lennox in her prison, it would never be seen by her. "But if she ever meets her lord again, he may tell her that he sent it," thought Master Secretary with precision.

He re-read the letter; it described events in Scotland too well to be ignored, and the marriage which Lady Lennox herself had fostered and to which the Queen of England's objections, she had stated once, were "full of affectations". Cecil smiled; my lady's grace had had the right of it. Under the devious twists and turns of Elizabeth's nature had been a determination that her cousin Queen should in fact marry Darnley, a young gentleman who would do her no good. They were married; had been so these seven months and more, and the news had been allowed to filter to the Tower by means of an old woman much about the Queen, who carried such gossip to Lady Lennox as she might be instructed to. But this letter should not go.

My sweet Madge [it ran],
    ... if ye should take unkindly my slowness in writing to you all this while (as I cannot blame you to do), God, and this bearer our old servant Fowler, can best witness the occasion ... it being not a little to my grief now to be debarred, and want the commodity and comfort of intelligence by letters that we were wont, passing between us during our absence.

No doubt the fellow loved his wife.

    But what then? God send us patience in taking all things accordingly, and send us a comfortable meeting, when we shall talk further of the matter.
    My Madge, we have to give God most hearty thanks in that the King our son continues in good health, and the Queen great with child (God save them all); for which cause we have great cause to rejoice the more. Yet, for my part, I confess I want and find a lack of my chiefest comfort, which is you; whom I have no cause to forget for any felicity or wealth that I am in. But I trust that will amend ... I do not doubt that their Majesties forgetteth you not ... else, ere you should tarry here any longer, I shall wish of God I may be with you ... I bid mine own sweet Madge most heartily farewell ... God ... send us a merry meeting.

The fellow certainly called a great deal upon God, Cecil had decided. Maybe an Italian singer named Rizzio had called on God as well, when they came for him and stabbed him again and again at Holyrood in front of the pregnant Queen, who was unable to save him. They said – by this Cecil meant Randolph, who had gained the love of one of the Queen's Maries, and sent prompt news – that young Darnley himself had, for jealousy, been in league with the murderers.

That marriage would not go well. Her Grace's hopes and his own could hardly be bettered. It was possible also – Randolph had not sent news of this yet – that the Queen of Scots would miscarry of her child, after the rough handling of the murderers, one of whom had been a Douglas. It was true that one could not rejoice openly over such news. But Cecil still awaited it.

MADGE WAS ODDLY CONTENT in prison after she had received word that little Charles was safe in the care of Lady Knevet, whom she knew. She had been ill, with a colic which sometimes troubled her, but was recovered now; and lately she had been sent some warm clothing. Moreover, there had come, through the gossiping old woman whom she did not altogether trust, good news; the Queen of Scots had borne a son after a long and terrible labour, but mother and child were safe. "So now I have a lord who loves me, a son who is King, many friends, faithful servants, a coat lined with coney fur, slippers, a farthingale and a grandson." Thinking in such a way she forgot that she was fifty years old; she felt almost gay.

Visiting her often, and renewing a friendship tentatively made in her former days in the Tower, were the two de la Pole brothers, Geoffrey and Arthur, younger sons of the martyred Lady Salisbury. They had white hair now, like herself. Together they and she would watch the shadows growing longer over Tower Green, but the sight had lost its terror. Her Grace would not take an old woman's life, as her sire had done. The de la Poles – Reginald, the Cardinal, had died the day after Queen Mary Tudor – were resigned after long years of imprisonment; they could hardly recall any other life now, except to remember their mother. Geoffrey, who had unwittingly helped betray her, had the aspect of a hunted hare, his pale Plantagenet eyes straining within their lids, and he met no one's gaze and spoke little.

257

R

Arthur was the more talkative, but there was not much to say here; only to remark on how the great bell above them still tolled, of an evening, to send them all back to their separate prisons, or to watch the river if one had a window on that side of the thick wall, and remark on the boats and barges passing. Then there were the sunsets, over the water and St. Paul's spire; surely nothing could destroy London. It still held its magic for her; and she had a sense of continuity now that her name would not be blotted out, unlike the Plantagenet stock.

She smiled; the word itself had reminded her of a saying of the old gossip, carefully looking back over her padded sleeve before whispering it. It had been after she brought Madge the news of the Scottish grandson, who had been called James.

"James the Sixth, he will be in time," said Madge, trusting that time would be long. She had heard reports of nothing but the happiness of the royal pair. "What," she murmured, "did Her Grace here say regarding it? Was she not pleased at the news that my grandson is born, and thrives?"

"Her Grace? She withdrew into her closet, and cried out – and cried out, my lady, this: *The Queen of Scots is lighter of a fair son, and I am but a barren stock.*' But never say I told it, my lady. It would come back to make trouble for me, maybe, if any knew."

So she was contented enough, while the days passed from winter towards spring. It was two years since Harry had ridden away. She thought of him distantly, as though in another life. She found that she remembered him most clearly in his childhood; the splendid young man who had come back from France was beloved, but no longer needed her. What a fine king Darnley must make, with his height and fair proud looks! One day, perhaps, they would all three meet again, herself and her son and his father.

"My place is here, as hostage for them," she told herself. "I am well enough; they cannot keep God from me." She remembered, again, the saying of Lady Salisbury, all those years ago, that suffering should be offered up to God. Had she, Margaret Lennox, truly suffered, except in the deaths of her children? There had been discomforts of the body and estate, it was true, apart from that; but little more. And she was not completely separated from Lennox and her son; her own letters were sent off by way of Flanders, reaching Scotland in course. How much news there must be awaiting her from there, if she could but learn it! Slowly, solely by way of the old woman who gossiped, she had learned that the marriage was made, and knew it must be happy; of course it must be so. If only a letter could reach her here!

"I would I knew how it was with them," she said aloud.

Overhead, the great bell tolled.

After it had grown dark two women came to her. She knew them both, and marvelled the more; what was Cecil's wife doing here, in her prison? And the other, she knew, was William Howard's lady. The Howards had always been there to watch her life go by...what were they saying? Why where they so pale, with lips compressed and trembling as if half afraid to speak? What terror could she manifest that they were in such fear?

They spoke of Harry. Harry dead...*dead*...A madman's tale, and her own lord dead also. It could not be true. A house blown up with gunpowder, somewhere near Edinburgh; what had Matthew and Harry to do with such a house? And the servants' bodies had been found after the explosion, mangled and burned, all except one, the man Taylor, naked save for his nightshirt, in the garden dead, and one other...

One other. Darnley's dead body, without a mark or a wound. Something was strangely wrong with the tale, but she could not think clearly...

"My husband and son are dead, then," he heard her own voice saying. Then, as if she had no control over her own body, other sounds came. They were the sounds of wailing, such as common folk made after their men were slain; perhaps such as her Douglas forebears might have made for their lords fallen in battle. But this furtive, violent death...Were the sounds coming from her own mouth? Was she still here, in a prison room, with the two women watching her with open pity? Matthew her lord, and Harry her hope, her darling, her King...

"No," she heard another voice tell her, "God is King." Harry and his father now were with God.

But they were dead and she would never see them more in this world, and now she was quite alone.

It was strange; at that time she felt that she had run mad, that hands were holding her down, that physicians came and bled her. It was like those earlier days when she had lain sick here and Tom in another place, and Tom had died. They had all died now except for herself and Charles, and he was not strong. She would be left a wandering ghost on the face of the earth, an old woman with white hair.

"Take heart, my lady; Earl Matthew is alive." The latest news came presently; it had been an error about the Earl's death, he was in Glasgow. Madge sat up on her bed in wild hope and fear, her hair streaming about her; was it, could it be possible that none of the tale was true at all, and Harry also safe?

But that part at least was true. Word came from the ambassadors, the newsmongers, the gossip and the rest. There was not a detail with which she was not fed, when she had recovered her reason. What was the thing they were trying to put into her head? It rotted there now like a monstrous growth, sending out veins of poison into her body and soul. Harry was murdered, and by whom? By the friends of his wife, the Queen. The Queen of Scots had killed her young husband, and why? Because he had helped to murder Rizzio, and because she was jealous of her crown.

Who had Rizzio been? Madge could barely remember. She had heard his name from the gossip once; a minstrel, that the Queen of Scots liked to have about her to sing to her, whom she called her secretary. A minstrel. Queens did not prefer such. Why, Harry had had his own band of musicians follow him to Scotland, it had happened before she herself left Settrington. But Harry would never think of setting any one of them up beside him, when he was King.

God will avenge gentle Henry, but a vengeance on Mary.

The gossip told her of that. It had been pinned on a church-door in Edinburgh.

"He is dead," she said again and again. It still did not seem that it could be true. All of her children who died, even the little girls, had been young. Darnley had grown to manhood, magnificently as he had promised, from being the strongest, the most learned, the tallest of them, the first to ride his pony and then mount a horse, and play a lute. "She had no need of Rizzio. Her husband could have played to her."

Darnley, her son. Later he had had the wit and daring to escape through London to France, while she and the rest of them had lain in prison. She cursed the very name of France now; had he never gone there, he might be with her today.

But he was dead. She must accustom herself to it and not run mad. Matthew, at least, remained to her, and would be in grief like herself. She must think of him, and pray for Darnley's soul.

"THE BITCH killed him, without a doubt," said Lennox, "or rather caused it to be done, which is the same thing."

He was seated nearby Madge's window at Westminster, through which the summer daylight came. It showed Matthew's features as harder, older; there was an indefinable change in him, which at first sight she had feared. Now she relied on it; it was as though he had shed, for all time, the illness of the mind which had afflicted him in their Yorkshire years. He was no longer afraid to be alone, or afraid of anything. He was a man made of iron, and her master; hitherto, she realised, it had been herself who ordered him. The change was welcome, but did not mend her heart.

"How did they – bury him?" She asked it timidly; so much horror had been told her that it was difficult to believe that Harry had had Christian burial.

"Well enough, in the chapel of Holyrood, beside James V. He will sleep sound. I will avenge him, never fear." He turned so that his back was to the light and she no longer saw his features. She watched him with weary eyes reddened with weeping. It seemed that she could not stem her flow of tears, as though, since being released from the Tower and brought back here to Westminster, she no longer cared that all folk knew her state; tearful, penniless – the lands were still sequestered and she had no income from them – and lacking her son. Yet her lord had been returned to her; she must be grateful for that.

262

"You talk of revenge, Matthew," she said to the dark shadow of his face. "You sound certain; yet you left Scotland to come to me."

"Matters are set in train there. I left when a false edict was put about that her lords advised her to wed Bothwell, who was her lover."

"Bothwell." She echoed the name, seeing in her mind's eye the Fair Earl who, with Lennox, had made a bid for the hand of Marie de Guise long ago; but that would be this lord's father.

"A one-eyed villain who has divorced his wife, that he and the Queen may wed. She left her child, our grandson, and went with Bothwell to his stronghold of Dunbar. He has her in a state where nothing will serve but that they marry. For disgust, I quitted Scotland."

"But you will return?" Her own feeling echoed his; a wanton and murderess, and their grandson in peril, and fatherless. "Ay," said Lennox, "I'm needed there. But I had to come south, Madge, to bring ye comfort, if I could."

"None other could," she said, and gave him her hand. Her tears welled up and began to fall again. "If only Harry could have ridden home with you, I – I had been content."

"He himself was so ill content with the way things were tending that he kept a ship waiting and ready to take him into France."

France, she thought; and not to his mother. "He was not happy?" she asked, and a clear picture came to her of Darnley as he must have been: young, arrogant as the young are, and dissatisfied with the position he held and with the royal bride he had married. "The pity of it!" she said. "And I unable to do aught; I heard nothing, nothing, until – "

"Ay. I would have spared ye the breaking of the news by any except myself, but I had to stay till the matter had been sifted, and some hint given that folk knew how it came about." He was looking down at his shoes, and the summer light shone on his hair. It was grey and thinning. Madge knew compassion for him.

"You have had as much suffering as I – maybe more," she said, "for you had to watch while matters went thus, while I – "

"No one could have guessed that matters would end as they did, though it was plain that he had enemies. Those in high places acquire them by being where they are; folk resented his having the Crown Matrimonial." Lennox did not add that Darnley's haughty abuse of the privilege had alienated more persons than his holding of it had done. Nor did he admit that he suspected Madge's own kin, the Douglases, of the murder; it suited him better to blame the Queen. By now he had almost made himself believe in Mary's guilt. Staring at his wife's ravaged face, he felt for her grief but could not abate it. He was troubled also over money; between them they owed more than three thousand pounds, and the Queen here would not bear Madge's prison charges. A bog of debt, and his son dead; but at least the child Harry had sired would be King. "Ay, and that quickly," Lennox told himself, knowing some part of what would happen; he had his enemies, but his friends also. The Queen would be made to renounce her throne once her lover and she were separated.

A messenger of Her Grace came in, to say that the Earl and Countess of Lennox were required to attend at Court. He showed no change of expression at finding the pair sitting hand in hand, like young lovers. They rose, and with the woman's hand on her husband's arm went down to Her Grace's hall, where their tear-stained grief made good the secret claim of Cecil and those in his employ. Such a sorrowing pair, to be seen by all the world, argued the worst possible guilt on the part of the Queen of Scots, whose name was beginning to be spoken of very doubtfully here and in Europe: when she had – as Cecil knew she would – taken the man for her husband who might well be blamed for Darnley's murder, a train of gunpowder almost like that of Kirk o' Field would be set alight, with results favourable to England. Elizabeth, whose own name had long been under a shadow as Robert Dudley's paramour after the death of his wife, saw it emerging now into comparative sunlight. The tragedy in Edinburgh over-reached all minor scandals. She smiled, and received the Lennoxes amiably.

THE QUEEN seemed to play fair and foul with them, as if she could not steer her mind to a straight course even of pity. She had sold their remaining goods at Settrington well below market value; she had kept the rents, and although she once promised Madge to restore them, repented of her promise as soon as it was made. Nor would she relieve the pressure of debt left by living in prison. But she did permit the Lennoxes to dwell in Cold Harbour, away from the constant eyeing and speculating of the Court.

The house stood in ancient decay above the river, its huge mulberry trees being almost the only thing about it not crumbling and ruined with damp. Their twisted branches reached down to the Thames like tentacles. They were too old to bear fruit. Dully, Madge remembered Syon, where young trees had now been planted, and the nuns had gone to Portugal to escape the new harsh Elizabethan laws. Such things gnawed at her remembrance, but she could take no heed of them; her whole being was swallowed up in horror and grief, which time did not lessen. It was as though the two sensations swelled and grew in her like a new life, in exchange for that which had been taken away.

She lay awake at nights in the wide bed they shared with its scanty covers; the furniture here was old, doubtless from Edward IV's time, and riddled with worm and damp. Lennox slept better now than he had used to do in earlier days, when he would often waken in the night and call for her. He lay now sound asleep, and she could watch the moon's light change with the scudding clouds before the wind, at times shedding light on his face. He, at least, was left to her; why had she this feeling of numbness, as if the facts he had himself told her were only half true?

The two bodies . . . found dead in the garden, untouched by burning from the blast. Taylor, the faithful servant, short of a slipper. He had stayed close to Darnley all of the boy's life, and was with him in death; that was as he would have wanted it, but . . . "Did they leave the house in haste before the explosion? If they had stayed, they would have been marked. The other servants who were dug out of the ruins were mangled and blackened with smoke."

She turned restlessly, keeping close to Lennox for warmth for the house was cold. Her movement half waked him, and he stirred. She shook his shoulder suddenly, and saw his eyes open.

"What – " he said drowsily, and would have slept again; but the sight of his wife's haggard face made him put out a hand to her, caressing her. "Get some sleep, lass," he said, "it boots nothing to lie awake in the night hours. The thing is done."

"Matthew – "

"Eh?" he was fully awake now, half resentful of being disturbed; to him also, sleep meant release from his thoughts. What was she saying to him? She'd taken the boy's death hard, harder than, even with her loving nature, he'd have thought possible. It was many months now since the thing had happened, and much had befallen; the Queen of Scots and her paramour defeated and separated, he to the north parts, she to Lochleven after a howling mob had cried at her for a harlot in the streets of Edinburgh. Harlot and murderess; his own men had added that last. She –

"Matthew, *what killed our son?*"

He thought she was wandering in her wits with grief, and said gently "Why, ye will remember the house was dung to dross with the blast of gunpowder; why ask more?"

"But *he* was not in the explosion. He had won to the garden, maybe somehow knowing that the fuse had been set. He and Taylor did not die of the gunpowder."

"There was not a mark found on his body, it is true. That is all I know, or any of us."

"Someone must know," she said, and began brooding on it,

266

as the night changed to day. Someone. Whoever they were, Queen's men or other, they had come in and – how could one kill a young strong man without leaving a mark? "And his servant was by."

Lennox had been made wakeful, and muttered again that it was that bitch, the Scots Queen herself, and Bothwell. "He would order her henchmen to do as they would; maybe they held a cloth to the boy's face to stop his breathing, or –" He dared not go on, to her, of it; he knew that the inquest on Darnley had found no trace of what killed him, but that someone that night had heard the boy cry out, "Pity me, kinsmen, for the sake of Him who pitied all the world."

But that was the last thing he dared say to his wife, a Douglas born. "And it might after all have been the Hamiltons," he thought. In any case there was no proof now; to him, Darnley's father, it had been repeated as hearsay, and he would include it in the speech he must make before Her Grace's commissioners, the enquiry begun at York about the death having shifted lately to London. But Lennox knew no more than the next man, though he had a right to his suspicions. It was best now to let things be.

He tried to turn his wife's mind from the murder. "Harry's son is King," he reminded her, for they had made the child so after his mother had signed her forced abdication at Lochleven. "May he reign long and merrily."

He began to talk to her of their grandchild, holding her in his arms; knowing that every detail of the baby's appearance, health, and promise of wit would please Madge even in the midst of her sorrow. Presently he saw her swollen eyelids close as if she slept, and he fell silent. The moon died at last behind its clouds and in its place there came a grey sunrise. All the world was grey for them now, Lennox thought; but there was that one hope, that his grandson lived, and was King.

James VI was not allowed to have his crown without war. Word came soon that Mary Stuart had escaped from Lochleven, and had raised an army which would fight. Later they heard that she had been defeated at Langside by her half-brother Moray and his men, and was in England at last, a fugitive. Moray had made himself Regent of Scotland for the baby King.

Lennox saw a change in his wife. From being a passive, grief-stricken creature she became a woman bent on vengeance, fired with what seemed almost the fighting spirit of the Douglases, and yet still in tears. She made Lennox attire himself for Court and together they went there and approached the Queen through withdrawn rows of courteous curious strangers who had already gossiped their sad affairs to death. Madge knelt before Elizabeth. The hooded eyes looked down; did they hold triumph, and did Her Grace remember a time when Lady Lennox had charge of a quiet-spoken, plainly-clad girl, in the Tower? Perhaps she had never forgiven Madge for that; if not, she had her revenge by now.

"How is it with you, cousin? What would you here?"

The cool, courteous tones mocked the tear-stained face, the faded mourning-gear. The Earl of Lennox and his wife had proved themselves of use beyond all expectation in the matter of blackening Mary of Scotland: no one could look on them without remembering the cause of their grief. But they were tiresome about money, and Her Grace could be close-fisted. After my lord's speech to the Commissioners which was forthcoming about Darnley's death, they could, Her Grace was thinking, be allowed to retire again to Yorkshire, where they would not trouble her. Certainly the red-eyed, threadbare creature before her seemed as if she would trouble few folk for long. A spasm of compassion passed over the Queen's face, but she hid it behind her paint. "Well, cousin?"

"I ask that Your Grace will take vengeance on my son's wife, who murdered him."

A flutter of agitation, ruffling lace and disturbing folds of stiffened satin, passed through the Court. It was not usual to speak so plainly; but it made a diversion. No one spoke. The Queen turned her thumb-ring, a diamond sunk in jet.

"You ask much, cousin. Such things are the province of lawyers."

"She is in Your Grace's dominions, and in your power. My son is dead. By her plottings and her harlotries she killed him in a foul manner, without mercy, and married the man who had aided her. What has justice to say to it but that she should suffer as she made *him* suffer ... as she made my son, who never harmed ..."

The courtiers regarded the floor. Lady Lennox was weeping

openly now, the tears running down her face like rivers to the sea. How many more tears could she have left to shed, they wondered curiously. She had reason, no doubt, but the world must go on. That family –

Elizabeth spoke, judicially, gently. "Such accusations must not be spoken against the good name of a Princess without further proof."

The curled beruffed head inclined itself, bade them take their leave. A babel of relieved talk sounded in the hall as Lord Lennox bore his half-fainting wife away on his arm. It was sad, it was shocking, without a doubt; but Her Grace had as always shown partiality to no one, in such matters. What would become of Mary Stuart now that she was over the English Border? Perhaps she would come to Court.

SETTRINGTON was ruined and despoiled, a sad mildewed ghost of the home they had known. The icy winds of January blew through the unhinged doors, the bare walls which once she had hung lovingly with tapestry made by her own hand; everything was clammy to the touch, and there were neither beds nor fire. At first sight of it she had almost given way to despair, thinking that she had no heart for any more. She had sunk down on the bare stones; the servants who had ridden north with them clustered about her, pale-faced from their own prisons; they had been put in Newgate or the Marshalsea, partly by reason of their faith, partly for their loyalty to herself. This remained; while she sat there desolate, two of them went and rubbed sticks together to make a fire, which smoked; but at last it gave out a little warmth. As though it had thawed her heart, Madge looked about her. They would stay here, somehow.

In the end she had compromised by making only one or two rooms warm and lived in, part by the servants and part by themselves. Charles was not with them; she and Lennox had seen him, long-legged and shy as a fawn, at Lady Knevet's, and had decided that until the house was made habitable he had best stay where he was. My lady had agreed, having grown fond of him. So Lennox and Madge made the best of it at Settrington that Yule, drying out wood to make a larger fire, on which by the end they were able to roast game the men had shot. Had they been younger and the season of the year more clement, they might have jested about it; but they had endured too much and had grown too old.

The time passed. Sometimes Madge would feel anxiety about her husband, who seemed to have fallen back into the moods of despondency he had been used to take before he went north. That that should happen was not surprising, she thought; but she essayed to cheer him, and ended by partly cheering herself. What was done was done; nothing could bring the dead back to life. Mary Stuart she had heard was a prisoner at Bolton. It did not seem as if she was to be shown any favour by Elizabeth, who had insulted her by sending her some old clothes when she was at Carlisle, and had not yet invited her south. So much they heard; but Madge was weary of rumours and predictions, and at last busied herself about the house to occupy her thoughts, which otherwise saddened her. Had she indeed begged the Queen for vengeance on Darnley's widow? "If it should be so," she thought, "I would feel that I had murdered her." So often, day or night, reciting the offices and prayers as she made herself do, it was brought home to her that in demanding blood for blood, she was betraying her faith. She said nothing of it to Lennox; it might anger him.

One day a rider came in haste, splashed with mud from his journey; he bore letters. At first sight of him Madge knew a sinking of her heart; were they yet again to set forth on a summons? But the letters themselves were for Lennox, and brought word from Scotland. What it might be she learned from the man as she plied him with food and wine.

"The Regent Moray is dead, my lady, killed at Linlithgow by a man of the Hamiltons who owed him a grudge." When she heard the place named, she feared lest Lennox would recall the murder of his father, which had taken place there. But to her astonishment he was standing erect, in appearance younger than she had seen him for four years. The letters were in his hand; he gave them to her, but before she could read them drew her apart. His eyes were shining and his face flushed above his beard.

"I did not care for Moray," he said, and she listened in silence; nobody had been overfond of James V's sour bastard son. "Now that he is dead – " Lennox let out a long, satisfied sigh – "they have asked me to be Regent, to govern the country for our grandson. It means power at last, such as I have waited for all my days. They promised it me when I first came out of France, and again when I went south to King Harry; and not till now has it come about, now I am old."

He turned to her and took her face between his hands.

"I must ride south," he said, "and obtain leave of the Queen's Grace to take up this task. Without that, I'd be turned back at the Border. She surely will not refuse." He talked on, excitement giving an edge to his tongue; his French accent slipped out in a way that had not been so marked for years. He was as she remembered him from earlier days, a man full of ambitious plans. She let him talk, glad to see that he had shed his burden. Suddenly his talk broke off.

'But what of you?' he said. 'I cannot ride away and leave ye here alone. And I doubt Her Grace will not part with both of us – and there is Charles," and his face fell, like a boy's. She soothed him.

"We will both of us ride south, to beg the Queen to free you. What should I do but rejoice for you in this news that has come? I would never chain you, Matthew; that you know well."

She would always remember the grateful look in his eyes. He took her by the shoulders, and set his lips to her forehead.

"Ye are the best wife a man ever had," he said. "If all were to do again, I'd choose no other."

MASTER SECRETARY was asked for his help, which he gave readily; the more in that the Lennoxes were housed this time not in Cold Harbour in the decay and mould, but in Somerset House, among the icy grandeur left by the dead Protector. Their risen status no doubt stemmed from the fact that Her Grace required some favour of Lennox once he won to Scotland. What this might be was put in the written petition Madge and her husband were advised to send to the Queen. It was worded by Cecil, whose shrewd eyes scanned it and then transferred themselves, for an instant, to my lady's face. Her husband followed where she led, Cecil knew well; no need to fear Lennox's default if his wife were kept safe in England.

Her Grace's "poor orators and suppliants" – ay, so they were, reflected Cecil, and advisedly; my lady plotted and schemed as soon as her fingers were among silver coin – begged the Queen to "cast her pitiful eyes on the great danger of her fatherless and desolate orphan kinsman, the young King of Scotland." That was reasonable enough; and if aught befell the boy there would be anarchy, which ill suited Cecil and Her Grace at this present time, having troubles enough in the south, and abroad. James VI must be safely kept, and so "beseeching Her Majesty of her goodness and pity to take measures for the safety of that little innocent, that he may be delivered into Her Majesty's hands" might well bear fruit. Cecil tightened his lips within his beard. A generation ago, he reflected, Henry VIII had been demanding

S

the presence of the infant Queen of Scots in London: and earlier than that, the guardianship of the infant James V. That no previous success had ever resulted from such demands made it all the more laudable if this last should be accomplished now. And the careworn grandparents, still shocked with grief, would be more pliable than Marie de Guise had been, or Margaret Tudor: though that last would have smuggled her son across the Border if she could, but had been prevented.

"It is well framed," nodded Cecil, who had framed the petition himself. He advised the Lennoxes to present it to Her Grace without delay. The sooner my lord set out for Scotland the better; ambitious persons there might soon seize the small body of the King and use it for their own purposes, which need not be those of England.

After they were alone again Madge took the paper and read it through, her eyes narrowed between their reddened lids. Always now she had a look of late weeping. Her lips moved over the sounds of the words, and at the last phrase faltered. "Delivered into Her Majesty's hands" . . . but surely no harm would befall him? Surely she, his grandmother, would be permitted to see him, if not to undertake his whole care till he should be older? So many things could happen ill to children; she recalled the loss of her own. A fever here, a wasting away or visitation of smallpox, or the dissolution of the bowels that came with drinking polluted water; so many things, and unless someone who loved him was there, the child might be exposed from lack of watchfulness. Perhaps she herself had undergone all agony in order to be made fit for guarding this little King. Perhaps she –

Lennox watched her. It grieved him to part with her, for he knew that they would not let her ride north with him beyond Yorkshire. All of their married life had been this, this separation and meeting again which, while it lasted, had been sweet, and now was bitter because of their dead son Darnley. But Darnley's son was Lennox's guerdon. He would allow the petition to go to Queen Elizabeth, not because he intended to implement all its clauses, but because without it he would never win free to be Regent of Scotland. Regent! It carried with it almost the power of a king; and he would win his grandson's heart, for the child had known no love since he lost his mother. Lennox's

mouth grew ugly at the thought of the imprisoned Scots Queen.
That bitch should never again be let out of her English kennel.
As for the boy – he raised a hand to his beard to hide his sudden
grin – the Scots would never agree to let their King come south,
but it would not do to say so, even to his wife. Madge was all
Englishwoman now, and had little reason to be other. She would
not understand the Scots way of thought, of life. That he, who
had spent his youth in France, should understand it himself did
not seem odd. There was more similarity between members of
the Auld Alliance than between two nations bordering one on
another. It had always been so, and no doubt always would be.
Lennox had no doubt of what his reception in the north would
be, or of his own ability to govern.

Her Grace was pleased to give ear to the petition, and without
delay Lennox made ready to ride north, in somewhat greater
grandeur to that which he was accustomed. Together he and
his lady rode towards Yorkshire; he looked upon the land as
if he were seeing it for the last time. Madge could not understand his silences.

"It pleases you to go?" she asked many times.

"Well enough." He disguised his elation from her, lest she
think he did not grieve at their parting. He placed his own hand
over hers where it lay, holding her palfrey's reins. She was old
for the long ride; many women would have demanded a litter,
which would have delayed matters by days, perhaps weeks. But
she had always put her own comfort in the background when
it was a matter of his welfare. She turned her anxious face to him
now, cheeks reddened with the wind against which they rode.
He remembered, oddly, at this moment, that she had spent her
youth as a fugitive, in all weathers.

"You will have a care to him on the journey south? You will
take him up in your own saddle?" It might, she knew, be a little
while before they could bring so young a child; best give him a
chance to grow, perhaps, and strengthen, and then –

"You will write and tell me what he looks like? I long to hear
of him," she said. She bit her lip. Letters could have come easily
to her at Settrington, but at the last moment before they set out,
Her Grace had sent for her; she was to have a post about Court,
and must return. "They mean to have an eye to me," she thought,

"but it is not to be the Tower this time." In a fashion, she was glad enough not to have to stay on at ruined Settrington, with its reminders of happy years. She was better in London.

"Ay," said Lennox, "I will write."

He was regarding her, and it was not the look of an old, accustomed husband, but that of a young lover; he had always seen her so. A rush of gladness suddenly came to her; what a blessing she had known in this handsome man's love, and he in hers! "It came strangely," she thought, "our love for one another. But it has endured."

She saw Lennox ride off beyond the Border at last, and, as once before, she waved him farewell, remembering the hard clasp of his arms about her, his rough bearded cheek against her own. "Have a care to yourself," they had both murmured. She would pray for him night and day. "Have a care..."

He was gone, with a last wave of the hand, and she was alone; alone for one night in the bleakly echoing house, and tomorrow again she must ride south, to be – she grimaced – first lady to Her Grace at Windsor.

Madge Was Walking in the Queen's autumn garden with Lady Cobham. Her Grace was absent, staying at present with Lord Rich at Lee. In her absence, a certain tolerance prevailed; of the two discreet matrons walking up and down, one chattered unceasingly, contrary to her usual habit. Madge stole a glance at Lady Cobham, attired as she was in wide farthingale and ruff, with a cap set sedately on her head; she is, thought Madge, a reflection of myself; we are both careful and elderly, and walk slowly. She let my lady talk on, occupying her own mind with the new sadness which had grown in it lately, after the news there had been of executions throughout the north of England. Every fifth man they said had been hanged in each village, and her own old friend Lord Westmorland had fled to Flanders, leaving his wife, a daughter of poor Surrey's, to play her hand alone. Jane Westmorland was a stout Protestant and no harm would come to her. The matter had arisen in the first place because of Mary Stuart and the fact that the Duke of Norfolk had fallen in love with her and wished to marry her. How much harm had come about because of that woman! Yet –

"And they say Anjou was angry that his mother had tried to wed him to Her Grace here, and do you know, my lady, what they say he said?"

Madge tried to simulate interest. Lady Cobham put her lips to the other's ear, breathing that one could not be too careful.

'He said *she is an old creature, with a sore leg*. It is true that

277

Her Grace has had an issue in it lately and has had to travel by litter, but to *say* so – " Lady Cobham raised her eyes and hands to heaven. "How little one can make known aloud!" she concluded, having registered the fact that Lady Lennox had made known nothing at all; no doubt her early tribulations had made her fearful of speaking openly. But when Her Grace was away surely one need not be quite so careful? Poor Lady Lennox always looked *distraite;* not that one could blame her.

Madge had been trying to solace herself by thinking of her grandson. Lennox's letters described James as a clever little boy, apt in speaking although his tongue was too large for his mouth; perhaps that fault would be outgrown. The ordeal his mother had sustained at Rizzio's murder while her child was still in the womb had done harm in such ways, and young James also had been slow in learning to stand and walk. But he progressed now, and was almost five years old, and Lennox wrote that the child had a mark on his side in the shape of a lion. That was a strange thing. Perhaps –

"It sounds as if there were a bustle without," said Lady Cobham, offended not a little at Lady Lennox's continued silence. One knew she had had her sorrows, but there was no harm in courtesy; she herself had been trying to cheer the poor woman by bearing her company. Surely the stir meant that the Queen had returned early? "My lady, we should be about our duties," murmured Lady Cobham, picking up her skirts to go inside. The day had turned cold and the leaves on the trees were sparse; walking was no longer a pleasure. "See," she continued as a servitor came in sight, "we are sent for."

"We were doing no harm," Madge told her. The man came nearer, and bowed. She herself was requested to go to Her Grace without delay. Even now, such a summons had power to frighten her; in all of her life it might have meant good news or ill, or questioning, or prison.

She excused herself to Lady Cobham, and outdistanced the other in reaching the outer door. Her Grace was abovestairs, she was informed, and awaited her.

Awaited her? What could the reason be? Of late Elizabeth had been petulant and difficult, having been disappointed in the Austrian Archduke who, having suffered rebuffs these many years, had at last made up his mind to marry elsewhere. And now, according to Lady Cobham, the young French prince also was unwilling. Well, it might be good news if Her Grace never married, but she would keep everyone guessing about *that* until she was an old woman "as old as I am now; and she will alter little in herself."

Elizabeth had not changed out of her riding-gear; she still held her gloves. Her back was to the light – lately she had forbidden painters to put shadows in her portraits – and one could only see her small hat and the blaze of the red wig beneath, with a drop-pearl in one ear. For instants they beheld one another, then Madge made her court curtsy. When she rose from it the Queen had come forward, and extended her hand.

"Cousin, I would ask you to prepare yourself. It is ill news, and sudden. I would allow none other to tell you than myself. Be seated, cousin."

Fear rose in Madge's throat. *"Be seated, cousin –"* the Queen never allowed her ladies to sit in her presence unless on very rare occasions, and now what awaited her? Bad news could mean – "My grandson?" she faltered, eyes fixed on the other's face. If that were the matter, then everything was at an end; her whole life had been for nothing.

"Not his young life, thank God. But you will hardly bear it. Your lord is dead."

The Queen averted her eyes from the older woman's face and went to the window, looking down upon the park. She told the tale as it had reached her. It did not take long. Lennox had been riding at Stirling when he was shot in the back. "It was the old feud with the Hamiltons; you will know as much as I." Her cousin did not answer or move.

"He would not dismount," said Elizabeth. "They brought him into the Castle, where the little King was. He said – his words were sent to me – 'If the babe be well, all is well.' Yet it was not so with him. They laid him down, and found that he could not live; his bowels were cut through."

She hurried on. How still and how silent the poor widow sat! It was as though all the tears she could make were already shed. "And yet," thought the Queen, "I know they were a fond couple." She went and sat down by Madge Lennox and took her hand. "He asked that such lords as were in residence might be brought round his bed. He said –" The Queen drew a letter from her glove, and opened it. "Here are his words, Madge; would you that I read them to you?"

She scanned the paper closely; like her sister she had short sight, but allowed few to know it.

I am now, my lords, to leave you at God's good pleasure, to go to a world where there is rest and peace. You know it was not my ambition, but your choice, which brought me to the charge which I have this while sustained.

If he said that, Elizabeth thought, he was a liar; his ambition never slept.

– which I undertook the more willingly, because I was assured of your assistance in the defence of the infant King, whose protection by nature and duty I could not refuse.

"He grudged nothing," said Madge.

And now being able to do no more, I must commend him to Almighty God, and to your care, entreating you to continue his defence, wherein I do assure you, in God's name, the victory. Make choice of some worthy person fearing God. [The choice, reflected Elizabeth, would probably be the Earl of Mar.] *and affectionate to the infant King, to succeed in my place. And . . . desire you to remember my love to my wife Madge, whom I beseech God to comfort.*

There was silence in the room. "Is there aught that you require, cousin?" said the Queen. For once she felt at a loss, and humble. A little wine, a soft pillow, would not go far to recompense such a loss. Suddenly she said openly, harshly, "You are fortunate; you have known a love such as I in all my days will never experience."

The other did not answer in words, but a thing happened then which had not been done for many years in the presence of Elizabeth of England. Without words, Lennox's widow lifted her hand, small and twisted with rheumatism, to her breast, and made the sign of the cross.

280

V

The House at Hackney, 1578

"And So, my lord, we come to the end."

The fire had gone out and there was no more wood. Leicester downed a feeling of sympathy for her, this old woman left alone in a cold house. She had plotted, he knew, had fingers in matters that she should not. He himself had had many occasions to set spies about her.

And yet —

"She has courage," he thought. That quality had shown again in the Cavendish marriage-plan after Lennox's death. Did she think the Queen's kindness towards her at the news of that had empowered her to make marriage for her second son as she would? Whatever the reason, it was done, and the young man dead. Margaret Lennox had nothing to live for now except the child here, and the young King in Scotland. That last was in the hands of her dangerous cousin James Douglas, Earl of Morton. The Douglases had triumphed in the end.

He heard his voice grow loud and bullying suddenly; it was as though he discounted any pity he might feel.

"You take me for a fool, my lady. It is not known to everyone that you have carried on a correspondence, all these years, with the Queen of Scots in her prison; but *I* know, as does Her Grace."

Her smile mocked him; reminding him that he no longer held all the Queen's favour, and would lose what remained on news of his marriage. She did not answer, and curiosity drove Leicester to question her further.

283

"How can you bear to maintain a friendship, for such it is, with Darnley's murderess? Have you no feeling as a mother? Or does your memory fail?"

"I have forgotten nothing."

"Then why—" He spread out his hands, which were elegant, with long fingers. Even at this moment he felt himself appraising them and the fact that they had not aged with the rest of his body. He and Elizabeth, he knew, were both egoists. Nothing was tragic enough to keep them from themselves, for long.

She said in a low voice, "You may well ask. There had been many lies told. I discovered some of them, at the first in small things. The man Nelson, who escaped alive from Kirk o' Field, saw a fragment of stuff I had which they told me was from Darnley's bed there. But it was not of the colours which had been said. If there can be lying in such small matters, it may well be so in the greater. And I had word from Denmark, by a man my lord sent. Bothwell was prisoner there, but he swore that the Queen of Scots knew nothing of my son's murder till it was done. And again there were poor men held in charge from the siege of Edinburgh, who told me certain things. But most of all I knew that she could not lie and love Christ, and in the end I believed in her innocence."

Her wits are wandering, he thought; she is old and tired. He said, to try her, "When you were at Rufford for the marrying of my Lord Charles, the Queen of Scots was less than thirty miles away, at Sheffield. Yet you have never admitted to visiting her there. Did you in fact meet the Scots Queen?" He felt the blood pound in him; had they met, those two enigmas, mother-in-law and daughter-in-law? What had the one made of the other?

She smiled, very sweetly. "There are some things, my lord, that you will never know."

He grew impatient; would she make a fool of him after all? "It is nothing to me," he said curtly. "What was the question you would ask of me?" It was growing late, and cold; he and his men must be on their way.

Lady Lennox took no heed of him; she was communing with herself in some secret place. She said very softly, "When I was in the Tower the third time, my lord, I had a pastime. I would make lace out of my hair, with pins. My hair has always been very long, and now that it is silver it makes pleasant enough lace. I sent a gift of it to my daughter-in-law, who cares for such things."

And convinced her that you believe in her innocence, he thought; an old, tired, bereaved woman, making lace out of her own hair with her own hand. Why did the tears prick at his eyes? He had not felt so for many a year. "You came safe out of the Tower at last," he said with an attempt at a smile.

"Why not? It is become a second home to me. But I shall never look on it again, and I am not unthankful."

She rose and came towards him, and laid her hands in his. He could smell the odour of damp, age and lavender that came from her garments. It was as though the dead had risen to speak. Courtesy prevented him from casting off her hands.

"My lord of Leicester, I have this to ask of you. I shall die soon, as I have said. Nobody but our two selves will know what is told in this room. But I say to you now, who is to succeed Her Grace on the throne of England? Is it to be my grandson? I cannot die till I am sure."

"How are you to know that I would not lie to you?" he said roughly. "I am no longer in Her Grace's counsels as I was once."

"I think you will not lie. Is it to be so? Are the two lands to become one? There has been war for so long; all my youth and the centuries preceding, since Bruce's time and beyond. It would be well if my grandson could become King both of Scotland and England." Her voice cajoled him. He put his hand over his beard, frowning. How could he say what Her Grace's caprice might not dictate? And yet . . . to give this old woman hope . . .

"There is – hope." The answer was difficult; he found he could not look into her eyes, and surveyed the rushes of the floor. She made no answer, but he felt her hands leave his and saw them fly to the jewel at her breast, and she smiled. He saw in the smile all the sweetness of her youth, as though the years and their burdens fled from her.

"Then," she said, "I have not lived in vain."

He left her soon after; perturbed within his own mind at the thing he had told her. No one except himself, and possibly Cecil who was now Lord Burleigh, knew for certain. Her Grace disliked talk of her death, and the succession. But compared to Jane Grey's sister's children, or the Lady Arbell, or a foreigner brought in to reign, the King of Scots was . . . feasible. Leicester had little doubt of the outcome. In any event the old woman he had just seen would be unlikely to live to see such a day, even if her prophecy concerning her own death did not prove immediately true.

He cantered off, followed by his train. He remembered that he had forgotten to ask her how Malliet, the reformer, occupied so friendly a place in her household. Something in his capacious memory recalled the fact that the man had been Lord Charles Stuart's tutor. The fact that he had stayed on with the Countess all these years argued leniency on both sides regarding religion. Leicester, who had none save that of expediency, shrugged the matter off. The old woman's old servants would look after her, and the Queen's Grace, when it came to that, would bury her. She would not have the money for her own funeral, princess of England though she might be.

After he had gone, Margaret Lennox stayed on in the cold room and told her beads. The regular exercise of them calmed and soothed her, making her feel in communion with her dead lord and her dead children. "We are all one in God's grace," she said to herself. As though she echoed Leicester's own thoughts, her own returned to Peter Malliet the tutor. He had been chosen by Cecil to bring up Charles, no doubt with the intention of alienating the boy from the old faith. Charles – she smiled – had been a handful for herself, a widow; she had been glad enough of anyone, Protestant or Catholic, who could control him through affection. He had never made a scholar, but had grown mannerly enough to please Bess of Hardwick's daughter, Elizabeth Cavendish. Their brief marriage had been happy, despite the trouble which came with the Queen's wrath at news of it.

The Tower. She herself had hoped never to see it again. Her life had narrowed now, since Charles's death; and as for the young King in Scotland, James Douglas, Earl of Morton, now that he had realised his ambition to become Regent, never wrote to her. They had once been friends, in the days before he was taken prisoner to England.

"I am a faded leaf, part fallen from the tree," she thought, and suddenly became aware of pain. It was familiar, being the old colic she had had at intervals since Settrington days. She put her hands over her abdomen and continued to walk, and recite the rosary; soon the agony would pass, as it had done often.

But it did not pass. In the end she called for Malliet and John Phillips, who came; she could see from their anxious faces that she looked ill. "I am going to bed," she told them. "If I am no better by tomorrow, fetch a priest." That would be possible, she knew, even in these penal days: those of the old faith knew where to seek. And now she would lie down, and rest. There was nothing that a physician could do, and they cost money. She made her way with difficulty into her bedchamber, and unlaced herself; she had no woman, except the wife of the spy Nelson whom she would not ask. She lay down, at last, with the pain gnawing at her. Suddenly it grew unbearable, then stopped. The cessation of agony was indescribably sweet.

It came to her that she was dying, as she had foreseen. The knowledge did not rouse any fear. She lay still in the bed with her knees drawn up to ease the place where pain had been; but there was no pain any more, only an awareness of drifting, until nothing any more seemed real; the carved posts of the bed wherein she lay were no more solid than the worn curtains.

She had been alone, but now there were voices about her; it was like that other time when she thought she had run mad after news came of Darnley's death. This time, though, her mind was clear; it set itself apart from, a little above her body, as though she could look down and see the priest come, with the Host borne under a white cloth. She heard a voice, her own, making her last confession; and felt the anointing oils of Extreme Unction, and followed the Latin phrases. She could even think, with a half smile, "I know less Latin than the Queen, for all I am a Papist," and then this and every other thing, the voices and faces clustered about the bed, faded and waned in presence of the supreme reality now within her. She was able to speak to them, those devoted souls who had stayed with her despite poverty and affliction and cold. Two of them were provided for; my lord of Leicester would take them into his house. The rest –

John Phillips was sobbing. She reached out a hand to touch his grey hair. "Weep not for me, for I am glad to die. I am going to those I love; I am going to God." There was so much more she should tell him, but her time was short; while it lasted she recalled the two hatreds in her life, which she had confessed and for which she had received pardon. One was hatred of her mother, now long dead. The other –

"The Queen of Scots is innocent," she tried to say to those about the bed. They included Nelson, the spy. A great freedom came to her; at this moment of dying, there was no punishment they could send for having spoken of what was in her mind; they would never again send her to the Tower. And yet she was beyond speech, and could not say what she would; and past and future ran together. The future held a great tomb peopled with figures, her own and all her children's, at Westminster. Nearby was that of Mary, Queen of Scots. They had been put there by the first monarch of Scotland and England both, him of the lion's mark, who would come south at last to claim a united crown. "Our resting-place is worthy," she thought with a smile. Then she travelled on to where her lord and children waited, with a light about their heads that was brighter than the sun.

The Queen was at the expense of her funeral. It was spread abroad that Lord Leicester, the wizard, had poisoned her. Like the other accusations against him it could neither be proved nor denied. It was let rest, and even the Wisest Fool in Christendom, when he came to London to claim his crown, did not resurrect the story when the monument to his grandmother was raised at Westminster alongside that of his mother, whose bones had been transferred from Peterborough where they had lain since her execution at Fotheringay. The two foes who had become allies would lie near one another, but the Lady Margaret had by far the greater number of kings of England in her pedigree. They were enumerated, but not her misfortunes; there were few left who remembered those. Beside her in the tomb lay young Charles Lennox, who was to give his name to a line of Stuart kings; but no one recalled that he himself had been named for his mother's lover, Charles Howard, who for her sake had remained single till his own obscure death.

288